Icejacked

Icejacked

Adrian L. Hawkes

iUniverse, Inc.
Bloomington

Icejacked

iUniverse books may be ordered through booksellers or by contacting:

iUniverse
1663 Liberty Drive
Bloomington, IN 47403
www.iuniverse.com
1-800-Authors (1-800-288-4677)

ISBN: 978-1-4620-4711-6 (sc)
ISBN: 978-1-4620-4713-0 (hc)
ISBN: 978-1-4620-4712-3 (ebk)

Printed in the United States of America

iUniverse rev. date: 09/13/2011

Contents

Thanks and Acknowledgments

To the editorial staff at iUniverse
To the creative rainbow community in North London
To my editor, Anita Brookes, at Technicolour Text, who shared my enthusiasm and helped bring the story to life
To my ten grandchildren, who I know are very creative
To my wife, for not moaning too much about me writing
To you, for reading a new fiction author

Foreword

With a fascinating premise, Adrian Hawkes's first novel makes its presence felt. Through the eyes of Gerhardt Shynder, a Swiss PhD student, we get up close and personal with Leddicus, a 2,030-year-old man. Has society really changed since Roman times? Of course, there's an overwhelming difference in our standard of living, but human beings, what is in us, and our capacity for love, joy, beauty, hatred, destruction, and selfishness seem to straddle all the centuries. So in Adrian's story, he is able to talk passionately about some of the ills of our society: slavery, detention centres, and the use and abuse meted out to an unprecedented one person every minute who is being trafficked. Adrian obviously delights in history, and his story has many interesting facts about the ancient world and the one in which we live. Implicit in the story is a challenge. Are we frozen icemen needing to melt and wake up and, in doing so, perhaps help change a little of the world where we live?

Ann Clifford, film writer and producer

Preface

When you begin writing a book, I always think you have to ask yourself the following question: "Why am I doing this?" With this book, the answer is, "Just because I wanted to." Will that do as an answer?

To give you a little background, how we all react to change fascinates me. We live in a time of rapid change that sometimes makes life difficult. The older you get, the harder it is to cope with change. But it is not just about the aging process. It is also about firsts. Here is a simple example. Have you ever been on a flight with someone who is flying for the first time? I have, and it's great fun watching their reactions. Have you ever watched people arriving at an airport? I recently watched a group of young girls who were obviously experiencing a moving walkway for the first time. It was hilarious to watch their little dance steps as they tried to deal with the idea of stepping onto a moving walkway. Have you ever been to a supermarket with someone for the first time? I accompanied a young lady from a small third-world village who was just astounded that you could buy ready-cooked chickens and you could sometimes "buy one get one free." She told me that for her to cook chicken, it was a full day's work. She had to collect the firewood and then catch, kill, pluck, and finally cook the chicken in water, the collection of which involved a walk of six miles there and back. Observing these things makes you think.

Ferania, a fourteen-year-old young lady who lived with my wife and me for many years, amused me. For my wife, I bought one of those old black telephones from the late 1950s. A sales company had homed in on the nostalgia for these old phones and manufactured them with modern technology on the inside. I showed Ferania my wife's present.

She said, "What is it?"

I said, "It's an old-fashioned telephone."

She replied, "It couldn't be a phone."

That response left me confused, so I said, "Why couldn't it be?"

She responded, "Look, it hasn't got any buttons on it."

I plugged the phone into the wall and showed her how to dial a number, put your finger in the hole, and twirl the device round.

Ferania looked disgusted. "I could never use that. It would break my nails!"

When my children were younger, they were fascinated that I might have remembered sixpence pieces. I didn't like to tell them that I could remember silver threepenny (thrupenny) bits and went shopping for sweets with a farthing.

One day, I was watching one of my ten grandchildren, a three-year-old, who was working hard on his father's computer.

I said, "What are you doing?"

"Well," he said in a matter-of-fact tone, "I am building a city."

I looked at the screen, and sure enough, he was, designating areas for schools, playgrounds, houses, and factories. He couldn't read yet, but he could type in "www," click his favourite sites from the computer history list, and build a virtual city. It's science fiction, isn't it? Or is it?

My friend Ferania asked me one day, "What TV did you watch when you were fourteen?"

It was hard to explain that, when I was fourteen, there was only one channel, and it came on a black-and-white screen. TV was only just beginning, and many people did not have one, my family included. To a modern teenager, that is almost unbelievable. These innovations we take for granted become so normal that we cannot imagine a time when they did not exist. The mobile phone I now use has as much computer power as the computers used to land the first spaceship on the moon. How times change.

Times change, and technology certainly does, but what about our values? Should they change with the technology? Some people believe there is no such thing as a God or spirituality and everything is about our neurons and chemical structure or those selfish genes. A bunch of miseries—love, peace, joy, righteousness, justice, and responsibility—are all meaningless. Just the result of chemical reactions. Errm!

So I thought my friend Leddicus might help us to look again at what is out there. Perhaps he will help us appreciate it—if we don't already—and maybe question if we need to and ask ourselves, "Have I got sight of a good value package?"

Chapter One

On My Way to Work

By tomorrow, my life would never be the same. Today was the start of a mystery that would echo and re-echo across the world of history and science. Oblivious, I pushed my specs up my nose, ran my fingers through my hair, and locked my front door.

Audis are such comfortable cars. This was my idle thought as I nosed out into the early morning traffic to drive from my apartment in St. Gallen to Universität Zürich, the largest university in Switzerland. It was my normal route, and today was no different, but for some reason, I was appreciating the comfort more than usual. I smiled fondly as I ran my hand across the steering wheel, remembering the gratitude I had felt as my parents proudly handed me the keys to the A4 on the successful completion of my history degree.

"Gerhardt," my father said, beaming first at me and then my mother, "you have made us so proud, and we want to show you just how much."

I was delighted to get my own car and especially pleased it was an Audi into which my lanky frame could fit with comfort.

I liked living in St. Gallen. I had a cheap apartment and access to the incredible library in the Abbey of St. Gall. This wonderful place contained books dating from the ninth century, and as a history buff, this was a magnet to me. When researching, the cleaners would often find me hunched over some dusty tome in a far corner of the library. They would bustle me out, muttering that the library had been closed hours ago.

When the jibes came from my fellow university students because some got there a year earlier, I avoided socialising at their facile events. They thought I was fixed in the past and a loner.

I always consoled myself with this all-consuming thought: *I will show them.* I was determined I would make it one day. One day, I would be rich and famous.

I wasn't thinking much about anything this morning as I navigated through the slow-moving traffic. It was a cold day, but I was cocooned and comfy as I flicked on the radio to catch up with the latest news and views. It was rare that news grabbed me, a history major. The nature of my work kept me buried in the Roman past, my specialty.

But that morning, as the radio chattered away, a news item suddenly caught my attention. I quickly turned up the volume. I didn't want to miss a word. A few days ago on a Tyrolean mountain, a search party, while seeking missing climbers, had stumbled upon a body totally encased in ice. The report went on to state that an investigation had been launched to discover the identity and origin, as no one was missing. The climbers being sought by the search and rescue team had been found safe and well. They had returned via a different route.

Ötzi the Iceman came to mind, and I wondered, *Could this be a similar find?* Ötzi was found in the Austrian mountains in 1991. At the time, I was still in school and read everything I could find about this ancient man. As long as I could remember, history had fascinated me. I wondered if this newly found body was perhaps from the same era, not a recently lost climber, but someone similar to Ötzi, who became encased in ice fifty-three hundred years ago.

The traffic was crawling, but my thoughts were racing. *Would this be an Ötzi II case? If so, would the university let me join the investigation? Would Archiv History be interested?*

I kept retuning the radio to Italian, French, and English stations to hear their take on the story. I needed to get some facts before I ran ahead of myself. *What if it is as I suspect?* My imagination was gripped, and my pulse was racing. I took a few deep breaths to calm myself and resolved to do some intense research on the story as soon as I reached the office. Anticipation filled me. I was full of thoughts about my iceman. I had claimed him already! I had even given him a gender, for heaven's sake. I needed to calm down.

Chapter Two

In the Car Again

Audis are such comfortable cars, aren't they? This thought encouraged me as I headed out of St. Gallen. I needed that comfort. I was at the start of a four-hour drive to Bolzano in Italy.

Yesterday, I felt as if I had the phone glued to my ear all day. *It's amazing how much you can do in a single day if you really try.* As soon as he was available, I met with the head of the university to discuss the iceman find and my plans to get involved. It was hard to keep a lid on my excitement. It quickly became clear that he shared my enthusiasm and was keen to have a representative from Zurich University on this case. He gave me the three-month release I requested and agreed it was fine to feed in material from wherever I am based and have it count toward my future studies and doctorate.

The thought did cross my mind that, once my name was all over the newspapers, my detractors would have to eat their words. Unlike Indiana Jones, who was able to roam the world at the drop of a hat or crack of a whip, no expense spared, in the real world, I had to face up to the boring and practical issues of how to finance my three-month trip.

I called up the guys at *Archiv History*, the small Schaffhausen-based magazine to which I regularly contributed, and explained my plans. I was delighted to discover they wanted the story. They quickly saw it was a big plus for them to have a man on the spot. This made my negotiations easier than I had expected.

They agreed to pay me three months up front. The deal was that I would continue to write my weekly column, plus a regular iceman special. I even squeezed a higher rate out of them.

I called my parents to give them the good news, and still more pieces of the financial jigsaw fell into place. They offered an early transfer of my quarterly allowance, gently extracting a promise from me to keep them in the loop with news of my iceman. When you add on the three-month break from paying my doctorate fees, I was in business.

It was long after midnight before I got everything completely sorted. I had never stayed so long at the university. *Who says men can't multitask?* I was talking on the phone, sorting papers, surfing different language websites, and making copious notes all at the same time. *I hope the researchers are correct that mobile phone radiation does not fry your brain.*

I achieved my main goal of becoming a member of the iceman team. I wasn't sure what I would be doing. It would probably be a very junior role, and I sincerely hoped it wasn't making tea. After a furious eighteen-hour scramble, my normal day-to-day routine was now on hold. I was off to Bolzano, where my man now resided in the local morgue.

From my extensive phone calls and research on the various language websites, the first impressions were that he wasn't as old as Ötzi. The description of the clothing and other items found alongside the body indicated he was a much more modern man, perhaps only two thousand years old. *My expertise should come into its own here.*

The blurry view they initially had of his clothing mystified the rescuers a little. They assumed he had died recently and possibly got lost on his way home from a fancy dress party. *But would you really go climbing in the Tyroleans dressed like that? Highly unlikely if you had any sense!*

When Ötzi was discovered, they dug him out very crudely with a small jackhammer. Unfortunately this punctured his hip. Ice-cutting technology has advanced dramatically in the last fifteen years, and this time around, the salvage team quickly cut this new iceman free, keeping him safe and sound. The extraction was simplified further because he was not completely buried, but in an ice protrusion requiring only one vertical cut. He was then winched into a helicopter and transported to Bolzano, snugly contained in the ice block.

Unusually, the epidermis was intact. This body still seemed to have its original skin on, which was extremely rare. Perhaps that was why they initially assumed he wasn't very old. It was incredible how quickly the bloggers, news feeds, and forums had gathered information about this new iceman. Some of it might have been conjecture, so I was keen to see for myself what was fact and what was reporting hype, hence my urgency to get there. Even after such a long day and a very late night, my adrenaline was still pumping, and I found no trouble at all in making an early start.

Since my childhood, I had been fascinated with Ötzi, so being part of a similar investigation would be incredible. Also perhaps it would make me famous. And as always, there was my underlying determination to prove my peers incorrect about my style of operation.

The drive, although long, was uneventful. When I finally arrived, I managed to book into an incredibly cheap hotel. It was just a bed and place to wash, but that was all I needed at the moment. I pushed open the door to my room and found there wasn't much room to move. It was long and narrow. The single bed was pushed against the far wall; a tiny shower room was in the opposite corner. Squeezed between the bed and the shower was a small desk complete with a reading lamp and Wi-Fi connection. Alongside that was the smallest wardrobe I had ever seen.

I unpacked my battered suitcase and carefully hung up its contents. I precariously placed my toiletries on the narrow shelf in the shower room. I glanced in the mirror. My blue eyes were red-rimmed with purple smudges underneath from lack of sleep. I ran my hand through my bushy, sandy hair and shrugged. I badly needed a haircut, but never seemed to have the time. I brushed my teeth, grabbed my notebook, and left for the morgue.

I was so keen to take my first look at the body, but as I pulled to a stop in the car park, I started to worry that all my phone calls yesterday might not give me the access I needed. I began fretting that the messages had not been passed on as promised. It would be tedious and terribly disappointing to have to start again.

My anxiety was raised further when I entered the reception and the girl behind the desk viewed me suspiciously. But after scrutinising my university ID and *Archiv* press pass, her demeanor changed dramatically.

She beamed and said, "Hello, Mr. Shynder. We have been expecting you."

She picked up the telephone, punched in a number, and spoke into the receiver, "Mr. Beck, Mr. Shynder is in reception." She replaced the phone. "He'll be with you in a moment, and I think you will find he has rather surprising news for you."

I was relieved that all the messages got through without a hitch, but a new worry now beset me. I had just completely altered my entire life and driven for four hours. Anticipation filled me at being part of this amazing project.

Are all my hopes about to be dashed at the outset? It all seems to be going far too smoothly. My genes, unfortunately, predisposed me to the half-empty glass syndrome. I sat restlessly, pushed my hair out of my eyes, and chewed at my nonexistent nails.

A tall, bearded man strode in and shook my hand. "Good morning, Mr. Shynder. Good to meet you. I'm Mr. Beck, the manager here." He turned to the girl on reception. "Could you please rustle up some coffee?"

I followed him to his office, and we both took a seat. He shuffled some papers on his desk and stroked at his beard. He eventually looked up.

"Well now. This is a very strange case."

"You mean because the epidermis is intact?"

"That is part of it, but there have been some rather curious developments, to put it mildly."

"Can we go and have a look at the body?" I tried to mask my impatience.

"Well, no. I'm sorry, but you can't. There isn't a body any longer, not in the sense that we in the morgue understand that word."

I was rather bemused. I opened my mouth to speak, but he held up his hand and stopped me before I could begin.

"Let me tell you what has happened. Then you can make up your own mind about what to do next. When the body came in, we put it in a specially prepared container in the morgue, and the ice began to melt. We noted the skin seemed to be normal. This could be clearly observed as the ice became thinner. The body seemed to be in very good condition. We were also able to observe the clothing that looked like a Roman tunic. Once the ice had fully melted, the body started to warm up. We had specialists on standby with the necessary equipment. You know how quickly these types of artifacts deteriorate when not properly preserved." He paused to gauge my reaction.

I simply nodded, keen for him to continue.

"As it warmed, we were very surprised at how supple the body was, so we decided we could actually remove the clothing, which I have to tell you we wanted to do as it smelt so poorly."

The receptionist discreetly entered the room and placed cups of coffee and biscuits on the desk between us.

"What did it smell of?" I asked.

She looked at me quizzically. I smiled at her confusion.

"Thanks for the coffee," I said. "Don't worry. I'm referring to some clothing."

She smiled with relief and left the room. I was grateful to get a caffeine fix and gulped at the hot liquid.

"Well, at a guess, I would say urine," he replied. "We have sent it to the university for the boffins to examine. We can't be sure at this stage."

"Urine would make sense if the body were of Roman origin, particularly if they were reasonably well-off Romans. They had a very strange custom of often washing their clothes in the stuff."

Mr. Beck nodded at my comment and continued, "After removing the clothing, we had placed the body on a slab, and I was dealing with some urgent phone calls. You could imagine the stir this is causing. I was speaking to the university and the museum and sorting out the details for your visit, Mr. Shynder."

"Thank you. I really appreciate how quickly you organised this for me, but please continue."

"One of my junior associates was with the body, carrying out some standard tests, and he shouted for me to come. He was so insistent that I cut my call mid-conversation. When I joined him, he had his hand on the heart of the iceman and looked at me in consternation. He told me he thought he could feel a heartbeat. Of course, I laughed and told him this was impossible. This man has been frozen for thousands of years."

"He was so agitated. He beckoned me to feel for myself. To humour him, I put my hand on the body, and to my amazement, Mr. Shynder, I felt something. It was weak, but it was definitely beating!"

I couldn't believe what I was hearing. My iceman dreams were melting away. I started firing off questions. "What are you saying? Is this is a recent missing person who has been found on the mountain? What fluke is this? How can he still be alive even though he was encased in ice?"

Again, he held up his hand to check my inquisition. "We don't know what to think. We have reached no conclusions. We have moved him to Bolzano General Hospital."

"He's been moved to the hospital!" I checked myself. I was close to losing it.

"Yes," he spoke quietly, as if trying to calm me down. "We packed up his stuff—the belongings we found alongside his body, his odd little purse, and the peculiar money—and put it into his strange little bag. We arranged for an ambulance to transfer him."

"I see." I regained control with great difficulty. "What now?"

"We only deal with dead ones here. For anyone with a beating heart, this is not the place to be. I'm sorry, Mr. Shynder, there is nothing more I can do for you. You need to continue your investigation at the hospital."

"Thank you for your time," I said and wandered out into the late afternoon.

I was confused, bitterly disappointed, and at a loss about what to do next. I suddenly felt utterly weary and ravenous. I drove slowly back to the hotel. The streets were busy with commuters on their way home. They all seemed to be walking with direction and determination. They had plans. They had homes to go to. They had fulfilling jobs and a sense of purpose and direction. The car behind me honked impatiently, letting me know the lights were green. I shook myself mentally and decided the best medicine for this pity party was to find a cozy restaurant, eat something comforting, and down a few beers.

The hotel room, which seemed so ideal for my purpose this morning, seemed bleak and comfortless this evening. I showered, shaved, and unsuccessfully tried to make my hair look less like an overgrown bush. I promised myself I would find a barber the next day.

The hotel receptionist gave me directions to her favourite eatery, and I headed off to find it. The menu was eclectic and my spirits rose a little when I spied a childhood favourite, bangers and mash, a most unexpected item to find on an Italian menu until I noted the owners were English/Italian. A favourite aunt of mine who used to visit us in the school holidays had introduced me to this feast when I was seven years old, and I had loved it ever since.

I was not disappointed. Big, fat, juicy onions were nestled in shiny, smooth gravy, swamping a large plate of the fattest bangers and smoothest of mash. As I ate slowly, my equilibrium returned. With a beer at my elbow, I began to wonder what I should do tomorrow.

Chapter Three

The Hospital

The sun shimmered through the thin curtains and gradually roused me from my tossing and turning into full consciousness. I remembered yesterday's confusion, so I sat up, put my head in my hands, and groaned. I needed to get some clarity and try to make some sense of the dramatic turn of events. I showered, dressed, and made my way to the hotel dining area. It was basic, but provided all the necessities spread out on a long, well-scrubbed pine table. I poured a large bowl of muesli, helped myself to a cup of steaming coffee, and began to muse over my predicament. I had driven to Italy to what I imagined was a big adventure and the chance to improve my ambition of becoming a professor of note, with high hopes that this ancient body discovered in the ice would be a great leap forward for me. I had managed to obtain excellent support from the university, *Archiv*, and my parents. But now, to my huge disappointment, I had discovered my iceman was alive and well at the hospital and, for all I knew, eating a bowl of muesli. Good for him . . . bad for me. My hopes and dreams of fame and fortune were fading as fast as the early morning mist.

He's one lucky tourist . . . but a rather odd one if the morgue were to be believed. A tourist, apparently wearing authentic Roman clothes that smelt badly of urine, carrying a little leather bag containing what appeared to be ancient coins. What on Earth was a tourist in fancy dress doing on the mountain? Why would anyone venture into the snow dressed in sandals and thin outerwear? And how had he survived being frozen solid in a block of ice?

My thoughts ran round in circles. I topped up my coffee and sat gloomily pondering what to do next. *Should I go back to St. Gallen?*

Tell the magazine it was all a mistake? Let the university know I would continue with my normal studies?

So many possibilities were crushed. So many hopes were dashed.

By the time I finished my second cup of coffee, I had made up my mind. I would go and meet this iceman for myself. I decided to go and take a look at him.

It was a cold, fresh day. The hospital, a short drive from my hotel, was set on the edge of well-manicured farmland, and beyond, I could glimpse a heavily wooded area. If I had more time, I would have loved to go and explore, but instead, I parked and headed toward reception with very little idea of how I would gain access for my visit. The receptionist was vaguely aware of the odd person who had arrived from the morgue yesterday and quizzed me about my connection to him.

"Are you a family member or a friend?" She looked at her clipboard.

"Well, neither really." I then launched into the only idea I could come up with. "I'm from *Archiv*. I've been sent to interview him for the *St. Gallen History Magazine*." I handed her my business card.

To my surprise, she bought it and made a call. "There's a gentleman in reception." She glanced at my card. "Gerhardt Shynder. He's here to interview the mystery man." She listened for a moment and then smiled at me. "Mr. Bernard, our press officer, is on his way. Please have a seat."

I sat down, but remained anxious. I'd heard how officious these hospital press officers could be. I didn't have to wait long. My fears were unfounded. A cheery-looking young man strode up and offered me his hand.

"Mr. Shynder, you're in luck. Mr. Beck from the morgue has already called me to let me know you would probably be popping in. We don't normally let the press in. In fact, we never do, but Mr. Beck told me that your main role is that you are a history professor working with the research team on this case. The standard procedure is that the press must remain off the premises, and when required, we brief them outside. Strangely, they have not arrived yet, but I'm sure they will. You mark my words."

"Thank you. Access to this man is vital if we are to get to the bottom of what has happened."

"This is a very curious case. I'll take you down to see him, although he isn't very communicative, but it should be all right for you to spend a little time with him. I'll let Sister Franz know who you are." I handed him my *Archiv* card and trotted after him as he scuttled down a zigzag maze of corridors.

The young man stopped outside a side ward. The door was open. Inside, a man with thick, curly, dark hair was sitting bolt upright in bed. He was slim and slightly built. His pallor was pale beneath his dusky skin.

"I'll just tell the sister you're here. Please let her know when you are finished." Mr. Bernard left the room and hurried away.

I stood quietly in the room for a while, but the man in the bed did not acknowledge me. I moved closer to him.

"Hello!" I put out my hand for him to shake, but he made no movement and gave no response. His dark brown eyes were veiled and empty. "How are you feeling? Did you sleep all right? Are you being well looked after?" As I kept talking, he turned to his head very slightly toward me, but said nothing. His eyes stared vacantly.

This would make excellent copy for Archiv and my uni reports, I thought gloomily.

A chair was in the corner of the small ward, and I slumped into it just as a tall, white-coated, angular man entered the room. He glanced at me perfunctorily and then busied himself with Mr. Iceman: temperature, pulse, and a quick check of his chest with a stethoscope. He poked and prodded the ears and throat. He meticulously noted the results onto the chart located on the clipboard at the end of the bed. He nodded at the silent man and headed out of the ward.

I jumped up and followed him. "What is the prognosis for my friend?"

He looked a little irritated. "We're not sure what's wrong, but he's quite possibly traumatised and has therefore been struck dumb. We are planning to get in a psychologist to run some tests and find out what is going on. I can tell you no more at this stage." He strode away before I could ask him anything further.

I walked slowly back into the ward. Mr. Iceman was still sitting to attention. Stark white sheets surrounded him. I dragged the chair up close to the bed and wondered what to do next. I started to play a little game to see if I could get any response.

I pointed to myself and said slowly, "Gerhardt." I pointed again and repeated, "Gerhardt." Then I pointed my finger at him and kept quiet. I did this about five times with no response.

Finally, he turned his glazed, unfocusing eyes in my direction and said quietly, "Leddicus."

Now I'm getting somewhere.

"Gerhardt Shynder," I said slowly, again pointing to myself.

This time, it was clear he understood the game. He pointed to himself and said weakly, "Leddicus Palantina."

"Hello." I took his limp hand firmly in mine and shook it gently. "Hello, Leddicus." I repeated it a few times. "Hello, Leddicus." His cold, dry hand still rested in mine.

A little frown developed between his eyebrows. "Hello, Gerhardt." He formed the words slowly in a monotone.

I grinned at him and walked over to the window. I pointed to myself. "Gerhardt Shynder." Then I pointed out of the window and said, "St. Gallen, Switzerland." Leddicus was looking a little more alert now. In fact, he seemed to be enjoying the game.

He slowly raised a pale arm and pointed to himself. Again, he said slowly, "Leddicus Palantina." Then he pointed out of the window as I did and said, "Caesarea Philippi."

My head jolted away from the window and I stared at him, my mouth open, I sat down in the chair with a thump. I felt as if all the air had been sucked out of the room. Now I was the one struck dumb. I knew where Caesarea Philippi is . . . or was. It was once a very great city. Today, it was an archaeological site located in the Golan Heights.

What could this mean? My thoughts were whirling in confusion. I then had a brain wave. I needed to find that doctor.

"I'll be back in a moment," I said to him while making indecipherable hand movements.

I walked out into the corridor and headed in the direction I thought the doctor had gone. I poked my head into each of the side wards as I went. I eventually caught up with him.

"Doctor, could you spare a few minutes?"

"I'm sorry, but I can't. I'm in the middle of my rounds." He began walking away.

"Do you speak Latin?"

He stopped and half-turned toward me. He did not look at all amused.

"I think my friend speaks Latin. He says he comes from Caesarea Philippi."

He turned directly towards me. His face was closed and hard. "Is this your idea of a joke. I'm far too busy for this," he said without emotion.

"No, no, truly, it's not a joke!" I shook my head firmly, but I could see my words were having no impression. He was checking his watch. "And surely his recovery will be helped if he can talk to someone." His shoulders slumped in resignation. His mouth was a thin, taut line as we walked back along the corridor the way he had come.

As the doctor entered the ward, his demeanour changed completely. He sat down close to the bed and placed his hand gently on Leddicus's arm. "*Latine loqueris?*"

Leddicus was suddenly alert. The veil dropped from his eyes. "*Sane, paululum linguae Latinae dico.*" A weak smile played at the corners of his mouth.

The doctor and Leddicus began talking together, quietly and hesitantly. After a few minutes, he stood up, said something in Latin to Leddicus, and made some notes on the clipboard. Without looking up, he said, "I really must get on with my rounds."

"Could you tell me what he said?" I called after him and then followed him out of the ward and down the corridor until I was eventually walking alongside him. His loud sigh of frustration made me acutely aware that I was hounding him, but I didn't care. I kept walking, and then he began to talk in clipped phrases. His voice was stripped of emotion.

"It was difficult for us to understand each other. The way we speak Latin is very different. As you said, he thinks he comes from Caesarea Philippi. As far as I can ascertain, he thinks he has died and is now in the hereafter. He also wanted to know how the little people survived in the box. I'm unsure what he means by that.

He obviously has big psychological problems." He turned down a corridor and stopped at a ward entrance. "I can tell you nothing more. Good day." He dived into the room and closed the door firmly behind him.

I stood in the corridor in confusion and frustration and then wandered slowly back to Leddicus's room. When I got there, I hovered in the doorway, feeling foolish. At which point, a nurse bustled along the corridor and pushed past me into the room. She began fluffing the pillows and straightening the sheets.

"He needs to rest. I'm sorry, but you need to leave now." She eased Leddicus into a more comfortable position of sitting bolt upright.

"Good-bye." I lifted my hand to wave.

Leddicus's tousled head turned slightly toward me as it lay against the fat pillow. Small creases formed between his eyebrows.

"I'm going home now. I shall see you tomorrow." As I spoke, I was also beckoning, pointing out the window, pointing down the corridor, and making little stepping movements. I got no response from him except I noticed the creases between his brows getting deeper. The nurse wafted her hand at me as if she were shooing away a fly.

As I was on my way out, I remembered the request the press officer made so I obediently went in search of Sister Franz to let her know I was leaving. I found her at the nurses' station, talking loudly on the phone and gesticulating to one of the nurses to sort out a patient who was wandering down the ward in just a vest.

She put her hand over the mouthpiece. "Mr. Shynder?"

I nodded.

She finished the conversation and started riffling through the files on the desk. "Did you get anything out of our mystery man?" She looked at the files, not me.

"Hardly anything. A very strange case. What is your prognosis?"

"We have very little to go on at the moment. Obviously traumatised, hence no communication. Seems to be in reasonable physical shape though."

A nurse rushed up and thrust a folder at her. "Excuse me, Sister, could you sign these off? The lab is waiting for them."

The sister bent down and started scribbling on the files. She looked up at me briefly, gave me a crooked half-smile, and shrugged her shoulders, her way of indicating the discussion was concluded.

I turned to leave, but as I moved away, I said over my shoulder, "His name is Leddicus Palantina." I raised my hand in farewell, but no one reciprocated.

I walked out of the hospital and noticed the sun slanting across the trees from the west. I had been there longer than I realised. I was disappointed, mystified, intrigued, and very hungry. My mobile began to chirrup. I flipped it open. It was my head of department.

"Gerhardt, I'm sorry to say that you're being pulled. A representative from the Italian Historical Research Centre called me. I'm sorry about this, but they reckon they have someone with more experience. I told them I doubted it."

I took the phone away from my ear and looked at it in disbelief. "Do you know who they have lined up? Is there anything I can do or say?" I rubbed at my temple with my thumb. I could feel stubble sprouting.

"If you want to give them a call, I'll endorse that. I'll text you the number."

"Where are they based?"

I could hear him riffling through papers. "They actually have a small office in Bolzano."

I checked my watch. Three thirty in the afternoon. "Were you speaking to a rep from that office?"

There was a pause. "By the look of the area code, yes, his name is Calabro. Eduardo Calabro. I'll send you the details."

I ran to the car. I was already pulling out the map as the text pinged onto my phone. I was soon driving through the late afternoon sun and praying he would still be there. The parking was horrendous, and when I eventually stood outside the heavy oak door, I was breathing heavily, hot, and sticky. I pushed my hands through my hair and straightened my jacket. Just as I was about to enter, a tall man with wispy grey hair came rushing out and almost walked straight into me.

I took a chance. "Mr. Calabro?"

He looked a little startled, but gave a single nod. "Yes. And you are?"

"I'm the Roman history specialist from St. Gallen."

His eyebrows shot up. "What are you doing here? I've already spoken to your head of department."

"I know. I understand that, but if you could just give me ten minutes, I'm sure I could convince you to keep me on this case."

He shook his head and looked at his watch. "I doubt that, and anyway, I haven't time. I have to be across town for five thirty. I need to catch a train."

"I have my car here. I could drive you, and we could talk on the way."

"Fine. That's appreciated. But I can assure you that it won't make any difference. I plan to take up this case." He clipped his seat belt into place.

"I'm sure you're eminently suited." I pressed my temple with my thumb to ease the rising tension. "But I doubt anyone has longed for this opportunity more than I have."

"Is that so?" He shrugged. "And why would that be?"

"I read my first Roman history book when I was five years old and thus began a lifelong love affair."

He gave a low whistle. "And what book would that be then?"

"Asterix the Gaul."

Mr. Calabro laughed aloud and slapped me on the knee with his huge hand. "And because you liked that comic, you think I should let you lead on this project?" He laughed again.

I had expected this reaction. I was ready with my comeback. The words tumbled out. "By eight years old, I had consumed every Roman fiction and nonfiction book in my local library. I then begged my parents to take me further afield to bigger libraries with more resources. By ten years old, I had spent every spare minute logging Roman history in copious notebooks. I had charts on every spare wall in my bedroom."

"Bit of a loner, were you?"

"You could say that." I agreed with him reluctantly.

He checked his watch, something he had done regularly throughout my monologue. "I make that eleven minutes, Gerhardt. Pull over. A coffee shop is at the end of this block. The place I need to go for my appointment is just around the corner."

We sat in the dimly lit café, he with his double espresso and me with my Americano. We chatted for another half hour. He finally drained his cup, steepled his hands, and looked me in the eye.

"I'm convinced about your knowledge. I can see you're obsessed. My main problem is your experience. I'm sure you would deal admirably with the research, but there are a host of other logistics in a case like this, not least the press."

"I'm keenly aware of your concerns, but with support from your organisation and St. Gallen, I know I'm the one to deal with this case, and I've already spoken to him."

"Who?" He motioned for the bill.

"The iceman. He can speak fluent Latin."

His thick eyebrows veiled his expression. His body language gave nothing away. After a minute, he threw some euros onto the silver tray the waiter had placed on the table.

"You are even keener than you led me to believe." He stood up, and I followed him out to the street. "I am also keen to get stuck into this. It all sounds too incredible, but I am already heavily involved in another high-level project. If I give this to you, you must keep me fully updated. At the moment, we have exclusive rights to this. We must keep that at all costs." He checked his watch. "I'm late. I need to go. Call me at eight o'clock this evening, and I'll give you my decision." He gave me his card. "We'll speak soon, Mr. Shynder." He took my hand in a viselike grip and shook it once. Then he was gone.

I watched him turn the corner. Then I went back into the café, ordered a large whisky, and downed it in one gulp. I was about to order a second, but changed my mind and picked up the menu. I needed to keep my wits about me. Mr. Calabro would not be employing a tipsy researcher. I beckoned to the waiter and ordered a dish of bucatini carbonara and a beer. He brought me my beer and a local paper, and now I became the clock watcher.

At seven forty-five, I was back in my meager room and regretting yet again how tiny it was. It was impossible to pace up and down. At ten past eight, I was on the phone to Mr. Calabro and silently punching the air. As soon as he cut the call, I took out my laptop and worked into the small hours.

Chapter Four

The Hospital and the Priest

The night before, I managed to write an article for *Archiv* and e-mail a sketchy report to the university with copies of everything forwarded to Mr. Calabro as agreed. I then made a list of what I needed to do today, including revisiting Leddicus and checking the research lab where the morgue had sent his clothes. My haircut somehow did not make it onto the list. At this rate, I would soon need to put it in a ponytail.

I also decided I must keep a journal, not just for my university research but also for personal reasons as who knew where this might lead. I had purchased a black Moleskine notebook, which fitted neatly into my inside top jacket pocket. I took it out now, wrote down yesterday's date, and made notes about all that had happed at the hospital and with Mr. Calabro. When I had finished, I slotted the elastic page holder around the cover, popped it back in my pocket, and patted it. I vowed I would do this every day.

I called up the lab and explained who I was and what I was investigating. They were most cooperative, and we had a long chat. So far, they had discovered that the clothing certainly had the style and appearance of the Roman era and could be two thousand years old, but radiocarbon dating was required to confirm this. They would be sending these artifacts to a local university who had the necessary equipment, but that could take some weeks. The strange smell, was, as I suspected, urine. Slaves who did the washing for the wealthy immersed the material in the repugnant liquid, and it came out sparkling white. The ammonia in the urine did the trick. But the downside of this washing technique was the lingering smell. The most notable Romans, although they looked bright and clean, must have smelled truly pissy. The stench would have been unbearable to the contemporary nose. The researchers at the lab and morgue staff had both complained about this overpowering smell.

The next item on my list was to find a way to rectify the communication problem with Leddicus. It was pretty obvious that I couldn't rely on the busy and very unfriendly doctor. I sat chewing on my pen, and then I had a brainwave. Perhaps I could engage the help of a Roman Catholic priest who must surely speak Latin. As far as I was aware, it was still the lingua franca of Vatican City.

I contacted the local Roman Catholic presbytery and located myself a fluent Latin-speaking priest who agreed to act as my interpreter, gratis! After breakfast, I jumped in the car and headed off to pick him up and take him to the hospital to meet Leddicus.

Father Patrick turned out to be a very friendly, multilingual Irishman who spoke Latin, Italian, and English so it appeared we had every base covered. He was short and round, and he had an unruly mop of ginger hair. When we arrived at Leddicus's ward, the room was empty, and we couldn't find him in the main ward. One of the nurses told me a nursing assistant had come to give Leddicus a break from the ward. She was going to take Leddicus for a walk, but his legs were too weak so she had to take him in a wheelchair.

Father Patrick and I went from ward to ward, but there was no sign of Leddicus. We then checked out the basement coffee shop and walked briskly around the garden area. He was nowhere to be seen. We began to make our way back to the ward by a different route. As we walked past the children's ward, we glanced in, and there he was, sitting in rapt attention as the children participated in an English lesson. He was leaning forward. Deep creases were between his brows. He was obviously paying very careful attention. As we hovered in the doorway, we caught his attention, and for a moment, I thought he recognised me. Perhaps he was pleased to see me, indicated only by the lessening of the frown.

I walked quietly into the ward, and as I did so, the lesson ended. I introduced Father Patrick in English, and then Father Patrick took over and spoke to Leddicus in Latin.

The nursing assistant, who until then had been sitting beside Leddicus, stood up and turned to me. "I was about to take him back to his ward."

"If it's all right with you, we'll make sure he gets back there safely."

"That's fine. Could you just sign here?" She pushed a clipboard toward me with a care plan form clipped to it. "We have to keep track of patients. You do understand, don't you?"

"Of course, no problem." I scrawled my signature and dutifully printed my name underneath. "Any other instructions we need?"

"You can leave him in the wheelchair when you take him back onto the ward. The nursing staff will get him back into bed."

I began pushing the wheelchair. Father Patrick walked along beside Leddicus and stooped down to chat to him. Every now and then, he would turn his head toward me and say, "Left here, laddie" or "Right will be grand." He was obviously a regular visitor to this place as he had no trouble at all navigating his way around the confusing corridors. We eventually arrived back at the right ward.

Leddicus seemed a little more relaxed, and I hoped he was pleased that I had found him another person with whom he could communicate more easily. This small meeting of just three people was but a microcosm of what was happening in the wider world, that is, the mass migration of traumatised war refugees into Western countries. They then had their trauma increased due to being unable to communicate with the local population.

Perhaps it was the presence of the priest, but I had a pang of guilt at my deep intolerance of people who cannot speak the local language. Perhaps I needed a rethink on that one. Seeing it firsthand might hopefully give me more patience.

It would be unfair of me to bore you with reams of Latin, but the priest seemed to be doing a great job. A fascinating picture began to unfold as Father Patrick chatted with Leddicus and then interpreted key information to me, switching easily between Latin and English. My pen scribbled away, filling up the pages in my Moleskine notebook.

"Could you ask him what he meant yesterday? About the little people in the box?" I said to Father Patrick, who relayed my question to Leddicus.

This a good place to start to help piece together this mystery man.

Father Patrick looked at me quizzically. "He means the people in the TV. He wants to know how they get in there."

This was indeed a curious question. I made a mental note to bring in my laptop tomorrow and educate him in the workings of a webcam. As soon as I had that thought, I realised that perhaps I was beginning to believe that he was who he said he was. I gave myself a mental shake to shrug off that preposterous and impossible idea.

"Ask him why he thinks he is dead and in heaven."

Father Patrick grinned at me. "For sure the boy is certain he is dead. He says the people here have such great power. They can create night and day at will."

I smiled at this strange notion, walked over to the light switch by the door, and switched the lights on and off. I then wheeled Leddicus over in his chair and beckoned him to repeat the exercise. He stretched up his hand and began flicking the switch up and down. His eyes widened as he gaped up at the ceiling as the lights went on and off. He seemed very excited and impressed.

The issues confusing Leddicus seemed to point quite strongly to him being from somewhere less developed, and perhaps he really was two thousand years old. My eyebrows shot up in surprise as I found myself thinking this again.

Father Patrick interpreted the response from Leddicus, "If I am not dead, then where am I?"

Father Patrick explained he was in Italy, in a place for sick people. Leddicus was keen to know what sickness he had. This was the most difficult to explain. It took Father Patrick quite a while to retell the story to Leddicus, of where he had been found, being taken to the morgue, and what ensued after that.

Father Patrick looked at me and shrugged. "Leddicus has no idea of how he came to be on a mountain. He does not remember."

"Ask Leddicus to tell us again where he's from and where he was going."

This gradually unfolded with Father Patrick interpreting the information to me, sentence by sentence. I was listening intently and scribbling into my notebook like a newbie journalist. Leddicus said he was married with two children. The family lived in Caesarea Philippi. He had been helping in the family business, which traded in a variety of cloth. He said he was a Roman by birth. His father had been a senior Roman officer, but had recently started a business in Caesarea, as he was now no longer part of the army. He said his mother was Greek.

He was trying to develop trade for the family business, and as Rome was such a large, important city, there was a lot of traffic between Caesarea and Rome. Caesarea was very much a Roman city. He explained many Jews were there, too, so he also spoke some Aramaic as well as his mother's language, Greek.

He had sailed first from Caesarea to Malet, which I guessed was Malta because that was a centre of the textile trade. From there, he planned to go to Rome, but he had instead gone to Gaul and then on to Helvetii. From there, he started to cross the mountains on his way to Rome, and that was as far as he could remember.

Father Patrick conveyed Leddicus's words to me, "Then I found myself here in this strange country, surrounded by very strange things! Where am I?" The priest placed a comforting hand on the arm of Leddicus as he turned to me. "Poor lad, he's so confused and distressed. He hasn't a clue what happened or what's going on. He's very worried that staying in this place is costing him a lot of money. He says he has money. He wants to count it to find out if he has enough. It's there on the bedside cabinet." Father Patrick reached over and handed Leddicus the small leather pouch, Leddicus untied the leather thong that secured the top. He then poured the contents into his lap. I quickly realised that the coins were denarius, aureus, and perhaps sesteritus. He started counting them back into the bag. After a while, he informed Father Patrick that he had almost four hundred Denarius.

Father Patrick and I exchanged an incredulous glance. The priest then reassured Leddicus, saying he need not worry about payment at the moment. I asked Leddicus if I could take a photo of the money. Leddicus looked at Father Patrick quizzically. The priest explained that it was a picture.

This made him more curious. He looked at Father Patrick and rattled away in Latin. He wanted to know where I would get an artist to draw a bunch of coins. I laid out some of the coins on top of the bedside cabinet, produced my mobile phone, and started taking pictures. I had my phone set to a loud click, and as I took each shot, this seemed to disturb Leddicus. He became anxious and gradually wheeled his chair as far away as possible. He ended up wedged against the window. Then I turned the coins over and took a few more shots.

When I was done, I walked over to Leddicus and showed him the pictures. His gasp indicated what he saw genuinely surprised him.

Just for a bit of fun, Father Patrick pulled out his phone. "Send me one of the pictures."

I punched his number into my mobile. A fascinated Leddicus watched as I sent Father Patrick one of the pictures. Poor Leddicus was completely overawed as Father Patrick's phone beeped to let him know he had a new message. Father Patrick beamed and held up his phone for Leddicus to see the same picture there on the phone. Leddicus let out what I thought was a stream of Latin expletives, but Patrick told me what he actually said was, "And you say I am not dead and in another world."

I was keen to ascertain Leddicus's age and what year he was born. The age was no problem. He said he was thirty-one and his birth year was "*Ab Urbe Condita seven hundred and eight five.*" Father Patrick reckoned he must be around thirty-five or thirty-six, as "*Ab Urbe Condita*" means "from the founding of Rome." Father Patrick tried to explain to Leddicus that, if this birth date were correct, then this made him two thousand years old, give or take a few years. His mouth open, Leddicus just looked at Father Patrick, then at me, and then back to Father Patrick. He then spread out his hands, covered his face, and began mumbling. Father Patrick gently pulled Leddicus's hands away so he could hear him better. Leddicus became silent and looked at the floor. All the colour drained from beneath his olive skin.

Father Patrick rested his large hand on Leddicus's shoulder. "He can't take it in, poor laddie. He was saying over and over, 'This can't be possible.'"

"I agree! It can't!" I said. "This gets stranger with every passing moment."

We sat there in silence for a while to let Leddicus gather himself. Just then, the door crashed open, and in bounced a jolly lady pushing a trolley.

"Tea or coffee?" She looked at Leddicus expectantly.

Father Patrick interpreted for him, but the crease in his forehead just deepened even more.

"Hot sweet tea," Father Patrick said firmly.

"Sorry. I can't serve visitors." She said, not unkindly.

Father Patrick smiled. "Yes, I know. This is for the patient. He needs an interpreter."

She clattered around, popped the tea onto the side table, and crashed back out of the room.

"Hot sweet tea." Father Patrick picked up the cup and offered it to Leddicus. "Tis grand at any time and never fails to comfort after a shock."

Leddicus took the proffered cup, held it to his lips, and took a gulp. He let out a yelp because it was so hot. He then sipped it more slowly, still frowning, perhaps at the unfamiliar taste. But the color gradually returned to his cheeks.

When he had finished his tea, Leddicus seemed calmer and asked Father Patrick what language the young children were learning, which he correctly guessed was a school language class. He was told it was English, but this just left him looking blank and wanting to know what country that was from. He then suggested that surely it would be better for the children to learn the more widely used Greek. It was now our turn to look bemused.

"How can we give him two thousand years of history in a sentence?" asked Father Patrick. "And is it actually worth the effort if this is some gigantic hoax."

"It's a tough one, but perhaps we could just keep going. Give it a try. Even if it is a hoax, it's a challenge for our brains, don't you think?"

Father Patrick chuckled. "Aye, that's one way of looking at it, I suppose." He beamed at me as we took up the challenge of giving Leddicus a whistle-stop tour through the last two thousand years.

We began by telling him that this area was originally part of the Roman Empire and that, over the last two thousand years, it had, in fact, become an empire of its own, probably bigger than the Roman Empire. Its capital city, which would have been called Londinium in Leddicus's 'era' and had a population of around sixty thousand, was now called London and had a population of around 15 million. It was now the largest urban centre in the whole of the European Union. English was the spoken language, and it was also an international language, so teaching it to schoolchildren was essential.

Father Patrick relayed the information we had discussed. I watched Leddicus. From his body language and expression, I could tell that he did not believe what he was hearing. It reminded me of a story I heard from someone who visited a tiny village in Ethiopia. One of the senior villagers took the visitor to the edge of the town and showed him a newly laid tarmac road.

"Have you ever seen anything like that?" he asked the young man, who happened to live just outside London.

"Oh, yes, I live near a road called the M25. It's about one hundred and seventeen miles long, and in some places, it has six lanes, and each lane is as wide as your road."

The old man glared at the young man and, with a derisory dismissal, said, "You're a liar!"

Our presuppositions of what we know colours how we hear and assess things. Leddicus did not say that we were liars, but the look on his face clearly showed that what he was hearing was hard to take in and even harder to believe.

A nurse popped her head round the door and tapped her wrist, indicating it was time for us to leave. I felt bad to leave now, and so did Father Patrick. Perhaps in retrospect, this could have waited until another day when Leddicus was feeling stronger and we had more time, but in our enthusiasm and perhaps naïveté, we now had to leave him with all that information churning in his head.

"That's a whole lot of confusion to land on this laddie's head, if he really is two thousand years old," he said.

"I know, but we don't have much choice now. The deed is done," I said.

The nurse hovered by the door, waiting to usher us out. I asked Father Patrick to let Leddicus know I would be back tomorrow.

As we walked across the hospital grounds, the late evening sun was dipping down toward the horizon. We had completely lost track of time.

"What do you think?" I asked Father Patrick.

"It's the strangest thing I've ever heard to be sure, and I don't know what to make of it."

"Me either, and if he is lying and it's a hoax, he is certainly doing a very good job of it. And if it is a big scam, what's the point?" I opened the car and climbed in wearily.

"It's a complete mystery to me. Would you mind if I came with you tomorrow? This has really got me intrigued."

"That would be marvellous. I was hoping you would have more time. I'm stumped without you." I edged out into the evening traffic and headed toward Father Patrick's presbytery.

By five thirty, I was seated in the local restaurant, eager to get to work and catalogue everything that had happened today. My thoughts were racing. I ordered the house special, gobbled it down, flung open my laptop, and started hammering away. After a couple hours, I sat back and ordered a large glass of red wine. I thought contentedly that I could relax and unwind for a couple hours before turning in. I would e-mail the uni and *Archiv* later from the hotel. There was a malfunction with the Wi-Fi at the restaurant.

My phone buzzed. It was a short, terse text from Mr. Calabro. "Remember our agreement. Daily updates by 8 p.m. via e-mail, or the deal is off."

I let out a frustrated sigh. I had completely forgotten. My watch said seven thirty. Depression descended. I thought I was set for the evening, but instead, I threw some euros on the table, left my half-drunk wine, raced back to the hotel, and fired up my laptop, only to discover that the hotel Wi-Fi was also on the blink. Back in reception with fifteen minutes to spare, I got directions to the nearest internet café. I felt desperate to meet this deadline, remembering Mr. Calabro's Mafia tone of voice as he had stressed the importance of this daily e-mail.

At eight fifty-seven, the e-mail sailed into the ether, and I breathed more comfortably. I slowly made my way back to the hotel, bought a beer, and watched CNN for an hour. I was hunched on my lumpy bed before collapsing into an exhausted sleep.

Eduardo Calabro sat down at his neat and tidy desk and cracked each knuckle individually. The blinds were closed against the darkness. He fired up his laptop and checked his e-mail. The last two months of e-mailed reports from Gerhardt were all filed neatly into their own folder. Eduardo opened a Word document entitled "The Leddicus Enigma." It was one hundred and twenty pages long in ten-point font. He checked the e-mail he had received today, and his long slender fingers began to fly across the keyboard.

It was after two in the morning by the time he leaned back in his chair and again began to crack at his knuckles with his thumbs. His shoulders were broad, and his chin bore a pale shadow of grey stubble. He lit a cigarette and smoked for a while. He tapped the ash carefully into an ashtray on the corner of the desk. After a while, he stood up, pulled up the blind, and opened the window. The small, enclosed courtyard was damp from an earlier shower. The air was sharp and fresh. He leaned out of the window and looked up at the sky, letting a stream of silvery smoke slowly escape from between his slightly parted lips. After he had finished his cigarette, he shut the window, shut the blind, and sat back at his desk.

He stubbed out the cigarette, saved the document, and shut down his laptop. He opened a narrow cupboard alongside his desk, took out a small glass and a bottle of Grappa, half-filled the glass, and carefully screwed the cap back onto the bottle, which he then replaced in the cupboard. He took a sip and let out a long sigh. A slight smile twitched at the corners of his mouth.

Chapter Five

Three Months On

The last three months had been hectic and hard work since the first day I met Leddicus, who was apparently icejacked from the past. My life changed beyond recognition, but I wasn't complaining. I was doing well with my living iceman. My university was making no complaints about my reports, the magazine was still paying me for regular articles, and on top of that, other papers and magazines were printing aspects of Leddicus's story, for which I was being paid. It got better all the time. Mr. Calabro had barely been in touch. The only thing he was picky about was his insistence that I blind copy him in to every e-mail I sent about Leddicus. Since I'd given him that guarantee, I had only heard from him about three times. His clipped tones questioned details in the reports, and he wanted the name of the hospital press officer and a contact number. Apart from that, I hardly gave him a thought except when sending e-mails.

Once it became clear that I would be in Bolzano for a while, I moved out of my hotel and rented a local flat on a short-term lease. It worked out cheaper than the hotel, and it gave me space to spread out a bit. It was a relief to leave that tiny basic room. It was becoming claustrophobic. I had managed to hang on to my flat in St. Gallen. Things could not have been better.

Bolzano was a fantastic place to stay, not least because it was the home of Ötzi. I'd spent some happy hours roaming the museum and reacquainting myself with my old friend. Often on Saturday or Sunday, I took drives out to one of the local castles. Runkelstein was astonishing, it was perched precariously on the edge of a cliff, as all good castles should be. On dark nights, when the mist was thick, I could quite imagine Dracula peering out from one of the windows, but of course, this was not his patch.

The surrounding countryside was full of woods and rolling hills. It was totally stunning and allowed me to indulge in long walks, my second love. I wasn't too keen on steep climbs, so, if the weather was kind, I got on a cable car and enjoyed the magnificent views without too much effort.

Leddicus had become somewhat of a celebrity, helped to some degree by my copy in *Archiv* and other articles I submitted to various publications. The world press loved this mystery man. Not a week went by without an e-mail or phone call from some publication wanting to get more information. I wasn't quite sure how I managed to retain my exclusivity on this story, but long might it continue.

Very early on, Leddicus decided that, if the majority of people spoke English these days, then he had better learn it. He started going every day to the English class in the hospital. It seemed he had a knack for language and picked it up remarkably quickly. We could now have basic conversations in English. He still made mistakes, but after only three months, he wasn't bad at all.

I bought him a mobile phone, and he called me now and then, sometimes speaking very loudly and sometimes very quietly as if testing its limitations. But unsurprisingly, the technology confused him.

When he first got the phone, he asked me, "How far can this machine make the sound stretch?"

It was very difficult to answer him without the jargon that his English did not yet encompass. I did have a stab at it and tried to explain about satellites, but his face was a picture of childlike confusion. So I just shrugged at him.

Even if the hospital did not believe he was two thousand years old, they were still puzzled as to how anyone could survive being frozen solid in a block of ice. After he had been in the hospital a while and his general health was stable, they discussed the situation with Leddicus and reached agreement that he should undergo a series of tests to find out if there were any long-term damage and to try to discover how and why he managed to survive. Poor Leddicus, he had been poked, prodded, x-rayed, scanned, and undergone many other tests, including the extraction of numerous DNA samples. Each day, another technician seemed to be whisking him off somewhere. When time allowed, I accompanied him. He was quite stoical as he sat there, wired to various buzzing, flashing, clicking machines. It would have been daunting for me, and I was used to technology. I couldn't begin to imagine what was going through his mind. I was ever hopeful that these tests could give us some answers.

I found, as each day passed, that what I initially dismissed as preposterous now hovered in my mind as a probable improbability. He could actually be telling the truth. Against all the odds, he could be who he says he was. Even as I followed this train of thought, it grated, and I pushed it away. I was sure there must be another rational and logical explanation.

He had been receiving intensive physiotherapy. Initially, he could not walk unaided. When he tried, his knees buckled under him, and his arms had no sustained strength. He could barely hold a knife and fork. Every day, his nursing assistant took him to his English lessons while the nursing staff investigated what appeared to be muscle wastage. He looked so forlorn when I left each day as the physio arrived to put him through his paces. I occasionally took pity on him and joined him in his workout. I encouraged him as he gritted his teeth and shuffled along.

I was concerned that some permanent damage had been done, but with the support of the physiotherapists, perhaps a little of my cheerleading, but ultimately, Leddicus's grim determination, he improved steadily. Halfway through the second month, he could walk unaided, and pretty soon, there was no stopping him.

Leddicus showed me his swatch. He had forgotten he had it with him, but the hospital had been efficient and kept it safe. They gave it back to him as he gradually regained his strength. It was a selection of the materials that he and his family traded. One was very expensive, a deep purple that was difficult to achieve and used a special and distinctive dye. He had some old-looking papers safely nestled in the middle of the material samples. Written on parchment type paper, one was in Latin. He told me it was to show people proof of his "free Roman" status.

Leddicus gave me permission to take the swatch and the papers to the university that had assessed the age of his clothes. The dating of these articles matched the clothing, being in the region of two thousand years old. The Latin paper, when translated, backed up what Leddicus had told me. It indicated he was financially secure, a cloth trader, and a free Roman. It seemed to be an ancient passport or reference, requesting those reading it to protect him and give him assistance in his quest.

Everything I touched with Leddicus seemed to verify his story. The more I got to know him, the more I liked him. He was a very special guy in more ways than one. In the face of such adversity and confusion, he was patient, pragmatic, and cooperative and still retained a sense of humor.

The other papers wrapped in the cloth were in Greek, ancient Greek, similar to the Greek that would have been used to translate the Bible. The university told me that they appeared to be greetings to different groups of people called "people of the way." The university was still working on the translations, so I would check back with them on this in a few weeks.

The time had come for Leddicus to leave the hospital. They had not found anything wrong with him. All the tests they had been carrying out had drawn blanks. There still did not appear to be any scientific or biological reason for the anomaly of why he survived being in a block of ice. They had also been looking closely at Leddicus's physiology. I was sure some of them thought he was just mad. But in every way, apart from his story, he seemed to be perfectly normal, apart, that is, from his complete lack of understanding of anything modern.

The phone, the TV, electric lights, and hospital equipment, everything seemed to be a complete mystery to him. His reactions constantly amused me. Once I took my laptop into the hospital and showed him a webcam. When he saw himself on the screen, he kept checking the picture and then looking at his body to see if it were all there. He probably thought I had stolen some of it and put it in the laptop.

But a hospital was for sick people, and he obviously wasn't sick, so he couldn't stay there any longer. He needed to find a permanent place to live. He thought he had a lot of money, but he would soon discover it was not legal tender. He would also discover that, legally, he did not exist. He had no birth certificate, driving license, ID, or passport, nothing to prove who he was.

In Switzerland, my home country, the exchange rate and the cost of living in other countries was brought into sharp focus for me in one of the stories my father regularly told me. He knew a young Polish migrant, Andrzej Pietraskievitch, who was working locally. His brothers planned to join Andrzej in Switzerland. At the time, Poland was still under the rule of the communists. Andrzej became extremely agitated when he knew their visit was imminent. He asked them to delay their trip to give him some time to save up so he could look after them. But they were adamant and assured him they had plenty of money. They had each saved up one year's worth of salary. Andrzej had his fears realised when his brothers arrived. Their first night in a hotel used up their entire year's salary. They were devastated and could not understand how this could be, and Leddicus would not understand either. My father, ever the socialist, helped them to find some cheap accommodation and get work. As a result, the two families became firm friends.

As a student, I did some voluntary work with an organisation helping refugees. I quickly realised how important bits of paper were to them. Passports, birth certificates, and identity cards are pieces of paper that give us our identity in our culture. Most of us take them for granted until we haven't got them. As history is my bag, I am aware of Fridtj of Nansen, the first refugee high commissioner of the League of Nations, the forerunner of the United Nations formed in 1921. He realised how vital a piece of paper was to a refugee and perhaps invented the refugee travel document. It looked like a national passport. This document became very important in 1951 when Europe was dealing with so many refugees after World War II.

Leddicus had a passport of sorts. Passports have been around in some form or other since the dawn of civilisation. Roughly four thousand years ago, it seemed that Moses, in his writings, inferred that, when Abraham sent his servant Eliezer to Mesopotamia to find a wife for his son Isaac, he gave him some sort of passport that provided him with "safe conduct." It is also on record that Augustus furnished Potaman the philosopher with a general passport, "Voyager dans les Pays etranger." The terms of that passport were significant. "If there be anyone on land or sea hardy enough to molest Potaman, let him consider whether he be strong enough to wage war with Caesar."

Leddicus's passport, without doubt, would not function in modern bureaucracy. I wanted to take him to Switzerland to meet the staff at *Archiv* and my colleagues at the university, but he wasn't going anywhere without a passport. In many unexpected situations, it is vital to prove who and what you are. A Tamil refugee friend from Jaffna, Sri Lanka, wanted to get married, but was unable to do so. The town hall containing the proof he needed of his single status had been destroyed when it was demolished in a bombing raid. Another resourceful friend managed to obtain the document from a local bureau . . . well . . . local in the sense that it was the corner shop where he printed up the document and stamped it.

"How awful! That's illegal!" I hear you cry, but perhaps the binding and restrictive bureaucracy is awful.

Travel documents for Leddicus were my immediate concern. I needed advice and help from friends. I decided to visit Father Patrick. He opened the door and shook my hand warmly. He beamed with delight. We hadn't seen each other for a few weeks. Now that Leddicus was speaking English, Father Patrick's role as interpreter had ended. He still visited him from time to time, but our paths rarely crossed. We sat and chatted through the passport situation over coffee and croissants. He was unable to help me in this instance.

I spent a couple days on the phone and called everyone I could think of to try to resolve the situation. A combination of support from the university and *Archiv* helped me achieve my goal. They pulled out all the stops. They were as keen to meet Leddicus as I was to take him to Switzerland. Leddicus was now the proud possessor of a special refugee travel document, and we could travel out of Italy.

I thought how useful it was to be in a place where you have connections that are powerful enough to make things happen. The refugees I worked with as a student didn't have powerful friends, and they were often totally alone. When assisting them, I would sometimes need to photocopy papers for them. But they would not give me even the most simple of official pieces of paper. Instead, they would accompany me to the photocopier and, once there, hand it over to me nervously. They watched my every move as I put it into the chute. I sometimes wondered if they thought I might eat it. As soon as the copy had been made, they retrieved it from me, visibly relaxing once it was back in their possession. At the time, I found this quite amusing. But having been through this situation with Leddicus, I now acutely recognised that those pieces of paper we take for granted were a lifeline to many displaced people.

Let the packing begin! Leddicus could now travel officially, and we were going places. Yes, sir! This guy could make me! What would it be like when he finally walked out of this hospital building into the big, wide, modern world?

I think I need a very good camera.

Mr. Calabro sat hunched over his laptop, his regular post-midnight haunt. *The Palanatino Enigma* was progressing well, far from finished, and many gaps remained, but he was encouraged. His mobile vibrated gently on the desk.

"Yes," he answered curtly.

He listened intently. He pushed back his laptop and drew a notepad from the drawer in the centre of his desk. As he listened to the call, he made brief notes in small capitals: Turkey—25-29,11/Philippines—20-31,11/Vietnam—50-4,12.

He laid down his pen and cut the call without saying good-bye. He leaned back in his chair and, with both of his slender hands, pushed his hair flat against his head. He sat for a while with his hands linked behind his head and looked at the ceiling. His pale blue eyes were deep in thought. He checked his watch. It was two thirty in the morning. He indulged himself in a cigarette that he smoked while staring at the sky out of the open window. The gardener had watered the huge terra-cotta flowerpots earlier in the day. The mellow smell of wet earth drifted upward and mingled with the cigarette smoke. Two stories down, a cat padded noiselessly across the courtyard. The automatic lights blinked on and dazzled, sending the cat scampering for cover. His eyes narrowed against the brightness that spoiled his view of the stars. He closed the window gently and prepared an e-mail.

Shipment requirement not met. Further goods being sourced. Delivery expected over four-week period. Confirm transport, holding bay, and finance is in place.

He read it through twice and clicked send. The secure server confirmed encryption, and the e-mail blinked away.

He poured his arbitrary measure of Grappa, sniffing at it as if it were a fine wine. He sipped it slowly and waited. The house was silent apart from the occasional settling floorboard, creaking as it cooled. Two floors down, his wife slept peacefully, accustomed and unconcerned about his nocturnal habits.

Chapter Six

Out of the Hospital

Leddicus was waiting for me. He stood stiffly alongside his bed and wore some of the clothes I had brought in for him yesterday: a pale blue polo T-shirt, a dark grey linen jacket, and classic navy Levi's. He fiddled with his collar. His short fingers with bitten nails picked at it nervously.

"How do I look?" he asked.

"Fantastic!" I said.

He frowned.

"It means you look very, very good."

He smiled broadly. Although small in stature, he was quite a good-looking guy, considering he might be two thousand years old. Or as Leddicus liked to say, "thirty-one and something."

"You're ready to go?"

"I am! Very ready!" He pointed proudly at the suitcase by the door. "It is full with the many clothes and other strange things you brought. They are all ready to come with me." He walked over and picked it up. "You are very kind!"

"Well then, let's get going. Zurich, here we come." I led the way out into the main ward for the last time.

We were surprised and delighted to see an entourage of nurses and support staff all lined up in the ward. One gave Leddicus a box of chocolates. The ward sister shook his hand warmly.

"We are all sorry to see you go. We will miss you. But we're so pleased that you are fit and well."

Then everyone was crowding round him, shaking him by the hand and hugging him. Their show of affection took him quite aback.

"Let's go the long way out this time," I said.

I usually went through the hospital grounds, but today felt auspicious, and I wanted to make the most of it. We walked along the maze of corridors, and it took us quite a while. Word had spread that Leddicus was leaving, and everyone wanted to shake his hand and wish him well. Heads were poking out of every doorway. Leddicus smiled and shook hands happily with everyone he passed. I doubt he had seen many of them before, but he was gracious and patient to a fault.

We headed toward the main exit, and as the automatic doors whooshed open, I could not believe my eyes. Dozens of people seemed to be mobbed outside. Cameras were flashing, mics were shoved into our faces, boom mics swung above our heads, and TV crews were running toward us with cameras rolling. Suddenly, everyone was shouting questions at us in every language except Latin.

Leddicus turned to me with utter confusion on his face. He was visibly shaken, and so was I. Reacting on impulse, I grabbed his shoulder and steered him back into the hospital. We raced down the corridor as fast as our legs would take us. As we ran, I heard peace descending as the automatic doors whooshed shut. A few corridors in, we stopped to catch our breath.

"What was that?" Fear filled Leddicus's eyes.

"Gerhardt! Gerhardt!" Mr. Bernard came running up the corridor toward us. "Wait up! I'm sorry! I'm so sorry!"

"What's going on?" I was breathing heavily.

"Communication mix-up. The press office asked the ward sister to request you leave by the back door. In all the excitement, she forgot. So sorry!"

"Where did they come from?"

"You didn't know?"

"Know what?" I shrugged my shoulders.

"The world press! You mean you didn't know they were there! They have been there almost from day one, but we are very strict. They know they cannot come past the main entrance. We always protect our patients. Our policy is security and privacy." He looked at my confused face. "You came almost every day. How did you miss them?"

"I had no idea. I always parked on a little side street. There's a small gate into the hospital grounds. I have never used the main entrance."

"Then you must leave that way today and quickly. Once they realise Leddicus is leaving for good, they will mob every exit." He turned and started walking quickly.

We followed at a trot and were soon cantering across the grass toward the small exit gate and safety. I glanced down the road and saw a few people on the corner. I flung open the car door, hustled Leddicus into the backseat, and stuffed his suitcase in after him.

"Get down!" I pointed to the floor.

He scrambled in and crouched down on the floor. I jumped into the front.

"Thank you!" I said over my shoulder to Mr. Bernard.

And we were off. I had been here so often that I knew these side roads like the back of my hand. I took off at high speed. In my mirror, I could see cars giving chase. I pushed the accelerator to the floor, almost taking corners on two wheels, nipping down tiny side streets, and doubling back on myself. After about ten minutes, the rear mirror was clear, and I knew I had lost them. We slowed to a more sedate pace until I eventually pulled into a quiet side road and parked. I peeked over my shoulder to see Leddicus's face, pale and full of horror, peering up at me from the floor of the car.

I got out and opened the back door. I grinned at him. "Come on. Let's get a coffee." I put my hand across his shoulder. He was shaking. "Don't worry. That's just the press." I laughed aloud with the exhilaration of giving them the slip.

"Press?" His voice was shaking.

I ordered up strong black coffee for me, apple juice for Leddicus, and a plate of croissants for us to share. We ate silently for a few moments and soon felt calm again and ready to face the world, if not the world press. It took a while to explain the concept of the paparazzi to Leddicus, but one thing that constantly amazed me about him was his ability to take in new information, assimilate it, and deal with it.

"Paparazzi?" He tested the word.

"The bane of modern life. They are a bunch of leeches."

At this, he smiled. He obviously knew what a leech was. I paid the bill, and we headed out of the café. While we were escaping from the mob, he had been flung unceremoniously onto the floor of my car and then jolted round a dozen back streets. As we walked toward the Audi, he hesitated, and those trademark creases crept between his eyebrows. He stopped and looked at me. The creases grew ever deeper.

"This animal, it makes no sense to me." He pointed at the car. "It growls like a tiger, smells like fire, and bumps me around like ten chariots."

"Oh, Leddicus, how can you say that about my beloved Audi. It's my pride and joy." I patted its bonnet and opened the passenger door for him. "Tell you what. You sit in the front with me, and I promise you'll enjoy it much more than being scrunched up on the floor at the back."

He climbed in reluctantly, and I helped him fasten the seat belt. His hands were gripping the seat even before I fired up the engine. I didn't think my driving was that bad!

As we drove on, I mused about what we had just come through. We had already talked about where to go and what to do, and I had given him some money and a wallet.

He had said, "But what is wrong with my money?" He looked at the Swiss francs I had got for him. "But this does not feel or look as if it has any real value."

"Trust me, it does."

Leddicus was still disturbed that his money wasn't going to be used. "I don't understand how the money will not be useful anywhere with all that Pax Romana has brought."

I hadn't heard that phrase for a long time. I smiled. *What a strange concept in today's world, but is it so strange?* It was going to be fascinating watching as Leddicus moved from the familiar hospital surroundings into the big wide world. If he were who he said he were (and so far, I had no reason to disbelieve him even though it went against every atom within me), from here on, everything he looked at was going to be new and alien.

As I concentrated on driving, he sat quietly. He watched the passing countryside with great interest and occasionally asked me to explain various landmarks. After driving for ninety minutes, I needed more coffee.

And here begins the first of many new adventures for Leddicus. I began looking for a service station.

Mr. Bernard sat in his office. He calmly sipped some hot tea and felt greatly relieved that Mr. Palantino was no longer his responsibility. He also felt a little smug that he had discharged the requirement to keep the press completely at arm's length. It had cost the hospital a lot in increased security, but thankfully, that cost was being covered. A text alert buzzed onto his phone.

Good work. Money being transferred to your account today. Keep me posted on further developments.

He fired up an e-mail to his boss to request some well-earned leave, and now he could afford to go somewhere exotic.

Chapter Seven

The Service Station

I knew that, as soon as we entered any new environment, Leddicus would bombard me with questions, but my need for coffee overcame my concern about getting bored with explaining the whole world and his dog to him.

"We need to find somewhere to eat, keep your eyes open for signs with a knife and fork on." Even looking for signs was an interesting idea for Leddicus.

My assumption that this was going to be a big adventure was not wrong. It's amazing how many things we do every day and take completely for granted. We don't even think about them. Leddicus got out of the car and stood a little away from it, waiting for me. I walked toward him, pointed my car key at the car, and pressed the automatic lock button. The car dutifully let out a peep and flashed its lights at me.

Leddicus looked startled. "What did you do?"

"Just locking my car." I passed him the key and showed him how to press the buttons for lock and unlock.

We could have been there all day. Leddicus was like a fascinated young child locking and unlocking my car.

"Come on," I said. "I need coffee."

We moved no further than the entrance to the service station, which automatic doors controlled. Leddicus was a little in front of me, and I thought he had been shot as he jumped in the air and let out a yelp as the door automatically opened. He stepped back quickly, and the doors closed, then, of course, he stepped nearer, and they opened again. I thought we were never going to get inside as Leddicus moved backward and forward, watching the door open and close.

"This is amazing," he said. "How does this work?" I pointed out the control sensor at the top of the door. I was sure Leddicus was unsatisfied with my brief explanation, but my urge for coffee was getting stronger by the moment.

We were finally inside, but I began to wonder if I would ever get my coffee. There were far too many distractions. Most service stations had game rooms quite close to the entrance. This one was no different, and Leddicus was drawn like a magnet to the flashing lights and electronic sounds. He wandered from machine to machine. A youngster chasing terrorists, blowing up buildings, and shooting people. There was a lot of noise and many explosions. Leddicus's mouth hung open as he watched transfixed. Further on, a spotty youth was squinting intently at the screen, gripping the steering wheel, and swinging it rapidly back and forth to keep his car ahead of the pack and on the road as he raced around the Le Mans circuit. Leddicus pushed his hand through his hair and shook his head in confusion.

In a stage whisper Leddicus asked, "Why would someone drive a pretend car when they can drive a real one?" Fortunately the youth playing the game was completely engrossed and didn't hear the comment.

We finally agreed to go and get that coffee for which I was so desperate and something to eat. The restaurant area of this service station was serving food buffet style. We picked up a tray and began to move along the counter to make our selections. It wasn't particularly busy. Leddicus was in front of me, and I could see his eyes were nearly popping out at the huge choice: cold and hot meats, vegetables steaming in big bowls, salads of every description, and potatoes cooked every which way. I took a couple slices of ham, some good Swiss Emmental cheese, and a little green salad. Leddicus, the poor guy, did not know what to do and just stood there looking from dish to dish.

I finally asked him, "Would you like hot food or cold food?"

"Hot," he said simply.

I grabbed a plate for him and began scooping up cottage pie, green beans, and chips. I then got us a drink each and headed to the checkout. Leddicus watched fascinated as I paid for the food and the girl chatted to me in Italian, punched in the cost of the food on the till, and gave me the right change, which I then put into Leddicus's hand. He studied it closely.

We finally made it to a table, and I took a sip of that long-sought-after coffee. We did not talk much over the meal. The food, displays, and surroundings distracted Leddicus too much, and his eyes darted everywhere with childlike curiosity, rather like a baby crawling across a carpet and carefully examining every piece of stray fluff.

Refreshed by lunch, I cleared the table, and we headed toward the exit. As we were about to leave, I thought it might be fun to give him a turn on an arcade game. I sat him in one entitled "Formula 1 Grand Prix." He looked a little reluctant and dubious, but I carefully explained what to do and told him nothing would actually happen because it was only a game. I wasn't sure he believed me or understood, but I dropped in a coin, and off he went, gripping the steering wheel and biting his lip in concentration as he steered along the video roadway. Once he got the hang of it, there was no holding him back. When the money ran out and the game was finished, he was like a child.

"I like driving this pretend car. I want to do it again!" He grinned from ear to ear.

I fed some more coins in, and off he went. After the second run, he wanted to keep going.

"Leddicus, I'm sorry. We really must go."

He looked very disappointed as he slid out from behind the wheel and followed me. We went through the automatic doors, much to Leddicus's amusement. I did wonder if I were in for another of those childish games, but he meekly followed me to the car. As we approached the car, I felt in my pocket for my key fob and pushed the button to open the doors.

"How did it know we were coming?" he asked.

"What?"

"The car? How did it know?"

I pulled open the passenger door and ushered him in. "Let's drive. I'll explain on the way." I sighed.

Chapter Eight

The Drive to St. Gallen

"How do they work?" Leddicus asked as I turned onto the motorway in the direction of St. Gallen.

"What?" I knew full well what he meant, but felt mellow and distinctly uncommunicative.

"The doors." He moved his hands back and forth to indicate the automatic doors closing and opening.

"They just do," I said.

I'm a historian, not a scientist! I tried to hang on to my mellow mood and not become surly.

He sulked quietly for a while. I hoped he was beginning to recognise when I had enough of explanations. The sun was still fierce even though it was late afternoon. It seared the patchwork fields and low mountains, relentlessly drawing moisture from their silent, unprotesting backs. The air-conditioner protected us from its stark heat. We sat in a cool, peaceful cocoon as we drove through the sultry day.

From the corner of my eye, I could see Leddicus glancing across at me from time to time. My conscience pricked me just a little.

"What's up?" I asked.

He grinned with relief. He hated to be quiet. "The hospital. What did they say is wrong with me?"

"Well, that's good." I turned to him briefly and grinned back.

"What is?"

"At least you want to know how you work, not the doors, the key, or the—"

"Okay, okay!" He gave my shoulder a friendly punch.

Do they have friendly banter in every era, or is he taking his cue from me?

"Tell me. What did they say to you? When I asked them, I didn't understand the answer."

"They don't know for sure. Without putting too fine a point on it, you are a one-off. The told me that they thought you had post-traumatic stress."

"Please!" He spread out his hands in frustration.

"I know you don't know those words, but try them out. Then I'll tell you what they mean."

"Post-traumatic stress," he said obediently.

Since he had begun to learn English, I had always pushed his understanding beyond the basics, even though he often got weary of me doing this. If he were going to make his way in this unforgiving era, he needed to broaden his vocabulary.

"Post-traumatic stress," he said again. "Please explain!"

"Calm down. I'm getting to it. It means that, after something very bad has happened, your brain and emotions can sometimes be badly affected. Let's take those words one at a time. Post means after, traumatic means something shocking or disturbing, and stress means pressure or tension." I paused and glanced across at Leddicus to see if he were getting this. I felt it was important not just that he understand the words, but that he fully understood what had happened to him emotionally. He looked back at me and nodded for me to continue.

"The medics think that being frozen on the mountain has caused your memory to blur, to get mixed up, and to shut out the shock of what happened. They think that's why you have started to imagine all sorts of odd things and why you think you are someone else."

"I see," he said calmly. "Thanks. That helps a lot."

"They think you have completely forgotten who you really are."

"And you? What do you think?"

"It doesn't compute. It just doesn't add up." I looked at him briefly. He was listening intently. I spoke slowly to be sure he understood. "If you are not who you say you are, then you are a fantastic fake. You know so much about that era, which, of course, you could have read in any number of books, but then there are the clothes you were wearing, the coins you were carrying, and your amazing grasp of Latin, Aramaic, and ancient Greek."

"No one can live for two thousand years. That's impossible," Leddicus interrupted. He rarely got agitated, but the pitch of his voice rose. "I know I don't belong in this world. It makes no sense to me." He clenched his fists and tried to contain his frustration. "And I know I have a family, children, and business. Where are they now? Who am I, Gerhardt? What has happened to me? How did I get here?"

"Leddicus, I wish I knew. I am as confused by this as you are. I have never seen or heard anything like this in my life," Sensing his mounting frustration, I said it gently. "What were those papers you were carrying?" I hoped to deflect his angst. "What were they all about?"

But my attempt at distraction only made things worse. He went from tense and talkative to stressed and silent.

I wasn't the most sensitive of people, but it was pretty obvious that questioning him about the papers had touched a raw nerve. We drove on a while. His hands were clenched, and the knuckles were white. I was intrigued.

"What troubles you so much about those papers?" I probed.

"Please, I cannot tell you. It may put my life in danger," he said quietly.

"I think I can safely say that whoever was after you is long gone."

He relaxed, very slightly. "Perhaps I can trust you."

"You can!" I said, not entirely sure I meant it, but willing to say whatever it took to get to the bottom of this new mystery.

"We must be very careful who we tell about what is in the letters. Many people cannot be trusted, and if you tell the wrong person, he will pass it on to the authorities, and we will be arrested, beaten, imprisoned, and perhaps even killed."

"What on earth is in the papers that is so life threatening?"

"The letters tell of the way."

"What way? Now it's your turn to help me understand." I smiled wryly.

His eyebrows shot up and disappeared into his lopsided fringe. "You haven't heard about the way? But it is talked of in the whole world! Everyone has an opinion on it."

"Well, I'm not one of them, so fill me in."

"There was a man in Israel, and many followed him because he always did so many good things. Some even thought he was the prophesied Jewish Messiah, but the Romans and Jewish leaders got together and lied about what he had done. As a result of their lies, he was crucified."

"Would this man, by any chance, be called Jesus?" I interrupted.

"He is the man!"

"You knew him?" I was on the edge of my seat now.

"No, not personally, but word gets around. We Romans love to discuss and find out what is happening."

"Why is there danger in having papers about him?"

"After he was killed, word got around that he came back to life." He spoke slowly and carefully. "When someone is crucified for . . . how do you say it . . . causing people to be against the leaders?"

"Political activist?"

He frowned. His struggle to find the right words frustrated him.

"It's okay. I know what you mean," I said to get the story flowing again.

"When someone caused a disturbance or said things that were not in line with the local laws, he was usually tried and killed. Afterward, the followers would melt away once the leader was dead." He paused, unscrewed the top of the bottle of Evian, took a long swig, wiped his mouth with the back of his hand, and continued. "That didn't happen this time. His followers disappeared for a few weeks. But then to everyone's surprise, they reappeared, more bold than ever, saying he had coming back to life." He still spoke slowly, searching out the right words and with reluctance. I assumed it was because of his fear. "I listened to what they said, and I was convinced they were telling the truth, and I became a follower."

"You still haven't said why it's dangerous to tell about the papers?"

"The Jewish authorities are furious and trying to stamp out the lies about someone coming back to life. Followers of the way also believe that this man was the Messiah, and that gets the authorities even madder." He paused and looked at me quizzically. "How do you not know all this if you know his name?"

"Go on," I said.

"The people in Caesar's household are in danger if the authorities find out they are following the way. I need to give them these papers in secret, and the message will encourage them to keep going."

"You're not thinking straight, my friend, but I won't hold that against you."

"What do you mean?"

"You are, understandably, very troubled and not thinking clearly. If you are as old as we both think you are, what do you reckon has happened to all the people in Caesar's house?" I paused to let this sink in. "And where do you think all the Jewish leaders are?"

He didn't answer. He just let out a long sigh and then breathed slowly and deeply a few times. As we rounded the next bend, the Swiss border loomed into view. My heart started to beat a little faster in anticipation of a long interrogation when they saw the papers on which Leddicus travelled.

"Border control." I slowed down. "We're about to leave Italy and enter Switzerland."

I pulled up at the checkpoint and waited for the official-looking guard to saunter to my car. I couldn't gauge his attitude. He had his peaked cap pulled low, and his dark glasses hid his emotions. A sliver of sweat trickled down from his temple to his jaw. He gave me a humorless nod as I held out the papers with my passport on top. He glanced at it, checked the motorway screen sticker and number plate, which was Swiss, and then waved us through without speaking a word.

I heaved a sigh of relief, pressed the accelerator, and watched as the checkpoint shrank to a dot in the rearview mirror. I was full of gratitude that I had an acceptable passport.

"Yes!" I punched the air.

"You are happy?"

"Indeed I am. If they had looked at your papers closely, there could have been a lot of difficult questions. I'm too tired for that. I just want to get home."

It was after midnight when I pulled into the underground car park. Leddicus was too tired to be surprised as I pushed a button on my sun visor and the garage door rolled up. The lights came on automatically, which was very comforting, but he just sat there in a daze and yawned every five minutes.

The lift whisked us swiftly up to my flat, and it had never felt so good to be home. I showed Leddicus to his room and gave him a quick tour of bathroom and kitchen, including the food in the fridge. *Ah, the joy of having a housekeeper as part of the rental agreement.*

He followed me slowly, not saying a word. He might have been sleepwalking. I opened the door to his room and popped the case on the floor.

"Get some rest," I said. "See you in the morning."

I was asleep before my head hit the pillow.

Chapter Nine

Universities and Magazines

I woke with a start, disorientated at being back in my flat. The sound of the TV blaring in the other room had jerked me awake. I stuffed the balls of my fists into my eyes, rubbed hard, and then checked the time.

"5:00 a.m." said the stark green oblong.

I got slowly out of bed and padded into the living room. Leddicus, washed and dressed, was sitting on the sofa. He gave me a cheery wave as I stumbled in.

"Look! I made your talking box work!" He was obviously very proud of himself.

"TV," I said grumpily.

"Yes, yes, and I stood in your rain machine and made it hot."

"Shower," I said automatically. "Do you know it's five in the morning. What planet are you on?"

Without waiting for an answer, I shuffled into the kitchen and filled the kettle. I sat at the kitchen table and drank a cup of scalding instant coffee while I waited for the real stuff to percolate. My sleepiness gradually started to fade.

Leddicus appeared in the doorway. "You are ill?"

"It's too early. I only went to sleep five minutes ago." I took another slug of coffee. Unfazed, he nodded. His excitement at being out of the hospital was not to be dampened.

"I am hungry, please."

I stood up slowly and began rifling through the cupboards, not expecting to find anything after my long absence, but the wonderful housekeeper had stocked them with a few essentials. I waved a box at him.

"How about muesli?"

"That is good."

I plonked dishes, spoons, mugs, milk, and sugar onto the table and motioned for Leddicus to join me. Leddicus helped himself to a huge bowl of muesli as I poured him some coffee. I pushed it toward him, determined to commence his education in this essential beverage. He picked it up and sniffed it. His nose wrinkled in disgust. He took a small sip and let out a yelp as he scalded his tongue.

"Here, have some of this and this." I doled out milk and sugar into his mug and stirred it vigorously.

He tried again. The nose still wrinkled, but not quite so much at the cooled sweetened version.

"It's essential. You have to drink coffee if you are to be part of the twenty-first century."

He nodded doubtfully, took another sip, and then began to spoon muesli into his mouth as I outlined our program for the day. I explained as simply and briefly as possible that I was furthering my career, earning money, and generally promoting myself because I knew him. I said I was his first point of contact with the rest of the world. I also went over what happened when we left the hospital with the paparazzi, telling him that it could happen again. He put down his spoon and looked quite worried at this point. I ignored this and forged on.

"Today, I am taking you to my university, where there will be a deputation ready to meet you." I knew there were words he would not understand, but hoped he'd get the gist of it. "There is a magazine I write for, and the editors want to meet you. After that, there will be a press conference. Newspapers and magazines are very interested in you, so this will be a chance for them to meet you in a controlled environment."

Archiv had been in contact with a number of historical publications, and everyone was keen to attend. E-mails had been flying back and forth between me, *Archiv*, and a broad spectrum of media outlets ever since I had implied that Leddicus would be discharged from the hospital. Mr. Bernard had been adamant that I should not tell them the date.

I poured more coffee and pondered the weird situation. Here I was, sitting over an innocuous bowl of muesli with an allegedly two thousand-year-old man, trying to prepare him for a press conference of which he had no concept. All he knew was that the people who would be there would be like the paparazzi who had chased him out of the hospital. I was pretty certain he thought they were going to kill him with their flashlights, boom mics, and video cameras. What he didn't realise was that they could kill him verbally and destroy my reputation if he got it wrong in a few hours time. Leddicus seemed sanguine about all the issues I presented to him and understood more than I expected.

"If you can make some money, that's good. You have helped me a lot, and you've been a good friend. If knowing me helps you do this, I am happy. You deserve it."

I wasn't so sure. Every now and then, my conscience would prick me slightly, but then I would imagine my name on the front of magazines and drift off into a fantasy of fame and fortune. I cleared the table and dumped the dishes in the sink. I was too preoccupied to deal with washing up now. My mind was racing. I wondered about the best way to brief Leddicus for the press conference. When I asked *Archiv* to set it up weeks ago, it seemed such a good idea. Now I was having second thoughts. To say I was anxious would be an understatement.

I left Leddicus in front of the TV while I showered and dressed. Then I sat down and, over my third coffee, made a list of all I needed to take to the university. I was so nervous. I didn't want to leave anything to chance. I systematically packed my briefcase and double-checked that my laptop had the files we needed, and then we set off to the car park.

Sometimes, the childlike fascination Leddicus had for all things modern was quite endearing. Today was not one of those days, and I had to bite my tongue as he pressed the button for every floor as we entered the lift. We made slow progress, eventually entering the car park in twice the time it should have taken.

Leddicus jumped a little as we walked into the pitch-black car park and the full glare of the automated lights kicked in. We headed toward the car, and suddenly, from behind a pillar, a young woman stepped in front of us. I jumped in shock. Leddicus sensed my alarm and stepped back nervously. She was tall, lean, and immaculately dressed in grey trousers and a red jacket. Her straight, chin-length blonde hair shone in the stark fluorescent glare.

"Hello. Are you Gerhardt Shynder?" she said in English

"Who are you?" I snapped, unnerved at the fact that someone had been deliberately standing still in the dark, tricking the sensors into thinking the garage was unoccupied.

She didn't answer. She stepped past me and stretched out her hand. "You must be Leddicus the Roman." She smiled brightly and pumped his hand with enthusiasm, much to his consternation and surprise.

I was furious. "Who are you, and how did you get in here?" I asked curtly in a low voice.

She smiled at me sweetly. "Sorry if I startled you. A car just drove out, and I dodged in through the door before it closed." She talked gently and soothingly. "I really wanted to meet you and Leddicus." She smiled at him again, and he returned her smile this time.

I was not smiling. "You're a journalist!" My blood was beginning to boil.

"Well, not quite. I'm a stringer for a number of UK newspapers. I'm currently based in Switzerland. I only get paid when I file a story, so I'm sure you will help me by letting me have a quick chat with Leddicus."

"Not likely!" I stepped in between her and my man. "If you want, you can come to the press conference at St. Gallen Uni at lunchtime today. Ask your questions there."

"Well, yes, I plan on being there, but I was hoping to have something a little more exclusive."

Leddicus unexpectedly joined in. "What is your name?"

"Julie. Julie Bright." She smiled and oozed sweetness.

"Why don't we have a talk later on? My friend Gerhardt wants to go to the university now, but perhaps we could meet somewhere. Perhaps you could come back here later."

I was desperate to take back the initiative. My heart was pumping, and I could see all my financial deals with the media slipping away, not least because of the instruction from Mr. Calabro of no exclusive contact.

I tried to buy some time and turned to Leddicus. "Let's make arrangements after the press conference."

Julie, still calmly in full control of the situation, also spoke directly to Leddicus. "I would like that, and I'll speak to you later." She again shook hands with him and then strode off toward the closed garage doors. She turned to look back at us, still smiling and waiting for us to drive out so she could leave.

Anger surged in me, at myself for being so unprepared and at Leddicus for being so friendly. I yanked open the car door, stabbed the key into the ignition, and fired up the engine. I revved it menacingly as I waited for the doors to rise. It seemed to take forever. The tires screeched on the ramp as I flew past Julie, who waved cheerily and then followed us out, ducking under the already-closing doors.

I sighed deeply. *This day is not going according to plan.* I fought valiantly to calm down as we drove to my university, and I was almost back to normal as we walked through the main doors. I was relieved to find no journalists waiting to pounce on us. When I entered my study area, I was not surprised to see quite a gathering comprising my tutor, the head of department, three of my fellow researchers, the university principal with his secretary in tow, and two of the editors from *Archiv*.

I introduced Leddicus to each one in turn, and then we sat in a circle of chairs that had already been positioned for this purpose. *This may help Leddicus to prepare for the press conference.* I instantly dismissed the idea. *These people will be polite and kind, unlike my vulture paymasters.*

My colleagues, as expected, were kind and patient. They took turns to ask Leddicus the questions I had asked him many weeks before. They didn't cover any new ground, but it was good they were finally meeting him. It would not do any harm to my credibility. After an hour, the secretary wheeled in the inevitable coffee and biscuits, a tradition to which Leddicus would soon become accustomed. He smilingly accepted the proffered cup of coffee. Only I would notice the slight wrinkle in his nose as the dark liquid flowed over his unaccustomed palate.

With the pleasantries over, my heart began to beat at twice the normal rate. It would soon be time to move into the big hall and participate in the dreaded, yet essential, press conference.

"Joseph, you are well?"

"Eduardo, my friend, I am very well. I have good news. She has made contact."

"Excellent, excellent. And the Roman? He is well?" Eduardo flicked open a silver cigarette case, extracted a cigarillo, placed it between his fleshy lips, struck a match, and lit up, all with his left hand. He squinted at his watch and took a long drag.

"As far as I could ascertain, he is, and she thought she was well received. She will push to meet them later."

"Well received? By Shynder?" Mr. Calabro's eyes darkened.

"No, he was furious. The Roman warmed to her."

"Good, good. We must meet for dinner soon, Joseph."

"Indeed we must!"

Chapter Ten

Meet the Press

We moved en masse to the university conference hall. The press was already assembled, milling about, gulping at uni coffee out of polystyrene cups, jotting in notebooks, adjusting cameras, clutching at mics, and taping down cables. The hall was full of all the clutter that is the press. George Christen, our press officer, was darting to and fro, confidently directing operations.

Our entourage entered via the stage door and filed to their seats at the long, gleaming oak table. We sat behind the names already placed there. The principal, Gianluca Wicky, sat next to Leddicus who was most definitely enjoying himself. He was goggle-eyed at the array of mics and crowds of people before him. The prebriefing session had done its job. He was relaxed and at ease. As we took our seats, so did everyone else, and the hall fell silent.

The principal stood up. "Ladies and gentlemen of the press, welcome to Zurich University. Thank you for coming. I am Gianluca Wicky, the principal here. I trust you all have copies of our official press pack. If not, please wave a hand, and our press officer, George Christen, will ensure you receive one." He quickly ran through the health and safety elements and finished by reminding everyone, "all mobile phones on silent, please. During the briefing, any calls received must be taken outside the hall."

I was breathing in short gasps, and my nails were digging into my palms. In an effort to calm myself, I tried to distract my angst by remembering the agony I went through night after night working with George to get that pack prepared. He was such a stickler for detail. He came up with stuff I never thought of, and he had a checklist as long as my arm.

Everything will be fine, I kept telling myself.George has dotted and crossed everything that needs dotting and crossing.

Gianluca went on to introduce each person on the platform and give job titles. "I would remind you, as stated in the press pack, that Leddicus has only recently learned to speak English. All questions should be directed through me. We have allocated twenty minutes for questions that are not already covered in the pack, but may add on a little extra time should it be necessary." He extended his hand to where George was seated at the end of the table. "George Christen, our press officer, will draw the questions to a conclusion at the appropriate time. I would ask that you are patient and bear in mind that this is all quite daunting for Leddicus."

Patience! Might as well ask a school of sharks to be patient at feeding time.

It started well enough, and once it got going, I began to breathe a little more easily. As the questions proceeded, it was obvious that the press did not really know what to ask. All the basic information had been covered in the press pack, including how old he was, where he said he was from, and his extraction from the mountain. The questioning kicked off with a focus on what he thought of the modern world with some very enjoyable discussions about technology. Leddicus was in his element on that subject.

He was then requested to compare the cultures. This was quite a struggle for him. He had only known the hospital and, in the last twenty-four hours, the motorway to St. Gallen. Gianluca swiftly moved them on from this subject.

A lull fell for a moment. A guy toward the back jumped to his feet and raised a hand. Gianluca nodded for him to proceed.

"David Yates, *Daily Mirror*, London. Is Mr. Leddicus aware it is impossible for someone to live two thousand years? And no one has ever been frozen in an ice block and lived to speak about it?"

After Gianluca conferred briefly, Leddicus answered, and I was so proud of him.

"I agree with you on both counts. It is impossible. Please note that I have not claimed anything. But I know where I come from, who I am, and how I got on your mountain. What happened after that, I do not remember or understand. If you will please explain it to me, then I am listening!"

A roar of laughter went up from the floor. David Yates sat down again and scribbled rapidly. There were a few safe questions about the tests and results of tests carried out at the hospital, which Gianluca directed to me for a response.

A woman in the centre of the floor raised a black-clad arm. She held it up rigid and still. Gianluca pointed to her. "Go ahead." He smiled.

"Pricilla Morrison, Vatican press corps."

Hells bells. I didn't think they had a press corps. But, of course, that was naïve of me. Had I been in the know, I would have been aware that they had a huge press corps of highly efficient and very experienced media staff. I shifted nervously in my seat.

"My question is to Mr. Palantino. Are you a Christian?"

After checking with Gianluca, he responded, "I am not aware what one of those is, so I don't know how to answer that."

Pricilla remained on her feet and jumped straight in with a follow-on. "Isn't it true that you Romans have been terrible to people who follow Jesus of Nazareth, you have been extremely oppressive, and you have many, many slaves?"

The palms of my hands were damp, and I wondered how he would deal with that one.

Gianluca and Leddicus talked quietly before Leddicus responded, "The ruling authority always needs to stay in control. Without it, there would be . . ." He hesitated and spread out his hands. He was searching for the words. "A lot of trouble. Anything that does not fit in with what the empire says will be dealt with firmly. But from what I have seen, ordinary people are very willing to acknowledge the claims of Jesus of the Jews. In fact, Romans, Jews, and Greeks followed him."

He finished speaking, but Gianluca spoke quietly into his ear. "Sorry, I forgot that bit. Yes, there are a lot of slaves, but what should I do about that?" Laughter rippled quietly across the crowd.

Pricilla still remained on her feet and quickly asked a third question. "So you must be a Christian then?"

Leddicus was just as quick. "I refer you to my previous answer."

Wow! He could be a politician.

Gianluca looked at his watch and started to fidget. I knew he would not be comfortable in this environment. His natural leaning was toward slow academic discussions, not the fast-paced, pushy media he faced today. George, on the ball as usual, scurried along the line of chairs and crouched behind Gianluca's chair. Leddicus sat smiling, enjoying himself enormously, and got ready for the next question.

It should have been obvious to the Morrison woman that her turn was over and things were being wrapped up, but the Vatican hack was very pushy and still on her feet. Her voice carried above the hubbub. "I have a question for Gerhardt." She used my first name as if she knew me. "You seem to be controlling this event and fronting the research into Mr. Leddicus. I would have thought you were far from qualified for this position."

My brain raced to try to find a response. She had really put me on the spot, and I had no idea how to answer this question. Before I had a chance to open my mouth, George stood up, clapped his hands, and announced, "Ladies and gentlemen, thank you for coming. We will not be taking any further questions."

Immediately, every press hack in the room jumped to their feet and started speaking at once. Some close to the platform attempted to get in one last question. Others gabbled into mobiles or live-feed mics. George just held up his hands and shook his head at the questioners. Then he began herding the platform party out of the hall.

We decamped to the study area. My hands were shaking as I poured myself fresh coffee. I half-heartedly waved the jug at the assembling group, and everyone nodded avidly. We all slumped into the chairs and clutched at our coffee mugs as if our life depended on it, that is, apart from Leddicus.

He was standing in the doorway, grinning. "That was good fun. What interesting people. When can we do that again?"

Never will be soon enough for me. I just managed to keep from saying it aloud. I let out a nervous laugh instead.

"Do you know who they were?" I said to him.

"No, who are they?"

"The ones who scared you half to death when you left the hospital!"

"Oh!" He continued to grin.

George summarised the session as a form of debrief and then made his exit in order to support the other press officers. "The phone will be ringing off the wall." He hurried away.

A few independent conversations broke out, and we let the tension seep away. I sipped at my coffee, and I was just starting to feel normal again when I remembered that leech Julie Bright. I had seen her lurking at the back of the hall. I was relieved that George had rescued me from that Rottweiler from the Vatican.

Who does she think she is? Her attack on me was personal. I guessed I had a lot to learn about frontline journos. That was how they worked. They rattled you so you let your guard down. I gave myself a mental shake and resolved to toughen up.

"Hey, want some of these?" I handed a plate of grapes to Leddicus. "You okay to hover here for a half hour?"

He took the plate with a nod of thanks. "Where are you going?"

"Need to do some planning with Serge Graty, my tutor. Shouldn't be too long."

"You come back here and get me? Then we can meet Julie."

Oh, dear. I had hoped he had forgotten about her.

Chapter Eleven

The Press in the Shape of Julie Bright

We finally climbed into the Audi and headed for home. I was drained. I didn't have a scrap of adrenaline left, but Leddicus was as high as a kite. I wondered if he had overdosed on grapes. He'd been up since four thirty in the morning, but he was chatting incessantly. Every time I tried to say something, he would talk over me. I was tired and frustrated. I needed to bring him up to date with the outcome of the meeting with my boss, but I opted not to push for a serious discussion. Neither of us was in the right frame of mind. I felt as if I had a very short fuse, and he was in no mood to concentrate. He was dazzled and delighted with all the attention, so I kept my mouth shut. I needed to keep him onside. Today had been out of control enough. Before I had a chat with Leddicus, I needed a double espresso to raise my game.

I forced myself to try to address the Julie Bright problem. I'd spotted her at the press conference. She sat at the back, asked no questions, and smiled serenely straight into Leddicus's eyes. I had a bad feeling about this stringer. *Could she be intent on stringing Leddicus and me along?* I consoled myself that I hadn't made any definite arrangements for the meeting, only my throwaway comment that we could meet after the press conference.

"Damn!" I spat as I turned into the entrance of my car park.

There she was, leaning contentedly against the wall while chewing on an apple. As soon as she spotted us, she smiled and waved. I scowled. Leddicus opened the window and stuck out his hand to wave back at her.

He leaned out and beamed from ear to ear. "Hello, Julie! Hello! How nice to see you."

My mind was in a whirl. I just wasn't prepared. If I were welcoming, she would take advantage of Leddicus. If I were gruff, Leddicus would resent it. He had really taken to her.

How could he be so stupid and not see through her cunning plan? How could I be so naïve? I should have realised she would stalk us. I knew I must keep her out of the flat. That was top priority, or I would never get rid of her. I stopped the car, blocking the entrance, and climbed out to chat to her.

"Nice to see you." I shook her hand. *Perhaps I could string her along.*

She pumped my hand vigorously and smiled her serene smile.

"Leddicus and I need to freshen up. We've been out all day."

"I'll come up and wait." She instantly suggested and bit another big chunk out of the apple with her straight white teeth.

"No doubt, but we need some space, thanks." I stepped beside her and pointed down the road. "There's a tavern down there on the right, about a block away. Can't remember the name, but there's only one. Meet you there in . . ." I checked my watch. "Twenty minutes," I said it as firmly as I could muster, but with a smile. I hoped she would be in no doubt that it was not open for negotiation.

"I don't need to freshen up. I'll go with her." Leddicus scrambled hastily out of the car.

"That's lovely." She took his arm.

My shoulders sagged wearily, and thoughts of a soothing coffee and a long, hot bath swiftly disappeared. *Damnation. I am going to have to be two steps ahead of this minx.*

"Let me park up, and I'll be with you." I jumped back into the car. I fumed as they started to walk off together toward the tavern.

I slammed the car into gear and skidded into the nearest space. That would upset the car park committee. All the spaces were allocated. Julie and Leddicus were only alone five minutes before I fell in step with them and joined the conversation.

We settled ourselves into a cozy corner table, and a waiter soon appeared to take our order. Julie settled for fresh orange juice. I ordered an excellent glass of red wine for Leddicus, and I had my usual lager.

As I had been unable to have a quiet word with Leddicus and I didn't trust this woman as far as I could throw her, I decided to put my cards on the table right from the off.

"Miss Bright, there is a problem with this interview. It can go no further until we set up a beneficial deal for Leddicus, plus there are exclusivity issues."

And what about what I want?

"Julie, please." She touched me lightly on the shoulder.

"I don't mind helping Julie," Leddicus chipped in.

"That's not the point." My heart sank.

I had blundered badly by not thinking ahead. I should have planned for such instances. I should have talked to George and got some mentoring on how to deal with such issues. Now I was in it, I would just have to wing it and hope for the best. And then there was the exclusivity issue that Mr. Calabro had so clearly laid down.

"What is the point?" he echoed back.

Yet again, Julie jumped in. "I don't want to spoil any deals for you and Leddicus." There was an almost-imperceptible emphasis on the you. "In fact, I think I can probably point you in the right direction. You need a publicist. I have many press contacts in London. I know just the right person to set good things in motion for you both."

Oh, she was good, so good. Cunning as a wolf, but in an angel's skin.

Before I could speak, she continued. Her voice was soothing and reassuring. "I would just like some more detailed background on stuff that is already out there." She laid her hand on my forearm. It took me all my energy to not slap it away. "I'm sure your story—or, rather, the Leddicus story—will continue to develop. Please let me ask Leddicus some personal questions. You listen in. If you think it will infringe your future deals, it will be off the record. I'll withhold that information, and in return, I will introduce you to an excellent publicist."

There is no such thing as off the record. George's mantra had been drummed into me over and over when we worked on the press pack.

I hesitated as I thought about the possibilities. A publicist might be useful. I opened my mouth, but before I could form the words, Julie plunged straight in. "What are your immediate plans?"

"Leddicus and I haven't even talked these through yet."

"No problem. Let me hear them, and we can discuss them now." Leddicus beamed.

I held up my hand. "Miss Bright, Leddicus, before we go any further, I need to make a phone call."

"Fine by me." She took a sip of orange juice and smiled at Leddicus.

"Do I have your word to not speak of anything that was not at the press conference before I return?"

She stuck out her small, well-manicured hand and shook hands with me. "Deal." She gazed up at me innocently with her sea blue eyes.

Out in the street, I called Mr. Calabro. I was a little afraid of him and expected a sharp rebuff when I explained the situation. I was more than a little surprised when he responded, "Is that so? I agree to this, but no one else. You must let me know exactly what is discussed."

"I will be unable to monitor the conversation and e-mail you by eight o'clock tonight."

"No problem. Let us not be so restrictive about that deadline, and it need not be every day. Now that you are in such a different routine, let us agree to three times each week." The line went dead. I stood looking at my phone. My breathing eased with relief at the tone of the conversation.

I rejoined Leddicus and Miss Bright.

"All okay?" she asked sweetly.

"All okay." I took a huge slug of my lager. "It's agreed, but I must see any copy before it is published. Now where were we?"

"I wondered what your plans were."

I felt a little easier now, so I relaxed. "I had hoped we could fly to Rome tomorrow. Leddicus is keen to go there. Then on to London. I'm setting up appointments at some of the London universities. Leddicus will be available to answer questions."

A light went on in Leddicus's mind. He let out a sound that I had come to recognise as surprise.

"Fly to Rome!" He banged the table with his hand. "That is the strangest, craziest thing I have ever heard. Shall we grow feathers and become human birds?"

The tension was eased as Julie and I laughed together.

"If you agree with the plans, then you'll see," I said.

"Yes, yes, I agree. This I must see! How very exciting!"

"Okay," I said to Leddicus, "do your interview. Afterwards, I'll discuss with this young lady about this London publicist friend of hers. Then we need to get to bed, and I still need to book the flights." I shrugged in defeat I realised I was fighting a losing battle. Without upsetting Leddicus, I seemed to have no choice.

I sat back and got stuck into my lager. Julie dived straight in, and as Leddicus responded, her pencil flew across the page with neat shorthand strokes. She questioned him about his early years, growing up, his family life in Caesarea Philippi, his wife, his children, and his parents. It was all stuff I had heard before. I guessed it was already out there, either on the Web or in a magazine. I was reluctantly impressed at her attention to detail, bringing out things I would not have considered. Leddicus was in his element, thoroughly enjoying telling his story. While this went on, I had ordered and almost finished a second round. I was beginning to feel intensely drowsy, and I hadn't said a word.

"I'm a Christian, and I know that, in your time, Christians often called themselves 'people of the way.' Perhaps we are saying the same thing but from a different time zone."

"Whoa there!" I came round with a jolt. "That's enough for tonight. It's late, and to be honest, I'm still recovering from that Vatican journo."

To my surprise, Julie complied, closed her notebook, and leaned back. "Mmm, she was a bit of a Rottweiler, wasn't she?"

Leddicus looked at me quizzically, but I just shook my head. I was too tired to get into an explanation. Julie, in her normal one-step-ahead style and taking advantage of my addled brain, offered us a ride to the airport in the morning. I gladly accepted, desperate to get home. I knew I still had much to sort out.

"We can discuss details on the way," she said brightly. "And if you let me know what area you are staying in London, I'll sort accommodation." Julie gave me her business card. "Text me your flight details. Then I'll know what time to pick you up."

Even in my weary stupor, I felt uneasy at the cozy relationship that was rapidly developing. Something nagged at the back of my mind, but I was too worn out to analyse it. We said our good-byes outside the tavern, and I was relieved that Leddicus finally seemed to be talked out.

Back home, I set Leddicus the task of rummaging us up a snack while I booked flights for Rome and London. I found a hotel near Rome airport, and it was far more than I should be paying, but I just wanted to get it sorted. I sat back from the laptop and massaged my neck and head, which I now felt I was in over.

I texted Julie, set the alarm, and sank into a dreamless sleep.

Chapter Twelve

Visit to Rome

The alarm startled me awake at six thirty. I knew that if I turned over for five extra minutes, I would not wake up again until the flight had flown off without us. I rolled out of bed and headed for the shower. The hot spray conjured me back to semi-normality.

Even in my somnolent state, I was quite organised this morning. I was sitting at the table with my requisite bowl of muesli and halfway down my second cup of coffee when Leddicus breezed in.

He sat down and gave me a broad grin. "Rain machine very good!"

"It's a shower," I said with a half-smile.

The TV news was prattling away in German in the background. I changed it to an English language station so Leddicus could be included. As it came into focus, there was Leddicus smiling back at us. He jumped up and ran to look closely at the screen. He poked at it. He still hadn't got to grips with modern technology, and he was fascinated.

"Yesterday's press conference," I said.

He ignored me and continued to watch intently. The news moved onto the next item, but he was glued to the screen, still enraptured.

"Come on. Shake a leg. We have to make a move." I hit the off button, and he looked quite crestfallen.

"More me?"

"Maybe later."

The news coverage surprised me. Although Leddicus has been around for months now, the newscasters made it sound as if he had appeared yesterday. The news could sometimes seem timeless. *I guess that's what sells. Old news is no news.*

We tidied up the flat and finished packing. On the dot of ten o'clock, the entry phone buzzed.

"Morning! It's Julie!" the speaker crackled.

I punched the intercom button. "Come on up. Floor four. Flat twenty-nine." I injected warmth into my tone, but felt reluctant as I buzzed her in. *What choice did I have?* It would be downright rude to keep her waiting in the lobby. She was, after all, saving us from lugging our cases to the Bahnhof and the cost of the fares, although I had a niggling suspicion that it would end up costing me much, much more.

She strolled through the door and looked cool, calm, and fresh. Leddicus gave her his best smile.

"Thanks for coming. Much appreciated." I tried not to be overly familiar.

Leddicus chatted to her while I made a careful check that I had everything we needed: passports, tickets, laptop, and camera. I checked each item off my list. Then I wandered round the flat, double-checking just to be sure I hadn't missed anything.

"Okay, I think we're good to go."

We each grabbed some of the bags. I double-locked the door, and we stepped into the lift together.

Leddicus claimed the front seat, and we settled down for the drive to Zurich airport. The caffeine effect was lessening, and I felt like nodding off, but I checked myself. I knew I should stay awake to keep track of the conversation. An animated Leddicus told Julie about seeing himself on TV.

"There will be more of that. You're on the front page of a heap of papers this morning." She maneuvered skillfully around a broken-down truck.

"I am?" He grinned from ear to ear.

"You are, in many different languages, and I managed to file my story late last night, just in time for the first editions of the London papers. They should be available at the airport."

The deeper I got into this circus, the more disconcerted I felt. I wanted the recognition and the financial rewards, but all the hassle of the publicity, paparazzi, and pressure did not sit well with this academic. I knew I had to get used to it, but I was a long way from that. It still made me groan. I wished I could just embrace it, but all

I truly wanted was a quiet life. I guess that was why I opted to study history in the first place.

I snapped back into focus. It suddenly dawned on me what she had just said. "You sent off copy? Have you forgotten that I asked to see any copy before publication?" My anger was rising.

"I know, but I didn't think a call at one in the morning would have endeared me to you. I have a hard copy in my briefcase for you."

I was still angry. "That's not the point. Couldn't it have waited?"

"No, Gerhardt, it couldn't. A day late on this story might as well be a year late."

I couldn't argue with that so I didn't try. "How on earth did you manage to get your copy in last night?"

"Bit of a workaholic. Just couldn't rest until it was in. I e-mailed it over at about two in the morning and then gave the night editor a call. We wrapped it up in about half an hour."

"Did you have time for a lie-in this morning?"

"Heck no. Was up and doing by six thirty. Had a mass of e-mails to wade through." She paused as a stream of brake lights flashed on in the three lanes ahead. She slowed to a crawl and then rummaged in her pocket. "Thought you would be interested in this. I have a cutting service subscription, and this popped through this morning." She handed me a crumpled piece of paper.

"It's from a free paper they give out at London Tube stations. I think it's called the *Metro*. My guess is that it's also appeared in other publications."

London Metro News
14 June 2009
Bug Resurrected after 120,000 Years
Scientists have brought a newly discovered bug back to life after more than one hundred and twenty thousand years in hibernation. It raises hopes that dormant life might be revived on Mars. The tiny purple microbe, dubbed *Herminiimonas glaciei*, lay trapped beneath nearly two miles of ice in Greenland. It took eleven months to revive it by gently warming it in an incubator. The bug finally sprang back to life and began producing fresh colonies of purple-brown bacteria.

I smoothed out the creases and read about a bug found in ice samples extracted from three kilometers under Greenland. A team from Pennsylvania State University, headed up by Dr. Jennifer Loveland-Curtze, carried out a range of experiments. Apparently, after what they calculated to be a nap of one hundred and twenty thousand years, they woke up the bug.

"Fascinating!" The article genuinely surprised me. "But this is a microscopic bug. Leddicus, well, he's a full-grown man."

"Mmm, I had noticed, but it's something at least, and there is ongoing stuff about cryogenics, which I think is a load of nonsense. At least I did until I met Leddicus. There are lots of things that science tells us are sorted and understood, but then they go and find something that stands it on its head." The traffic was still at a snail's pace. She was rummaging in her pocket again, and she handed over another dog-eared press cutting.

"From one of the German papers, a flute made out of the tusk of a prehistoric monster. I thought they existed before people were around. Yet here we find they are making music from its tusk!"

"Weird. Whatever next." I folded up the paper neatly after I had skimmed the article and smoothed down its curled corners. "Perhaps the Italian researchers will suddenly find all the answers to the curiosity that is Leddicus, and the world's press will turn from cynics to believers and be all over us like a rash. We'll never eat or sleep again. You included!" I laughed.

She laughed with me as she swung on to the slip road leading up to the drop-off zone for departures. After parking neatly in front of the Alitalia airline section, Julie popped open the boot and helped stack our bags onto a trolley.

"Thanks for the ride. Much appreciated." I shook her hand.

Julie hugged Leddicus and kissed both cheeks. He just grinned and attempted to return the kisses, but just got in a muddle and bumped her nose. She stepped back from him and gave him a friendly shove on the shoulder.

"You have fun now!" She turned to me. "I'll see you in London!" As we walked toward the terminal, she called after me, "Don't forget to text me your flight details, so I can collect you from Heathrow."

The huge automatic doors gobbled us up, and we stepped onto the moving pavement and glided along through the busy airport toward the escalator. I pushed the trolley onto the gently sloping grid. It gripped into place, and we were gradually transported up to the mezzanine. I loaded my credit card into the check-in machine, and it spat out the sticky tape for the luggage. I fixed these on our cases and popped them onto the conveyor, which transported them away to the appropriate loading bay. I was very smug about the whole Swiss airport experience. *We are pretty slick us Swiss.*

Leddicus was starstuck. The sights and sounds so overwhelmed him. He kept stopping and looking around. His mouth was wide open. I was constantly grabbing his sleeve so he didn't get lost. He was so amazed that he was struck dumb. There was too much to see and experience, and he didn't have the capacity to question me about anything. I couldn't begin to imagine how it must be feeling to see all this for the first time. In a strange way, I envied him.

We were finally on the main walkway running the length of the airport. The massive windows gave a panoramic view of the airfield. He stopped and glued his face to the glass. It misted up, and it was a full two minutes before he turned to me.

"Big cars!" he said breathlessly, full of wonder and adrenalin.

"Not cars. Planes. We're going on one of those to Rome."

"How will it get there? The roads? They are too small!"

I bent my arm level with my waist, extended my hand flat, and then gradually moved it forward and upward. "They fly."

He pinned his face to the glass again and then looked back at me, incredulous. "They flap those bits at the side? That's not possible. How can they fly?"

I laughed aloud at his simple logic. "I don't know. I'm a historian, not an avionics engineer. But trust me. They do. Sorry to drag you away. We're on a schedule here."

He walked alongside me. His eyes never left the airfield for a second. He stopped a few times, and when I grabbed his wrist to hurry him along once, I could feel his pulse pounding like a sledgehammer. The only adrenaline rush I got at an airport is my fear as I watch my case being trundled away on the conveyor belt. I worry I will never see it again. I usually packed my whole life into that one medium-sized, battered case.

We arrived at the departure lounge, and I sat as far away from the newspaper sellers as possible. I had seen enough smiling pictures of Leddicus and grumpy ones of me for a while. I thought perhaps I should hunt down a paper with Julie's copy in, but she had given me a hard copy. I wanted to keep as low a profile as possible. I rounded up some strong coffee. Even though it was early, I got Leddicus a small glass of wine. He looked more in shock than when I first saw him at the hospital. He gulped at it gratefully, and he was still lost for words. Every now and then, he would turn to me, open his mouth, say nothing, shake his head, and take another sip of wine.

Our flight was called, and we headed toward the Alitalia gate. We walked along the boarding corridor, and the only hint that might tip off Leddicus that we were getting onto the plane was the smiling, welcome hostesses. I found our seats and parked him by the window. I fiddled with the hand luggage, stacking it carefully in the overhead lockers, while he, still bemused, gazed out of the window. I helped him fasten his seat belt. Then he watched fascinated, without comprehension, as the hostesses went through their safety procedure dance.

He still had not spoken. The engines, which had just been purring quietly as we gradually maneuvered into position, now roared and throbbed to full throttle, getting louder and louder. Leddicus looked at me, panic-stricken. He could feel the pressure building as the engines revved up notch after notch, moving to optimum thrust. Then we were suddenly galloping down the runway. The airport buildings flew past as the Boeing 747 pummeled down the tarmac. I pointed to the window, keen he did not miss a thing.

"Look! Look!" I said as the runway began to shrink away.

He gasped and held his breath. His hands gripped the armrests. His face turned white. He bent his nose against the glass. He stared and stared as the airport and city rapidly shank to Lilliputian size. Soon all that could be identified was patches of green, slivers of blue, sparkles of ice white, and arching far to the endless horizon, the vivid azure sky. Then the cork popped, and he did not stop gabbling. The questions gushed out of him and tumbled over each other. They were mixed up and all wrapped in a heady ten-year-old-boy excitement. My head began to ache, but I was not complaining. His animation was intoxicating and infectious, and unless he had an Oscar for acting, it was the real McCoy.

The flight passed swiftly as he jabbered on, pressed every available button, and visited the toilet seven times just so he could walk up and down the aisle. He chatted to everyone he passed and never once ceased to grin like a Cheshire cat.

The plane began its descent to Rome airport, and Leddicus became silent again. The view from the window held him spellbound. Rome customs and passport control were simple and straightforward. Fortunately, my fears were unfounded as our cases came shuffling toward us on the conveyor belt.

We stepped out of the airport into the midafternoon sun, and I gave Leddicus a gentle punch on the arm. "Welcome to Rome, mate!"

He just stood there and gazed around, looking bemused and astonished. He lapped up the view from the window as the taxi transported us to the hotel. I was pretty exhausted, but Leddicus, although having a lull in questions, was as full of bounce as a six-week-old puppy.

Even though it was the last thing on my mind, once we had stowed our cases in our room, we went back out and wandered around the streets for a while. He had so many questions and yet more questions. I patiently answered him for about fifteen minutes, and then I stopped and held up my hand.

A mock frown was on my face. "Enough, my friend." I put my finger to his mouth. "Zip it for a bit, okay? I've run out of steam for today."

He shrugged, looking a little crestfallen, and then smiled and nodded. We wandered silently around the back streets for an hour or so. I eventually found a small, quiet tavern in which we ate a delicious supper. As we chatted about the plans for the next few days, we polished off a bottle of excellent Chianti, and I finally managed to get an early night. I was snoring by nine o'clock.

Ready for shipment. Outlets all agreed. Finance transfer to Swiss repository scheduled for tomorrow morning.

Eduardo hit reply and typed rapidly. His slender fingers flew across the keypad.

Further seventeen items acquired as requested. To be included in third shipment. Confirm acceptance. Finance is double due to extended journey time and minimum length of production. Will call at 1:00 a.m. tonight with further details.

The encrypted e-mail blinked away. Eduardo checked his watch. He had two hours before the call. He opened the ever-growing manuscript document on his laptop and began to work. The new copy received yesterday was most excellent. This would help to fill in some of the gaps and put a bit more meat on the bones.

Chapter Thirteen

The Tour

Leddicus and I strolled down to the hotel breakfast room and arrived at a leisurely nine o'clock. We wandered along the buffet table and selected a plate of hot croissants, some tasty-looking jams, and a cafetière of coffee. Although Leddicus opted for orange juice, his taste buds were still making up their mind about coffee.

The coffee was exquisite. *Nobody makes coffee like the Italians.* I drank it contentedly as I munched through two croissants, spread generously with the jam that was as delicious as it looked.

"We are going sightseeing today." I reached for another croissant. "I'm going to take you all around Rome." Leddicus just nodded thoughtfully. "We'll get a bus. We can sit on the top deck and get great views."

I ate thoughtfully for a while and relished this relaxing breakfast. My spirits were high, and I was feeling in holiday mood. "Some of the places I want to take you, we'll get a taxi, and of course, we'll do some walking. So eat hearty. You need the calories." Leddicus just gave me a half-smile. "This is modern Rome, but we will see some buildings that were here when your father lived here. I plan to finish up our tour at the Coliseum and then the Vatican."

I hope we don't bump into that obnoxious journo.

Leddicus remained unusually quite, but I was in such a good mood that I didn't really pay much attention. I was just enjoying the opportunity to relax. I polished off a fourth croissant, mopped up the crumbs, and pushed my chair away from the table.

"Ready for another little adventure?" I said.

Leddicus dutifully followed me out of the hotel, and we stepped into the teeming, noisy hurly-burly that is modern Rome. We crossed the road and got on a bus opposite the hotel. It was heading in the right direction for the centre of Rome. Horns honked incessantly as cars, buses, and taxis jostled each other for space on the busy roads. The pavements were crowded with people, smiling, dawdling, rushing, chatting, and sitting in pavement cafes sipping coffee. It was a riot of colour, sound, and movement.

Leddicus finally broke his silence with a long, loud sigh. I looked over at his gloomy face. He sighed again.

"This is not what I expected." He looked out of the window. The twin creases between his brows looked like two deep scars.

"What did you think it would be like then?" I was a little irritated at his gloomy persona, as I was looking forward to our day out.

"I expected to see people dressed like me, well, not like I am dressed now, but how I used to dress."

"Hmmm, we unfortunately came in a Boeing 747, not a time machine," I said a little flippantly. I had tried as best I could to explain that this Rome was two thousand years further on than the Rome he knew.

"I know what you told me about the time gap, but I somehow really thought . . . I guess I hoped I would be at home . . ." he tailed off with another long sigh.

I put my hand on his shoulder and tried to imagine how he felt. My irritation evaporated as I realised that perhaps his excitement on the plane was not just about flying, but perhaps also because, in his limited understanding of what had happened to him, he had thought he would find something familiar, something he could recognise. But all he found was more confusion.

"I'm sorry. Can't imagine how hard it is for you. I hope Rome will help you get a grasp of things. This part of Rome is modern and bustling, but I'll show you some of your Rome, not the people, of course, but some of the buildings at least."

We got off the bus outside the Pantheon, the temple to all gods.

"This was built between 118 and 125 AD, a bit later than when your father was here. I think Hadrian, the Roman emperor, had a hand in its construction, so it appeared after your ice encasement."

Leddicus tried a smile and failed. His gloomy frown dominated. A look of hopelessness crept into his eyes. I gave a mental shrug.

Nothing I can do. He'll have to get on with it. This place is amazing. I wandered around, absorbed, with Leddicus trailing listlessly after me. I was revelling in the wonders of this ancient structure. I stood gazing up at the huge bronze doors as we moved into the cool, marbled, cylindrical main structure. The massive dome arched above us.

"Do you know this was the biggest dome in the world for almost fifteen hundred years?" I was so animated that I didn't notice his little shrug.

We moved on to look at the Forum.

"I know you haven't been here before, but I understand this is a huge complex of ruined temple arches and basilicas. Apparently, this was the ceremonial, legal, and social centre of ancient Rome. It was a sort of business centre at that time."

Leddicus gave a wan smile. "I guess I would have been here with my swatches of cloth."

This trip was not turning out to be much fun. Nothing seemed to stir him out of his apathy. I had my camera with me, and I rummaged it out of my backpack.

"Hey, let me take your photograph. Stand by that pillar." I was tempted to say, "So you can show the folks back home," but caught my undiplomatic words before they spilled out.

Leddicus showed a bit of interest in the camera, and after I had taken a few shots, he had a go at taking a picture of me in front of the ruins. The first attempt chopped off my head, but he got the hang of it after a few more attempts.

The midday sun was starting to sizzle so we ventured down a shady side street and found a quaint pavement café. I intended to introduce Leddicus to the inevitable Italian pizza. He decided on the fish one with anchovies placed artistically across the bubbling cheese base.

He bit into it tentatively, chewed a little, and then smiled broadly for the first time all day. "It's good!" He bit off another huge chunk. He said something else, which I couldn't decipher because his mouth was so full. "Do they make oyster ones?" he asked once he could speak more easily.

"Oyster pizza? Now there's an idea, but I doubt it."

He sipped at his wine and looked into the middle distance. "When we went to the baths, oyster sellers would always be there. We used to get so hungry after a long bath, and we would eat lots of them."

I wasn't keen on oysters or anchovies, but I was pleased to see that the pizza was cheering him up. I pondered why this deep melancholy had enveloped Leddicus since our arrival in Rome. Perhaps his sense of loss was beginning to take hold, but I was no counsellor, especially not of ancient defrosted men.

I paid the bill, and after his mention of the public baths, I thought it would be good to make that our next stop.

"These are the Baths of Diocletian, and they once covered thirty-two acres." I tried to get the conversation going, but realised he probably had no idea what an acre was.

"Very interesting. I like them." But his brow remained unusually furrowed. This was quite a dramatic change of attitude for someone who was normally bright, happy, and inquisitive.

We walked around in silence, with me clicking away and pointing out various interesting features, but getting little or no feedback from a leaden Leddicus. The midafternoon slump was hitting me, and the only solution was coffee. I squinted at the guidebook and stabbed at a page.

"That's where we need to go, a recommended eatery just opposite the Coliseum, our next port of call." I hailed a taxi and showed the driver the page. He nodded and started gabbling away in Italian.

The taxi stopped right opposite the Coliseum. The driver shrugged placidly as a barrage of horns blared at him while we alighted and paid. We climbed up the stairs and went out onto the veranda. The immense building loomed into view. Its pillars and porticos stretched far above us. We both caught our breath at the size of it.

Leddicus sat down facing the building. Buses, cars, and scooters went hurtling past below us, but he just stared at the Coliseum. He was so absorbed that he simply nodded when I suggested coffee.

I was enthralled, and monologued enthusiastically at Leddicus. "Even compared to modern stadia, it is still an amazing feat of building expertise. It was built around 80 AD and held fifty-five thousand spectators. It was constructed to Emperor Vespasian's great plan without modern machinery, although there was undoubtedly an endless supply of slave labour to enable its completion."

"I heard about this building. The plans were being discussed everywhere. The news even reached us in Caesarea Philippi. It was causing quite a stir." He sipped his coffee and screwed up his face at the taste. I pushed the bowl of sugar toward him and offered him a spoon, miming to him to add some. He did so and then stirred it slowly.

"Why do you say AD when you say the date? Does it have a meaning?"

"Yes." I reached into my pocket for my sunglasses. The sun was dazzling up here. "It means 'after Christ.' In your language, it's *Anno Domini*."

"*Anno Domini* means 'in the year of the Lord,' not 'after Christ.' Or as I would say, *Anno Domini Nostri Iesu Christi*. In the year of our Lord Jesus Christ. How strange. Do you believe he is still alive?"

"I'm afraid, Leddicus, that the conversation has now lost me. Let's go and have a look inside the Coliseum."

"We can go in?" He looked surprised.

"We sure can for a couple euros."

We bravely dodged the murderous traffic, arrived safely on the other side of the road, and followed the signs to Coliseum tickets. I bought a couple, and we shuffled along behind a gaggle of Japanese tourists as they photographed everyone and everything at every step. The arena opened out before us. The enormous size of it had me in awe. I took a few pictures and then turned to point something out to Leddicus, but found him looking more miserable than ever.

"Whatever is the matter?"

"This place, so incredibly big, such an amazing structure. But I feel so much death, death of slaves, death of animals, and death of people. For what purpose? As a spectacle, just for entertainment? We are so wicked. It makes me very sad." He put his face into his hands and bent his head.

Today, I had no idea what to say. I normally got worn out giving explanations to his constant inquisition. Today, I had only watched him become more and more sad. He had given me no explanation of why, and I had no idea what was in his head.

“Do you want to go back to the hotel?” I felt helpless and more than a little frustrated. I very much wanted to get a good look at this amazing place.

“No, no, I should see what you have brought me here to show me. Where to next?”

Outside, I flagged down a taxi, and we clambered in. “St. Peter’s Square.” The car zoomed off with the horn honking loudly at every opportunity.

“We’ll just go to Vatican City. Then we’ll call it a day.” The taxi screeched to a halt at a red light, and I gripped my seat tightly. “It’s the smallest country in the world.” I could tell that Leddicus was only along for the ride and to please me, but I soldiered on. “The official language is Latin, your language. The population is only eight hundred. The people who live there have their own Vatican City passport. It even has its own post office.”

Leddicus looked out of the window and paid little attention to my monologue.

“The Pope lives here. He’s the head of the Catholic church, so I guess you could say this is the centre of Christianity.”

Leddicus picked up at the mention of Christianity, “Christian? Like Julie Bright?”

“Oh, did she say she was one?”

“Yes, but she didn’t explain much. She said she would tell me more in London.”

“Well, I guess she knows more about it than me. Anyway, this is its centre. Unless I’m mistaken, here we are.”

The taxi drew sharply to a halt. “Vaticano.” The driver snapped. The meter showed the fare to be twenty two euros.

I handed him twenty five euros and switched seamlessly into Italian. “Grazie, tenga il resto.”

The Vatican must be the most perfect mix of ancient and modern Rome. There were superb fountains and the vast marbled square for official papal occasions, but beneath each beautifully sculpted ancient statue were subtly positioned equipment to ensure a flood of light when the sun went down. And as we walked, I noticed CCTV cameras, blossoming on every convenient high point.

We strolled around St. Peter’s Square, past the obelisk, and into the shaded area at the edge of the square. We eventually ended up in the main auditorium. Obviously, a service of some kind was in progress. I heard music and saw lots of people in very large hats. It was all a little lost on me. I didn't know how to explain it to Leddicus, but as he was watching it all so dispassionately, I doubted he wanted an explanation.

A procession began its slow progress from the rear of the building with censers of incense swinging. The pungent scent floated through the building. The guy at the head of the column looked haughty and grim-faced. He walked erect despite his huge headgear. Many men followed. Their long black robes swished against the marble floor. There was so much pomp and ceremony that it wasn't really the place to have a chat. There appeared to be many people with scrunched-up faces as they concentrated on the rituals. I wondered what Leddicus was thinking. I wondered if a scrunched-up face was a prerequisite for being spiritual.

I was getting bored and hungry, but I thought it might be disrespectful to leave mid-service. I could see smart-suited men dotted around, Vatican security no doubt. They apparently mustered very quickly in the event of misbehaviour or even innocent friendliness, according to a friend of mine who was swiftly ejected when he smiled at and patted one of the priests on the shoulder. Leddicus stood still and listened intently. The ceremony was eventually over. The column of dark-robed men snaked slowly out of the building, and we were back in the sunshine.

I broke the silence. "What do you think of it so far?"

He took a deep breath and seemed to be choosing his words more carefully than usual. "That was very interesting. The ceiling in that building we were just in, the painting was amazing. How did the artist do that?"

"It took him years. I don't think his neck was ever the same afterward."

"The soldiers? Are they soldiers? They dress very strangely compared to everyone else."

"Swiss Guard. They're from my country. That's their traditional dress. Wait until you see the Beefeaters in London."

"Beefeater?" Leddicus scratched his head.

"Doesn't matter. Go on."

"The ritual in that place, the singing, the talking—I don't understand it. Is this the Christianity that Julie spoke of?"

It was my turn to scratch my head. "Sorry, Leddicus. I have no idea. Julie is the one to ask. I don't understand it either. My Latin is—"

"No, no, that's not what I mean. I understood most of it, but it was what they said. I didn't like it. They did not seem like the people of the way." He shook his head dismally.

"Your Latin held up then. That's good. Why didn't you like it?"

"So formal, so controlled, so controlling, all those strange clothes. They talked about Jesus the Christ. That I know . . . but . . . but . . ."

"What's wrong? Go on." I had no clue what he was on about, but I was trying hard to understand, if only to try to help him out of his gloom.

"It's as if they want to control us, the way that Rome does. Rome watches over every aspect of our lives. We are controlled with very tight boundaries. That is how those people in there spoke, but perhaps I have misunderstood."

"I'm sure Julie will be able to help you understand a lot better than I can. Let's put this to one side now until we get to London. I'm tired. Let's go back to the hotel, get some rest, and then see what tomorrow brings."

"I'm ready for that." Leddicus gave me the best smile that I had seen from him all day.

We grabbed a taxi, and I felt relieved to be back in the cool hotel foyer. I suggested we turn in early and left Leddicus at the door to his room. I ordered up a snack for supper from room service and caught up on the news as I ate. I snuggled down into bed and fleetingly wondered what Leddicus had eaten and if he even knew about room service, but sleep rapidly overwhelmed my conscience.

Chapter Fourteen

Change of Plan

I sat and ate breakfast, thinking of nothing much, except how unusual it was that Leddicus was so late. He invariably arrived well before me. By the time he wandered in, I had eaten my fruit and muesli, and I was on my second cup of coffee.

"You okay?" I reached for a croissant, but noted his frown.

He sat down opposite me and shrugged. "I think so. I found yesterday a hard day, although I am not sure why."

I found all this emotional soul searching enormously tedious, but thought I had better at least try to get inside his head, if only to keep him onside. "What was so hard? The walking?" I ventured.

Leddicus gave me a wan smile. "No, no, that was fine. I can't explain what it is, even to myself." He reached for the cafetière. I always knew he was distracted when he opted for coffee. "Not sure how you say it in your language. Lost, I think. Yes, that's it. I think I felt lost, or perhaps I feel I have lost something." He absentmindedly kept spooning sugar into his coffee. "I don't know what to think or feel. Nothing was as I expected. I know you showed me things from, as you put it, my time, but it was all strange. And the Christian thing, in that little country, I didn't get that either. Nothing makes sense to me in your world."

I didn't speak for a while. I looked at him in what I hoped was a calm and confident manner, but inside, I was casting around for some words of comfort and trying to keep a lid on my patience. "Sounds hard for you. You must feel quite mixed up," I said rather lamely. "We could tour around again today and see more of the sites, but we don't have to. Obviously, you can't deliver your letters to Caesar's court. It's not there anymore. What would you like to do? See more sites? Go shopping in Rome? It's your call."

Without any hesitation, he shook his head. "I think I have seen enough of the stuff from my time." He slowly stirred his coffee. "It upsets me, confuses me, and makes me afraid and lost. What else could we do?"

My great idea to visit Rome, which I hoped would be fun and fascinating for both of us and especially Leddicus, was turning out to be quite the reverse. Instead, fear and confusion filled him.

"We could go shopping." I hesitated from expanding on this suggestion, as I saw his quizzical expression. I guess shopping two thousand years ago did not have the broad appeal it did in the twenty-first century. "I originally planned we would be in Rome three days, but as you are not keen, we could go to London earlier."

A broad smile finally lit up his face, "Yes, that is good. I would like that."

At last, something had calmed him down. He was so pleased with the idea that he instantly got his appetite back and started lashing butter onto a croissant. As he ate, I explained what I needed to do to make the change of plan happen. I would have to Google cheap flights. The adverts dotted around the hotel indicated that Stanstead rather than Heathrow would be the cheaper option. And, of course, I would need to check with Julie to ensure these new plans would fit in with her schedule.

I wasn't sure if it were the mention of Julie, but Leddicus, now tucking into a huge bowl of muesli, stopped with his spoon halfway to his mouth, grinned from ear to ear, and nodded. "Yes! Yes! Let's do all you said."

"Okay!" I drained my cup. "Give me a couple hours to sort stuff. Can you amuse yourself? I'll come and get you at about . . ." I checked my watch. "Midday. Then we'll grab some lunch and at least have a bit of a wander round modern Rome."

Leddicus nodded and gave me a genuine smile. "After I finish breakfast, I'll watch TV."

At last, I am on the right track.

It didn't take me long to set up the flights to Stanstead for the next morning.

"Hello, Gerhardt. Nice to hear from you. How is it going in Rome?" said a chirpy Julie when I phoned her office.

"Not too well. I think Leddicus is suddenly facing reality and feels miserable. He wants to change the plans and come to London earlier."

"Oh, sorry to hear that. Poor guy. When are you coming then? Hope it's not today. I'm manic."

"I've booked the nine forty to Stanstead tomorrow. Don't worry about coming to get us. We'll make our own way. Isn't Stanstead a bit off the beaten track? So it's probably a long way from you."

"No, not at all. Stanstead's great. Much closer. You should be landing at around midday, yes?"

"Something like that, but, really, it's fine. We can get a taxi."

"No, I insist. Hang on. Let me check." She put the phone down and came back a minute later. "It's fine. I can rejig my eleven thirty, and I'll bring forward the hotel booking to tomorrow night."

"Thanks. That's great."

"Oh, yes, remember I mentioned my publicist friend. I'll check and see if I can fix up a meeting early evening at your hotel. Also, I should also be able to show you around London for a while if you like?"

"Well, if you're sure, thanks for everything." We said our good-byes, and I sat there bemused. Yet again, Julie had taken over.

No matter what I want to do, I always end up doing what she wants me to do. What is it about her that is so irritatingly compulsive?

The afternoon was pleasant and uneventful. We wandered around the centre, dipping in and out of a variety of shops. Leddicus got some of his old curiosity back and bent my ear with questions about the many strange wonders he encountered. We took an early supper in one of the many restaurants on the bustling Roman streets and then jumped in a taxi back to the hotel. I decided we had done Rome.

"Londonium and Julie tomorrow." I opened the door to my room. "Breakfast at eight. Can you be packed and ready to leave as soon as we have eaten?"

"I am happy," said Leddicus as he walked down the corridor to his room.

"Eduardo, I have good news."

"Joseph, I was going to call you later, but the day has been intenso."

"A meeting is set for tomorrow. I will finally meet our Roman."

Eduardo pressed the phone to his hear and spoke quietly, "The copy I have received is excellent. I am making good progress. I will e-mail you at length on the issues that need fleshing out."

Eduardo leaned back in the chair, away from his desk, and tossed a small ball of paper into the wastebasket in the corner. His office was Spartan, but he liked it that way.

"How is Marguerite?"

"She continues to nag me to get air-conditioning, but still I resist."

Joseph chuckled. "Still as stubborn as ever."

"What can I say?"

"I look forward to your e-mail and the suggestion of a date when we can have dinner."

Eduardo smiled thinly. "Yes, I should be over in about three months unless the circumstances change."

"I will call you in a few days when I see how things are panning out."

"Until then, ciao."

Chapter Fifteen

Londinium

I was texting Julie exact flight details as I wandered down to breakfast and walked slap into Leddicus on the stairs. He grinned and gave my shoulder a friendly punch, a trait he had picked up from me. He then started wiggling his thumbs, imitating my very slow texting skills.

"Oi! Cut that out." I was pleased to see him in better humour. "This is your get-out-of-jail-free text."

"I'm going to jail?"

"Yes, if you don't hurry up!"

We didn't linger over breakfast, and we were soon on our way to the airport in the hotel courtesy coach, which Leddicus insisted on calling "a very big car." The coach meandered from Hotel to hotel and filled with those who, like us, were airport bound. We made slow progress, stop-starting through the early morning Roman traffic.

I had checked in online and printed off our boarding passes, so there were no holdups at check-in. We were flying Cheapojet. *How I hate these discount airlines, but, as I'm not on a limitless budget, I must grin and bear it.*

Walking past the newsstands, I was relieved to see no pictures of Leddicus, once again confirming the fickleness of the press and its customers. Leddicus was excited about flying, and he was beginning to get hyper again, so I avoided buying him anything caffeine impregnated as I purchased some drinks while we waited.

"No coffee for you." I joined him at the table where he was guarding the cases. "Apple juice okay?" Leddicus nodded. "That's good. That's what you've got."

"It's not called Londinium anymore. Just plain old London now."

"I think I heard about it once from a Roman centurion who bought some of my materials for his family. He had been stationed there for a short while."

"It's a lot bigger now, huge in fact. Fifteen million people live there."

"It must be very busy."

"Certainly is. Lots of traffic jams. Never quiet. Julie has offered to take us sightseeing if you fancy it."

His big smile said yes before he vocalised it. "That's good. Very good."

"It's very different from Rome. Even though it was a Roman base, you can't see much of their influence."

Takeoff; once again, thrilled Leddicus, and he stared out of the window in fascination and awe. He calmed once we were above the clouds, so I thought I would have a little fun and introduce him to Coke. He made the strangest face, just like a child when he first samples a new taste or texture. He was unsure at first, but the sweetness sold it to him.

I was rambling on about how much money the company made from selling Coke all over the world when the mention of finance sent him off on a completely different track.

"I am so upset I could not deliver those letters, and I have not done any business for my father and family."

I was sorry that, yet again, he was disturbed by something that was so long ago and far away and about which he could do nothing. *But I guess that's the way the mind works when it can't quite grasp the present reality.*

"I did take some orders for cloth in Malet. It was a good order. I hope the messenger I used managed to get the details back home, and I hope my family made a good profit."

I was only half-listening, but my keen interest in history caught the tail end of what he said. "How did you send word to your family about that transaction in Malet?"

Leddicus regularly surprised me. This was one of those times. He suddenly went into a strange mood and clammed up. A slightly fearful look was on his face.

"What's wrong? What's worrying you?" I urged, but he looked out of the window and began curling the flight magazine into a tight tube.

"Leddicus, what's up?"

"I do not want to get people into trouble," he said.

"Of course not, but help me out here. Why would people get into trouble for taking information from Malet?"

He didn't answer. He stared out of the window for a couple minutes and then, looking decidedly glum, turned to me.

"I really do not want to get people into trouble," he said hesitantly.

"I don't understand how someone could get into trouble for taking a message?"

"The thing is—" He stopped and looked at me. His eyes were wide.

"It's okay. Go on."

"The thing is that there are official slaves from Caesar's palace who carry messages for the emperor to high officials around the empire. Some of them are in the way. Because I, too, am in the way, I know them through my father, who was a centurion. I knew who would be going where and when. For a few denarii, these slaves carry messages for other people."

"Sounds like a great arrangement to me."

"I met one of these slaves at a meeting, and he was happy to do me the favour of taking my message along with the message from the emperor. But you do not understand. They are on official empire business, and they would be in bad trouble if anyone found out they were carrying messages for my father."

"Ahh, now I get it. Moonlighting."

"What!"

"It loosely means doing other work when you should be doing the work for which you are paid."

Leddicus nodded solemnly. "Yes, that is exactly it."

"I'm sure he'll have been okay. Try not to worry. Even though it's very recent to you . . ." I tailed off, not wanting to finish the statement.

Fortunately, he was distracted as the landing gear clunked into position. Leddicus immediately looked out of the window and gazed at the patchwork quilt of Essex countryside unfolding below him.

Cheapojet flights often disembarked directly onto the tarmac. This was one of those times. Leddicus stood looking up at the aircraft with his mouth open.

"One of the smaller ones." I gently took hold of his elbow and steered him toward the terminal buildings.

Stanstead was heaving with midweek passengers, and the cases took forty minutes to arrive on the conveyor belt. We waited and waited until it seemed that everyone else had taken their cases and moved on. I was beginning to think my fears were bearing fruit. Then I spotted our cases, mine battered and his pristine, jerking drunkenly toward us. I sighed with relief as we headed for passport control.

A grim-faced clerk sitting in the booth made a point of looking very carefully at the travel documents, especially Leddicus's. My heart was skipping a beat with visions of being held for hours. But he was just being thorough and eventually handed back the paperwork with a curt nod.

We walked into the main arrivals area. There to welcome us was a smiling, waving Julie Bright. "Hey, what was the holdup? I've been here for hours!" She said with mock fierceness. Then she hugged Leddicus warmly and shook my hand. "I'm so pleased it's not Heathrow. I've spent many unhappy hours hunting down my lost car in those endless car parks. Okay, let's get this show on the road."

Julie was not talking much at first as she navigated through the various roundabouts, but we were soon out of the airport and into the heavy lunchtime M11 traffic.

"I've booked you into quite an upmarket Brentwood hotel. It's not London exactly, but it's near here, so it's very handy."

"Thanks for that. Good to know it's close. Why is the traffic so heavy?" I asked.

"M11 is always a nightmare, apart from late evening."

"Needs more lanes, doesn't it?"

Julie laughed. "Then there would be even more traffic. Anyway, Joe Simmons is already at the hotel. I've given him some background, and he's done a stack of preparation and planning. I can't believe what he's achieved in such a short time. He's keen to meet you both. Are you okay with that? To meet up straightaway? Or are you too tired from the journey?"

"Fine by me. Just give me a jug of coffee, and I'll be ready. Okay with you, Leddicus?"

"Whatever pleases you, Gerhardt. Thank you, Julie, for sorting it all out and coming to get us."

"My pleasure!"

"Did you sort it all out with your talk machine?" Leddicus put his hand to his ear.

"Mobile," I said automatically.

"That's right. I wonder what we did without them." She turned into the hotel car park.

I wondered how they set up such meetings in Roman times. I wondered what had happened to the slave carrying the message for Leddicus.

Julie parked, and we piled out of the car and headed for reception.

"I think you'll like Joe. He's not your usual PR chap, more honest than most."

We checked in, threw the cases into our rooms, and arrived in reception in record time. Julie was sitting on a plush sofa, deep in conversation. As soon as she saw us, she stood up and did introductions. Joe Simmons stood up. He was slightly built and had a huge shock of pure white hair. He seemed friendly, but had eyes that took in every detail. I was sure he was assessing the business situation even as he smiled and shook our hands.

We made our way to the hotel restaurant. A very smart, attentive Polish waiter ushered us to what seemed to me to be one of the best tables in the place and handed round, large, leather-bound menus. The wide variety bemused Leddicus, but Julie was soon walking him through the choices. No prizes for guessing what he eventually chose. It was fish, of course. He couldn't get enough of it. We all put in our requests, and Joe ordered a bottle of expensive wine.

Once the orders were placed and the wine uncorked, Mr. Simmons got straight down to business. Julie didn't get involved in the conversation, at least not the one between Joe and me. She and Leddicus were chatting away like old friends. I tried to pay attention to what both Joe and Julie were saying, but failed on both counts. Joe thought I wasnt interested. I mentally pulled myself together and apologised to Joe, giving him a feeble excuse about being a little tired. I then gave him my full attention as he explained the facts and figures on what seemed to be a new business empire focused around Leddicus.

Joe had planned a month-long tour to many of the major UK cities. The tour included seminars, discussion forums, university lectures, and small group sessions. My head spun as he showed me the prices he was charging for the pleasure of our company. To me, they were exorbitant, but he assured me everyone had agreed without complaint, and the tour was almost fully booked. All expenses were taken care of: hotel, travel, and food. He was taking a cut, which did not appear to be excessive, but I was being paid a very generous fee as project manager.

It took a great amount of willpower for me to stay in my seat. I wanted to jump onto my chair, punch the air, and yell, "Yes!" Instead, I nodded sagely and said to Joe, "Thank you. You have thought of everything."

My thoughts were racing. I was calculating madly. With my research allowance from St. Gallen University, the contract I had with *Archiv*, and this, I would be financially comfortable for the foreseeable future. I ran a very brief summary past Leddicus as we all tucked into the biggest bowl of fruit I had ever seen outside of a market. Thanks to Leddicus, someone had allowed him to decide on dessert for all of us. As he piled his plate with grapes and melon, he smiled from me to Julie and back again.

"It's all good to me." He sliced off a chunk of pineapple. I wasn't sure if he meant the tour or the food.

"Joe, I think Leddicus should have his own bank account and be included formally in the contract?" Julie said this kindly, but her tone left no room for doubt on my part or Joe's that this had better take place or there would be trouble.

What a bossy, interfering girl.

But Joe just nodded thoughtfully and agreed.

"Yes, yes, of course. I will draw up the final version today. It will be ready for review and signature tomorrow." Joe bent down to his briefcase and slid in the wedge of papers. He then topped up our wine and raised his glass. "To a successful tour!" He beamed. We clinked our glasses together and smiled at each other a little self-consciously.

The whole afternoon had drifted away most pleasantly. With good food, excellent wine, and the possibility of a big, fat cheque winging its way to my account, I sighed with contentment. The restaurant, which at one point was almost empty, was now starting to fill up again with evening diners, many of them suited, booted, and tapping away on their smartphones. I assumed they were businessmen, certainly not out for a romantic evening. We moved from the restaurant to the coffee lounge. Apart from us, everyone seemed to be on their own, clicking away on laptops or talking loudly on mobiles, oblivious of their surroundings as they set up their next big deal.

With coffee over, Joe Simmons took his leave. "Good to meet you, Gerhardt, Leddicus." He shook our hands warmly. "Julie, I'll call you tomorrow. We can arrange where to meet to get sign-off for the contracts."

He strode off toward the car park, and we were left adrift in a sea of clinking coffee cups, beeping laptops, buzzing phones, and the gentle lilt of canned classical music. Leddicus yawned, and I stood up to stretch my legs.

"Is the hotel to your liking?" Julie asked Leddicus.

"It is most wonderful. It's all a little . . . well, it's overwhelming."

"What are your plans for this evening, Gerhardt?" Julie got to her feet.

"I must write my copy for *Archiv*, or I will miss the deadline. I have some uni work to catch up on. Perhaps, Leddicus, you could watch TV?"

"Fine by me." He was always eager to please.

She signalled to the waiter for the bill. He was at her side in an instant.

"The man who left, he paid already, ma'am."

She smiled at him and gave him a tip. I couldn't quite see why. "Would you like me to show you round London tomorrow?"

It wasn't my first time in London, but a local guide always made things easier, even if that guide was Julie Bright. I smiled. "Yes, that would be most helpful. Shall we see you around nine thirty tomorrow. Is that Thursday? I'm losing track of time."

"Fine by me." She turned to Leddicus. "Do you really want to just watch TV? Are you hungry? I don't know Brentford too well, but I know a couple good places to eat if you would like a change of scene."

Leddicus did not need asking twice. "I am a bit hungry."

"You're always hungry," I said.

"Gerhardt, I don't mind entertaining Leddicus for a couple hours while you do your work."

And there it was again. The trap snapped tight. I didn't want to let Leddicus out of my sight with anyone, especially not to the care of Julie Bright. But I felt at a loss to explain why. Without seeming small-minded, I could not come up with a good enough reason to prevent this unwelcome outing. Yet again, I was painted into a corner.

"I guess that's okay. He is a grown man of two thousand and thirty, so I'm sure he can look after himself." I smiled weakly.

"Don't worry," she said. "He'll be just fine, and I'll bring him safely back to the hotel." Her tone was relaxed, but carried a hint of condescension. Leddicus was already heading off toward the exit. Julie patted me on the shoulder. "He'll be fine. See you in the morning." She followed Leddicus through the revolving doors.

Everyone was happy except me. I headed off to my room and laptop with an inexplicable sense of foreboding.

Eduardo read the document for the third time, checking and rechecking every detail. He attached his slightly adjusted version to an e-mail and began to type.

Joseph, There are no loopholes in this that I can see. Is there no time to run it past a lawyer for a last sweep to make sure it is watertight? Are you sure you can't delay the meeting? E

He clicked send and then turned his attention to the growing manuscript. There was no e-mail from Shynder today, but no matter. There was more than enough research material to keep him busy.

Forty-five minutes later, a response pinged into his inbox.

Eduardo, I have already done that. Have you forgotten Charles? I had him check every line. Fear not. It is watertight. I confirm my e-mail is encrypted. No worries on that score. J

Chapter Sixteen

Tour Two

Good grief! She's here already! Julie Bright, large as life, was sitting with Leddicus and scanning the menu.

I was feeling a tad groggy. Maybe a little too much wine while I worked, so I was not as alert or good humoured as usual. I was not in the mood to be sociable before I even had my first coffee.

"Good morning!" they said in unison.

I pulled up a chair and mumbled something incoherent at them. They smiled at each other with a hint of conspiracy. I poured some coffee and drank half a cup before I spoke.

"You're here already," I said to Julie

Julie nodded and smiled her broad, perfect smile. Her blonde hair was scooped up, framing her flawless elfin-shaped face. She was casually dressed in faded jeans and a simple black T-shirt.

"I hear it is a big city, so we have to get started early. Julie promised to introduce me to a full English whatever that is."

What the heck. If you can't beat them, join them, and it's a good hangover cure.

"I'll go for that, too, and then I won't need to eat for the rest of the day." I poured another large coffee and held it in both hands to comfort and steady me.

Two huge English breakfasts were soon placed on the table. Julie didn't indulge and settled instead for healthy fresh fruit. Leddicus's eyes widened at the plate of food.

"Wow! What is all this? I know that's toast." He dumped a large dollop of marmalade in the middle of the plate. "What's so funny?" He looked up at Julie, who was laughing at his choice of condiment.

"Welcome to a full English. Sausage, bacon, eggs, mushrooms, beans, tomatoes, fried bread." I pointed at each item on his plate with my fork. "But I'm not going into more detail. I'm suddenly ravenous."

The food was delicious, and I surprised myself by clearing my plate. I began to feel more normal as the food mopped up the alcohol.

"What's the plan then? You pair have obviously been plotting."

"Well," she said, "I'm driving us down the North Circular to the nearest Tube station. Then we can head into Leicester Square and walk to Trafalgar Square and down the Mall to Buckingham Palace. Maybe you would like to go to the Palace of Westminster?"

"Palace? We're going to a palace?" asked Leddicus.

"Two actually. One where the queen lives, and the other where our government meets. It's also called the House of Commons and Parliament."

"Let's not get bogged down in explanations this early. We can fill in the details as we go." I finished my second coffee. I clapped my hands and jumped up, suddenly wide awake as the caffeine kicked in. "Come on, you slackers. Let's move."

I signed the bill, and we were ready to go.

"We need to fit a meeting with Joe into our schedule," Julie said as we headed out through reception. "I've already spoken to him, and he can fit us in around lunchtime. Will that be okay?"

I nodded. *Let's get this thing sewn up.* I hoped the London tour would be a better experience for Leddicus. He was certainly in a much better mood. I was not quite sure why. Perhaps because it was not Rome. Or it was a place he had never been. Or, most likely, it was the Julie factor.

We parked and headed into the Tube station.

"I've got us some oysters," she announced

"I'm still full from the English, but I can always eat an oyster," Leddicus responded.

Julie giggled. "No, not the edible kind. These." She handed us each a blue plastic wallet with the word "Oyster" emblazoned on the front. "These are very handy and cheap for Tube travel. Watch and learn."

"I don't think I want to eat this." Leddicus turned it over. A slight smirk was on his face.

Julie marched toward the barriers and patted her Oyster wallet on the round yellow pad. The barriers obediently snapped open. Leddicus trotted swiftly after her, but the barrier snapped back and clouted him in the groin.

"The pad, Leddicus. Hit the pad." Julie pointed.

So hit it he did. We heard a resounding clunk, and he joined her in the seething melee of people. I brought up the rear, and we stepped onto the packed escalator.

A grumpy commuter snapped at us. "Right! Keep to the right!" He barked as he pushed past and ran down the stairs.

We meekly obeyed, and the long escalator trundled us down, down, down. Leddicus looked across at the opposite escalator, and his mouth fell open as he watched everyone rising upward. He looked back at me. His mouth opened and closed. Trying to get the words out, he was goggle-eyed.

"They are flying! How? What? How can that be?"

It was too noisy to give him a proper explanation, so I pointed to our escalator and then briefly explained that they weren't flying. There was another escalator opposite us, doing the reverse of the one we were on, taking people up instead of down. All the way down, his mouth stayed in a small surprised circle. His chocolate button eyes remained glued to the crowded escalator opposite.

We reached the bottom, and Julie scurried into the rabbit warren with us pounding after her. She stopped occasionally to glance at the maps on the wall. It was so crammed with people that I kept a close eye on Leddicus. I didn't want us getting separated. I did wonder why Julie was in such a rush. I was sure she was hyperactive!

We got to the platform just as a Tube pulled in. The doors opened, and people flooded out, jostling to get through the waiting crowds. We could only just squeeze into the packed carriage before it hurtled into the tunnel.

"Wow, so hot, so busy."

"Perhaps it was not a good idea to catch the tail end of rush hour," Julie said over the clattering din.

"What's rush hour?" said Leddicus.

"The hour when everyone rushes to work."

We stepped out into the fresh air in Leicester Square and paused to catch our breath.

"That was amazing, so amazing!" Leddicus gabbled. "And I thought our festival markets were busy."

Julie smiled. "It's mad, isn't it? But so quick. It's a Tube, a train that goes underground. There are trains that go above ground, too."

"How did you know where to go?" he asked.

She pulled a Tube map out of her pocket and handed it to him. "All the Tube lines are colour-coded. You decide where you want to go and see which line the station is on."

"How come all the tracks are so straight? The Romans must have built them!"

We laughed at his candor.

Julie explained, "Not quite. The Romans were long gone by the time the Tube was built. A guy called Harry Beck drew up simple maps at the beginning of the last century, ironing out all the wiggles." Leddicus, obviously impressed, handed the map back.

So many concepts, new ideas, and strange technology constantly bombarding him. It's a good job he is so laid back, or it could send him mad.

"Let's get across the road. I want us to get on one of those." She pointed to a topless bus with a huge union jack painted on the side.

We settled into our seats and relaxed. The tour guide described all the points of interest as we drove slowly through the heavy traffic. Leddicus craned his head over the side and listened intently. Julie helped by adding a comment here and there. I could tell it was going to be a good day. I let out a sigh of contentment. After forty-five minutes, we hopped off the bus and onto a boat for a trip down the Thames. Leddicus was as happy as a kid in a sandpit.

As we got off the boat, we decided to take a black cab to Piccadilly Circus for our meeting with Joe Simmons. Leddicus was pleased about everything today, even by the spaciousness of the back of the taxi.

"This is like a Roman chariot. And he . . ." He dropped his voice to a whisper. "Drives like a charioteer who is late for the battle!"

We stepped out of the cab, and Leddicus caught his breath, dazzled by the array of electronic advertising that enveloped the area. I wished I had brought my camera to catch his expression. He was so bowled over he couldn't speak. He just stood staring with his mouth wide open. Julie and I grinned at each other,

"I wonder if this is what is like to have a kid," she said to me.

"We'll come back tonight," I said to Leddicus. "It's even better then."

Joe's office was just off Piccadilly Circus, at the bottom of Jermyn Street. It was small but classically expensive. Joe had all the paperwork ready, neatly contained in a smart folder with a subtle corporate insignia on the top left.

"It's all as we discussed. I'm here until three thirty. It would be good if we can get this signed off today."

I shook his hand. "Thanks for turning this round so quickly. We're going to have a working lunch to go through it. Then we'll come back to sort out the signatures."

"Great. I'll see you later." He buzzed through to his secretary, "Lisa, please send in my next appointment."

We found a table in Prezzo's. While we waited for the pizzas to arrive, we started reading through the contracts.

"You were right about Joe. He knows his stuff. I'm impressed." And I was. Even though I had many doubts and misgivings about Julie, she had certainly come up trumps by introducing me to Joe.

Julie sipped at some iced water, and the food arrived.

"Mmm, this looks even better than I hoped," I said.

I sliced up the pizza and ate with my fingers so I could keep reading. I was careful not to splodge the paperwork with tomato sauce. Alongside the venue details, there were contact names, numbers, and e-mails, but these were only backup contacts. Joe's office would be doing all the follow up, the reminding, the chasing. The tour sessions he had arranged were based on the format of me introducing Leddicus and giving the background and other pertinent details for thirty minutes. Joe suggested this be done using PowerPoint and offered help in its compilation. After that, the session would be handed over to Leddicus for questions, with a wrap-up session from me. Each session would probably last roughly ninety minutes. Most of the venues were universities or colleges with one exception. In Liverpool, we were booked into a Roman Catholic seminary for priests. I was unsure what to make of that one.

I was still amazed at the booking costs that covered expenses and accommodation. There appeared to be more money out there than I had ever imagined. With Joe's office taking care of all the details this meant I would only need to concentrate on keeping Leddicus fit and healthy and making sure we were both well prepared. The tour commenced on Monday of the following week, so not much time was left for fun and relaxation. The latter part of the contract detailed all the financial arrangements. It was all as we agreed the previous evening. He was very thorough. Joe was also working on plugging the gaps with more bookings for the vacant dates, plus dealing with the accounting side, income, and payments that would be channeled through his offices.

Once we were all satisfied with what we had read, we headed back to Joe's office and spent a while with him getting more information on practicalities including weekly allowance, bank details, and mobile numbers. Finally, we signed and headed back out to grab a little more sightseeing while it was still light. It was all happening so quickly.

Will this make me famous? I hope so. Will it make me rich? Perhaps not, but I will not need to worry about finance for a few weeks.

We caught the Tube to Westminster, took a tour of Parliament, and then joined the long queue to see the crown jewels in the tower. It was getting dark so we headed back to Piccadilly. Although I was beginning to get weary, I wanted to keep my promise.

Leddicus stood gazing around, absorbing the wonder that is Piccadilly Circus at night, until finally he announced. "I'm hungry."

"I'm in the mood for Chinese," I said.

"That's handy. I know an excellent buffet just off Leicester Square." Julie said.

"What's Chinese?" asked Leddicus.

"Another adventure for you in gastronomy." He looked at me quizzically. "Food, new stuff you haven't tasted before," I said simply.

"Oh, good. I like trying new stuff."

Neither Leddicus nor Julie seemed as weary as I was. At least if they were, they didn't say so, but I was very pleased to take a seat once I had heaped my plate high at the buffet table.

It seemed to take forever to get back to the hotel, probably because I was now very tired and my feet ached.

Julie came in for coffee. "What's the plan for tomorrow?"

Julie now just assumed that she should be included in everything we do. How did that happen? Before I knew it, she was reeling out suggestions. Leddicus's eyes were alight with anticipation, and I was nodding reluctant agreement. Apparently, we were to visit some more sights in the centre and then take in a matinee. Julie assured me she could get some tickets.

Is there no end to her talents? I thought cynically.

"In the evening, would you like to go to the cinema?" she asked Leddicus.

I was sure she knew he had no idea what it was. I blurred over while she explained, and then she dropped her bombshell.

"On Saturday, I am wondering if you and Leddicus would like to come to church with me."

I was suddenly wide awake and responded quickly, "No, we can't fit that in. We need to prepare before we start touring."

As always, she looked to Leddicus for a response.

"I'm not sure. I didn't like the church in Rome, but you did say that yours is different, so maybe I would like to go. If Gerhardt doesn't want to come, perhaps you can take me?"

Back in the corner I go! I can never get control of the situation. Between them, Leddicus and Julie always call the shots. I am, once again, trapped.

"It's not my scene, but I guess I can tag along. But why a Saturday?"

"I'll explain later. I need to get going now. What about tomorrow? Early start?"

She is not going to win this time.

"No," I said with finality. "I'm having a lie-in. Breakfast at ten tomorrow. You're welcome to join us."

"Thanks. That would be good."

"You are coming tomorrow?" Leddicus said to Julie, grinning. The conversation was sometimes a bit too rapid for Leddicus, but he caught up eventually.

I had slept like a log and felt refreshed as Leddicus and I tucked into another full English.

"Where to first?" I said through a mouthful of sausage and beans.

I noted that, yet again, Julie was eating only fruit and cereal, undoubtedly how she maintained her slender figure.

"We must show Leddicus Tower Bridge. I checked the schedule, and it's due to be opened today. I've managed to get tickets for *Sister Act*. It starts at two thirty. Then we could grab McDonald's and head for the South Bank to see the Eye that's amazing. Have you seen it?" She didn't wait for an answer. "Then we must take Leddicus to the IMAX. I've been once. It blew me away. I've booked *Walking with Dinosaurs in 3-D*!" She paused to nibble on a strawberry. "Does that sound okay?"

I shook my head.

"Oh!" Her excitement was evaporating.

"No, no, it's all fine. I am just bemused at when you find time to sort this. Do you ever sleep?"

She smiled, relieved when she realised I was only teasing. "I sorted a lot of it out before you came, but no, I don't sleep much."

"And *Walking with Dinosaurs*? I have my doubts about that."

"It's got great reviews." She sliced a sliver of melon and bit into it.

"Leddicus has just been catapulted into the future, and now you're going to dunk him into the middle of the Jurassic era?"

"Oh, yes. Of course, sorry. Wasn't thinking. Got a bit carried away. It is educational." She tailed off. "Well, it's booked now. If we are going to send him crazy, we might as well do it in style."

Leddicus grinned at us. "I'm not crazy, although I feel like it sometimes." He tapped his head. "All sound in here. I just go with the flow. Is the only way to stay sane."

"Okay, my friend, on your head be it," I said.

"He sounds like you." Julie observed, which made me feel rather smug.

Julie had planned well, and the day sped by in a happy blur. Shortly after we left the theatre, Joe called to let me know about additional bookings. The first month had become so packed that he had decided to extend it to a second month. Booking requests were still coming in. I asked him not to run the tour beyond three months. I had it in the back of my mind that I ought to take Leddicus back home to Caesarea Philippi, if he were to be believed.

We arrived at the IMAX with little time to spare, got issued with our 3-D specs, and purchased the obligatory popcorn, Coke, and ice cream. Leddicus tucked in with gusto. Not long ago he had been polishing off a big Mac, and I was beginning to think I would have a rather sick young man or very old man on my hands before the film was halfway through.

The lights dimmed, and we donned our spectacles. I had never been to a 3-D film so the concept intrigued me. The screen was as high as five double-decker buses. Although almost impossible to do, I wanted to watch the film and Leddicus's face. A huge, drooling Giganotosaurus lumbered across the Patagonian landscape and slowly turned his head in our direction. The sound of his feet pounded our ears as he stomped toward us. Full of menace, he bared his teeth, roared, and then lunged toward us with his mouth gaping. The 3-D effect brought him right up to our noses. Leddicus shrieked, threw up his hands to protect his face, scattering popcorn far and wide, and then jumped up out of his seat. Before I could stop him, he was scrambling for the exit, stumbling and tripping over people's bags and coats. Julie and I leapt up and followed as quickly as we could in the dark.

We finally caught up with him, sitting on the carpet in the corridor, breathing heavily. Julie was stricken with remorse and kept apologising to me and then Leddicus and then me again.

I just laughed out loud. "Thought you said you could handle it, buddy!"

Leddicus, visibly shaking, stood up quickly. He brushed at his trousers and jacket.

"I dropped the popcorn," he said forlornly.

We thought it wise not to venture back into the cinema. Instead, we found an upmarket restaurant where I teased Leddicus relentlessly and he took it on the chin. We also had a huge debate about dinosaurs while we introduced Leddicus to fine cuisine.

"Champagne anyone? I think we have a lot to celebrate." I beckoned the waiter.

"Here's to a successful tour!" I said as we clinked glasses.

"Here's to never seeing another dinosaur," said Leddicus.

Back at the hotel, I was heading for the stairs when Leddicus placed his hand on my arm. "Gerhardt, I have a favour to ask."

"It's late. Can't it wait?" I regretted the words as soon as they left my lips when I saw his crestfallen face.

"Okay, it can wait." He turned to go.

"No, I'm sorry. Come on. Let's get a nightcap. The bar is still open, and you can tell me what you want." I was tired, but a pang of guilt stabbed at me. Leddicus had never asked for a favour before.

The barman delivered us a glass of wine each. I took a sip and turned to Leddicus. "How can I help?"

"I feel bad to ask, but it's important to me. I think from the meeting we had with Joe that I will be earning some money. At least that's what Julie explained to me."

"You will. You'll get paid for speaking at the tour seminars."

"Is it possible that I will earn enough money to buy a laptop?"

My eyebrows shot up in surprise. "What on earth do you want one of those for?"

"I hope it will help my English, and Julie said there is something called e-mail. I think that's what she called it. A letter that can magically go from one laptop to another."

"It's not exactly magic, but okay, if you want one, we'll get you one, but I don't quite know why you had to tell me that this last thing at night," I said in mock sternness.

Leddicus grinned at me. "I want it quickly. I want to take it with me on the trip we are going on, and we haven't much time before we leave. Do you think we can do that?"

"Not sure I can manage that, but I know a girl who can."

I lay in bed staring into the darkness. *The man filled with wonder at a light switch now wants a laptop. How times are changing.*

Eduardo unhooked his car keys from the hall stand. His wife was already asleep in the quiet house. He wore black, well-tailored trousers and a black fitted shirt. It clung to his lean, large frame. The night air was still warm as he stepped out into the darkness. He opened the boot of his Mercedes CLS500, placed a large leather case into the voluminous space, closed the boot silently and slid into the driver's seat.

He had only had the car a month, and its sleek lines still delighted him. He loved the smell of the leather seats. He eased out of the long driveway and turned the car toward the edge of Bolzano. Very few people were on the streets this late at night. He drove for twenty minutes, and was eventually on the road which snaked alongside the tree line. He slowed his speed and began scanning the road to the left for the turnoff. He spotted a small track barred by a gate, obscured by fir trees. He left the engine running as he pushed back the gate. Once he had driven through, he got out, checked the road in both directions, and closed the gate behind him.

Thick clouds were obscuring the moon. The headlights picked out deep ruts in the narrow track. He cursed as branches scraped at the sides of the car. He was jolted around even though he was driving very slowly.

The headlights highlighted a white van parked in a small clearing two hundred meters ahead. He killed the headlights, got out of the car, and waited a moment for his eyes to adjust to the darkness. His contact was leaning against the van, smoking. He took the cigarette from between his lips and flicked it onto the floor. Then he walked toward the back of the van, opened the doors, and beckoned to Eduardo.

Eduardo opened the boot of the Mercedes and removed the large case. Then he joined the other man at the back of the van. He laid the case in the rear of the van and clicked it open.

"Excellent shipment. My boss is keen for a repeat, and he is willing to maintain the payment per unit. You have excelled in the smoothness of the operation." He began stacking euros into the open case. Eduardo counted silently as each bundle was stowed away.

"Fifty, as agreed." The man snapped shut the case and nodded at Eduardo.

"Can you keep the units coming?"

"I can, but not to order. It must be when I say. Any pressure from your boss and I will place the units elsewhere."

The main scratched his dark, stubbled chin. "What do you mean? Pressure?" He lit another cigarette and held out the pack to Eduardo, who held up his hand in decline.

"I am making it clear at the outset. I have come to your organisation having withdrawn from my previous liaison due to heavy-handed tactics. This I will not tolerate. Requested units will be delivered, but I will have no truck with being told what and when."

The glow of the cigarette hung in the dark air. The dim light from the back of the van cast deep shadows across the faces of both men.

"I will pass on the message, but rest assured that the boss doesn't go in for bully boy tactics. If the units keep coming, then you will be well rewarded."

The man reached into the back of the van and took out a small packet. "Use this phone to contact me when the next shipment is ready. E-mail, even encrypted, is causing some concern."

Eduardo frowned. "Why? I've never had any problems. My system is very secure."

"You'll have to trust me on this one. There are strong forces out there who are opposed. Two shipments were recently intercepted. An irritating setback. The only conclusion we could reach is that the e-mails were hacked."

"Right." Eduardo dragged the heavy case out of the van and walked toward his car. The other man slammed the van doors shut and gunned up the engine.

Chapter Seventeen

Saturday

I purposely slept late this morning, wandering down to breakfast well after ten o'clock. As expected, Julie and Leddicus were there already, nattering over croissants and orange juice. I joined them feeling decidedly moody. I wasn't looking forward to going to some boring church service. But I had agreed, and there was no way out of it now without losing face.

As we got into the car and set off, my mood had not lifted. "What is it with this Saturday church? All a bit weird, isn't it? Are you some kind of Seventh Day-ist or Jewish or what?" I confronted Julie, but she didn't bite. I could see her face, smiling calmly, in the mirror.

"Why don't you ask Leddicus when his followers of the way had their meetings?"

I couldn't see his face, but knowing him, he would also be smiling. The fact he always sat in the front normally didn't bother me, but it childishly riled me today.

"We meet each other as often as possible in people's houses, in the woods, or all sorts of places. But we do have a regular meeting each Sunday, very early before it gets light. It would be about four o'clock your time."

"Blimey, you were keen," I said.

"Yes, we are," said Leddicus, "but it isn't just that. A lot of followers are slaves, and they have to start work as soon as the sun comes up, sometimes even before that."

I was unrepentant and still goading. "You're all weird."

Leddicus ignored my comment. "We have to meet where we put the dead people. In fact, I met the man who took my message to Caesarea at a meeting I went to in Malet, or Malta as you call it. They also meet where the dead people are."

"Catacombs? Why?" I snapped.

Julie's calming tone interjected. "It was very dangerous to be a follower, so they had to pick places that were as safe and isolated as possible. Not many people would be around a graveyard before dawn."

"Leddicus wasn't a slave," I said.

"No, I'm a free man, a Roman citizen, but we all, the slaves and everyone else, want to be together. The only time we can do this is to meet very early."

"Okay, fair enough," I conceded grudgingly, "but that still doesn't tell me why Julie's bunch meets on a Saturday."

"We don't own a building, and we've struggled to find a place to rent on a Sunday. The community centre we use on Saturday is ideal. We can all meet up, spend time together, and afford the rent."

Sullen, I sat back in my seat. I was all out of clever or annoying questions. I watched the rows of houses and shops slide past as we drove toward our North London destination. We eventually made our way through what appeared to be a housing estate, and Julie was soon parking at the community centre. Many other cars were parked or parking, and as we walked toward the entrance, I could tell they were all headed for the same place. As we entered the hall, I could hear a buzz of greetings. People were milling around chatting, and they all appeared to know each other.

Julie introduced us to several people, whose names I instantly forgot. A smiling, plump woman asked if we were hungry and pointed to a long table of food, soup, salad, and all kinds of bread. It was quite a spread.

Julie handed us both a plate. "It's lunchtime, and we like to eat together. Please help yourself." I put my hand in my pocket and pulled out £10. Julie laughed. "Don't be silly. It's a meal with friends. It's free."

Julie took Leddicus off to meet some of her friends, and I enjoyed a bowl of hearty soup and some delicious bread.

A guy wandered up and started chatting with me. "Hi, I'm Peter. Don't think I've met you before."

"Gerhardt. I've not been before."

"Where are you from?"

"Switzerland. You?"

We were soon chatting away like old acquaintances, and I discovered he was a scientific high flyer.

"You're a scientist and interested in religion!" My startled response didn't faze him.

"Not really. Religion leaves me cold. I'm more interested in community and getting to know God."

"I'm not sure about all of this," I admitted.

"I know what you mean. I've been there. The question people kept asking me was if there were such a thing as God and could you know him. What would change? It changed my perspective, starting a long exploration for me. I've come a long way." He laughed and shrugged. "I still have a long way to go. I still have a lot of questions, but I've had a lot of answers, too."

"Meeting Leddicus has made me wonder about many things. Perhaps I will give it some thought."

"Leddicus, yes, fascinating case. I've been following it avidly. You know him well. Do you think it's genuine? Although I can't imagine how it could be."

Before I could answer, someone was speaking into a mic, "Hello, everyone. Hello and welcome. If you want to grab a seat, we can get started with some updates."

The hubbub died down, and they got going on what I expected to be the more formal part of the gathering. But it wasn't formal at all.

The guy with the mic threw out an invitation to the group. "Anyone with anything they want to share?"

A young girl at the front raised a hand. He smiled and beckoned her to come forward, and she took the mic.

"I'm a member of a dance group, and we needed somewhere to train. We asked to use the local school, but they wouldn't let us." She hesitated. She only looked about nine years old.

"What happened then?" the mic guy encouraged.

"We asked people to pray a month ago, and now the school has changed its mind. Our class starts next week. Thank you for praying."

The whole group clapped, and some even whistled. *What a poor misguided youngster, as if God would intervene about a room for a dance group.* A few others got up. Some had apparent stories of answers to prayers; others had requests for prayers for problems they were facing. After this, they did a bit of singing. There were no hymn books. They used an overhead projector. I didn't know any of the songs, but everyone else seemed to and sang with great abandon. Then someone got up and did a Bible reading. He chatted about what he had read. It all seemed very low-key and informal. Even though I didn't want to come and didn't want to be there, it all felt quite welcoming and unthreatening and wasn't boring at all. It was not in the least what I had expected.

Quite soon, someone else was chatting about future plans. I didn't quite catch what was said. I was losing interest by then, as I didn't know who they were talking about and it meant nothing to me. Someone was sick or pregnant, and they were all planning to supply meals for a month or so. I grudgingly admitted to myself that it was a very caring act.

Leddicus was sitting with Julie and some of her friends. He was in my line of vision, and I had glanced at him a few times during the more formal proceedings. He seemed perfectly at ease. He appeared to speak the same language. I didn't mean English. I mean he seemed to be on the same wavelength.

Someone said a brief prayer, and then people started milling about again, chatting and laughing.

I made my way over to Leddicus. "Well, matey, what did you make of church?"

"I am very much at home. I think these people understand what I have been talking about." He seemed happier than I had seen him in a long time. "I would say they are people of the way. It's very strange because it's not my time and the problems are all different, but they have the same love and care for each other that we had in Caesarea."

"Uh-huh," I responded, "It's all a mystery to me."

Leddicus was about to launch into a deeper explanation, but Julie, who came bustling through the crowd, saved me. "Ready to go?" She also had that same strange happy face that I had noted in Leddicus.

We made our way slowly to the exit. It reminded me of when we left the hospital. Everyone wanted to hug Leddicus, kiss him on the cheek, or shake his hand. We finally climbed into the car and waved good-bye. As usual, Leddicus sat in the front.

"Did you enjoy our get-together?" Julie said to the air.

Leddicus responded enthusiastically, "Yes, yes, very much. A community I understand. Not like my time in Rome."

Julie laughed. "I know what you mean, but I'm sure some of the people at that place follow the way as you know it. But I'm with you on this one. I'm not keen on structure and ceremony. I like community and reality."

I joined in before it became the usual Julie/Leddicus tête-à-tête. "I don't understand any of it, but quite liked the informality, although a bit of theatre is often entertaining." I remembered my time in Rome and my one other very odd experience of church.

"Well, that's something at least." Julie almost read my thoughts. "Although church isn't something you go to, it's actually something you are."

The conversation was getting too deep for my liking, and I was relieved to see we were swinging into the hotel car park. I swiftly changed the subject.

"Julie, are you coming in? It would be good to get some input about plans for tomorrow. In fact, I could do with some help for the whole tour, if I'm honest, and Leddicus has a request. We need you to work some rapid magic before we leave for the tour."

"Sure, no problem. I'll help as much as I can. Do you want a ride to the station tomorrow? Or rather the nearest Tube to get you into King's Cross. I think that's what Joe said he had booked for you."

We sat at the hotel bar, me with my coffee, Julie with her juice, and Leddicus with his statutory glass of red wine. We made plans for the next three months.

Chapter Eighteen

Talking Our Way around Britain

My heart was pounding, the room was full, and it was hot, stuffy, and claustrophobic. The professor who had ushered us in ten minutes earlier was now at the microphone, introducing Leddicus and me to the one hundred-odd people who had packed into the hall. He turned to me. I stood up, and as I walked over, I took some long, slow deep breaths to calm myself. A host of flash cameras went off as I took my position at the podium.

"Hello," I began rather croakily. I took a quick drink from the glass of water on my right and tried again. "Hello. It's very good to be here." I was having to wing it. The wretched PowerPoint would not function. After approximately ten minutes of gabbling about I know-not-what, I introduced Leddicus and sat down. Shaking and exhausted from the trauma, I was sweating profusely and groped thankfully for the cooling coffee that had been placed in front of me. Perhaps public speaking was not for me.

The fear I experienced at the first few venues had long since receded, and I was now becoming an expert at public speaking, and I had got the PowerPoint show down to a fine art. The UK tour felt like a blur. We had not stopped since Julie dropped us off at the Tube to King's Cross on a Monday morning almost three months ago.

On that first train ride, Leddicus had bombarded me with questions, "How fast? How long? How it began?"

I was happy to pass the time with a history lesson beginning with George Stephenson's rocket. After all, history was my subject.

Now on train journeys, he sat quietly in his seat, totally at home, tapping away on his laptop or watching the scenery fly by. How Julie managed to get hold of a brand-new, fully configured laptop from when she left us the evening before the tour commenced to when she collected us in the morning remained a mystery.

Leddicus's English had dramatically improved. He was a smart guy and a very quick learner. Now he used the language almost like a native-born Brit. He would eventually be better than I was. He was beginning to pick up cultural nuances and getting his head around English humour, in that he was ahead of me. Perhaps that was due to my German roots.

The organisation and support from Joe Simmons's office had been fantastic. Every two days, I received an updated schedule, either by fax or e-mail, sometimes both, covering every base. We had been staying at the best hotels. We hadn't had to think about transport, either from rail or bus stations. A nice person was ready and waiting to whisk us to our hotel. On the whole, the venues, which were usually universities, but also included colleges, schools, and historical societies, had been well organised.

Leddicus had developed into a confident public speaker, fielding questions with clarity and precision. My nerves had long since ebbed away, enabling me to give clear details about the story so far, his discovery on the mountain, his stay at the hospital, and what studies were currently being carried out about him.

The money we were making was very, very good. I was still amazed at what people were willing to pay to hear us speak. Joe really knew his stuff. Every detail of the trip was covered, so we were not spending anything at all. Our UK bank accounts continued to increase by impressive amounts. I wasn't sure Leddicus understood what it was all about, especially not the financial aspect.

Leddicus, alongside his fluency in English, had also become an avid user of the mobile phone I bought him all those months ago. In any spare moment, he was either texting or calling. You could guess who most of his contact was with. Julie Bright. I didn't know why she bugged me, and I supposed I should have been grateful. She did after all introduce us to Joe Simmons, who had come up trumps. I didn't mind in the least if our tour had turned into a gravy train for his company and him. I didn't begrudge him that in the least.

Leddicus had also taken to computing like a duck to water. I found a training website for him, the idiot's guide to the web dot com. He worked through each session again and again until he grasped the concepts. Each evening after supper, we would both sit in the hotel lounge on our laptops, me working flat-out to keep uni, *Archiv*, and Mr. Calabro abreast of developments and Leddicus doing who knows what, but always with a very intense look on his face.

The whistle-stop blur of a tour was now over, and we were on our way back to London. Most of the time, I didn't know what town I was in or even if it were Scotland, Wales, or England. We hadn't touched Ireland yet. One of the places that stuck in my memory was Bristol. First, Julie joined us that weekend or, should I say, joined Leddicus. Second, Priscilla Morrison from the Vatican press office turned up. Third, we had a day off.

The presentation at Bristol University went like clockwork. I was sitting on the platform listening as Leddicus concluded his talk on his experiences since he had woken up in the morgue, and as usual, he threw it open for questions. A hand went up, and Leddicus indicated the questioner had the floor. I immediately recognised Priscilla Morrison as she stood to her feet.

"Do I conclude that you, your family, and all your relatives were in possession of slaves?" Her tone of voice was hard and bitter, and as she continued, she implied that Leddicus was responsible for the actions of the whole of the Roman Empire.

I groaned in dismay as I looked at her standing there. Her face was set. Her demeanour was as frightening as a cornered Rottweiler.

"Thank you very much for your question. I seem to remember you asked something along similar lines in Switzerland, am I correct?" Leddicus disarmed her with his broad smile.

"Yes, you are correct," she replied curtly.

"Slavery is disturbing in all its forms, and I cannot answer for the whole of the Roman Empire, although I appreciate my privileged position as a free and educated Roman citizen." He paused and took a drink of water, pacing himself. "I am still struggling to understand your world. Please forgive me for calling it your world, but I still do not totally understand where I am. However, I have researched some of your history. I know, for example, that you celebrate in this country what you call the end of the slave trade and the first abolition bill was passed in 1807. At that time, four million people were enslaved. Today, the number is estimated at twelve million. So are you staying you have a better world today?"

Leddicus looked across at Morrison and waited for her to comment. She opened her mouth, but no words came out.

Leddicus continued, "Two girls are taken as slaves every minute, and well-researched statistics state that between two and four million men, women, and children are trafficked across borders and within their own country every year."

I noticed Morrison was looking rather peaky. She had turned from a cornered to a cowering Rottweiler.

"More than one person is trafficked across a border somewhere in the world every minute. This equates to five jumbo jet plane loads every day. Financially, this trade earns twice as much worldwide revenue as that dark, fizzy drink I have just discovered. What is that called?"

Someone in the audience called out, "Coca-Cola!"

Leddicus was now in full control of the situation. He knew well enough the name of Coke. He drank it every day. He smiled and nodded. "Yes, that's it, and I would like to add that I don't want to protect my society, but I think you need to think about yours, too. I understand I am the headline person here today, and of course, my world intrigues you, but we need to think of the current global picture, don't you think so?"

Morrison crumpled into her seat without saying another word. The audience gave Leddicus some extended and enthusiastic applause, and I had to work hard to keep my mouth from dropping open. I was astounded at his complex, detailed, and articulate response. Then I spotted Julie right at the back of the hall with a big grin plastered on her face, giving Leddicus the thumbs-up. I looked across at Leddicus, and sure enough, he was returning the grin.

I thought back to earlier in the day when Julie arrived. I had been stuck in the corner of the lounge on my laptop, finishing an article for *Archiv*. I had left Leddicus and Julie to their own devices. I occasionally glanced over at them, and every time, they had been deep in intense conversation while poring over Julie's laptop with Leddicus frowning in concentration. The light dawned. The little minx had briefed Leddicus and accurately anticipated Priscilla's line of questioning from the first encounter in Switzerland. As much at Julie irritated me and frequently grated on my last nerve, I had to hand her this one. She had enabled Leddicus to pull off a masterstroke.

I was jolted from my reverie as the wretched Morrison woman recovered her composure and made a second attempt, but she directed her question to me this time.

"May I ask a further question?" she asked curtly. "This is directed to Gerhardt."

There it is again. She's using my first name as if she knows me.

She glared at me. Her eyes were hard and emotionless. "I would like to know why you are fronting this tour, what is your precise qualification, and why you think you are any sort of expert in history?"

I was stuck dumb. *What does she want me to say?* There was no George to rescue me this time. I sat there trying to conceal my panic. My brain raced in a hundred directions, but came up empty. Rescue swiftly arrived in the form of Leddicus.

He stood up and smiled sweetly. "Although your question is directed to Mr. Shynder, I need to stress that Gerhardt is my friend. He has been alongside me from day one, ever since my traumatic time in hospital in Italy. In my opinion, that is qualification enough for him to front this tour. I trust that is a sufficient answer to your question. As you are aware . . ." He paused, smiled sweetly, and met her steely gaze. "Our time here has now overrun, and we must bring this session to a close." He swept his hand theatrically across the auditorium. "Thank you everyone for your questions. I trust you have enjoyed your time with us." He tilted his head forward with the merest hint of a bow.

The crowd applauded, and I was off the hook again. As we had made our way back to the hotel later that evening, Julie and Leddicus confessed they had spent all afternoon swatting up on the history of slavery to enable Leddicus to do what he did in the event that Morrison asked the anticipated question.

"Well, mate, I can't thank you enough. You were fantastic. I'm especially grateful to you for jumping in to rescue me from that nut job."

"Gerhardt, my dear friend, I could not let you be tossed to the lions, not when I could rescue you!"

We all laughed at how well he had pulled it off. Leddicus laughed louder than I had ever heard him laugh before. Tears were streaming down his face.

He eventually wiped his eyes and looked at us both. "I haven't had so much fun since I can't remember when."

He put his hand on Julie's arm and looked her in the eyes. "Thanks for your help. I couldn't have done it without you." For the first time ever, I saw Julie appear a trifle embarrassed. She looked at the floor and giggled softly.

As planned, the next day was a rest day, and as usual, Julie had everything in place for a tour of Bath. The highlight was a visit to the Roman Baths. In the entrance is an exceedingly clever piece of theatre. Behind a huge glass panel is a computer-generated scene, looking realistically like ancient Romans making their way across the terrace to the baths. Part of the panorama includes a young boy driving a goat.

As we rounded the corner and Leddicus caught sight of it, he almost jumped out of his skin. He let out a yelp of shock. Julie turned, caught sight of his stricken face, and rushed over to put a comforting arm around him.

"What's wrong, Leddicus? What is it?"

He leaned his head against her shoulder, took a few deep breaths, and put his hand over his eyes in confusion. "For a minute there, I thought I was back in my own time," he said softly.

Julie hugged him. I gave him a shove and told him to pull himself together. Then we moved on. The incident was quickly forgotten.

Later that evening, after a relaxed meal and some excellent wine, we bid good-bye to Julie, who needed to be in London early the next morning. Leddicus looked rather forlorn as we made our way back to the hotel lounge.

In the last few days, Joe and I had chatted regularly about his plans to promote Leddicus in different fields. I hadn't mentioned any of this to Julie, mainly because I expected that Joe would be keeping her in the loop. To date, there had been approaches by a TV company who wanted to produce a documentary and a publisher with a ghostwriter on standby should we agree to an autobiography, although Joe was keen to push the writing work in Julie's direction. A company also wanted to produce a movie should the proposed book be a success.

As Leddicus and I settled down with a nightcap, I briefed him about the proposals, but I didn't think he grasped the concepts, plus he was not giving me his full attention because he was checking his mobile every five minutes. I gave up, topped up my lager, and decided not to worry about it. The tour was ending, and in a few days, I could talk it all through with Joe face-to-face.

Chapter Nineteen

Talking on a Train

Although I loved my Audi and I missed the independence it gave me, I did enjoy travelling by train, and of course, the trains in Switzerland are the best. The UK trains are not so bad; the newer models are reasonable, comfortable, and fast.

The final day of our tour had been in Glasgow. Ahead of us lay a five-hour journey to Euston station in London. Julie was meeting us there and taking us to the hotel she had already booked for us. The train was full. Possibly many were headed to the same destination as us. We piled our cases in the luggage area and settled into the comfortable seats. We sat opposite each other, a table between us. I had work to do, but I didn't feel like getting out my laptop. Instead, I thought it would be a good opportunity for Leddicus and me to have a decent catch-up.

The train eased silently out of Glasgow, and I was content. I had managed to juggle an extra large fresh coffee on board, and now I sipped at it, savouring the time to relax.

I looked across at Leddicus. "What a trip! How did you think it went?"

Leddicus turned to me and smiled. "I have enjoyed it, and I'm pleased with how much my English has improved. But I am surprised at how differently everyone seems to speak English. So many ways on such a small island. In this city, it was a real struggle. I had to listen very, very carefully and ask them to repeat things often. But they are kind people, and they have been nice to me. What did you think of it all?"

"I've enjoyed it a lot! I also got a heap of work done for my doctorate. I'm pleased I managed to fit that in and send it back to

Switzerland. It's been fun being with you, and we've earned lots of money." I leaned back in my seat and stretched my arms up to the ceiling. "Maybe I will yet be a famous historian!" I folded my arms and stretched out my legs. I did feel decidedly like the cat who got the cream. "I don't think there was any part of the trip that I didn't like. Even those two church meetings we went to. Can't remember which places we were in at the time, but they weren't so bad. I bet Julie put you up to that, didn't she?"

He nodded and tapped his hip pocket, where his mobile was stowed. "Julie called me with the suggestions." He and his mobile had become inseparable. During the trip, he'd been chatting with Julie regularly. She had called me from time to time to give me updates and act as an intermediary for Joe and me, but she and Leddicus spoke almost every day.

"I think the best bit has been Lisa."

"Who's she?" Leddicus shrugged.

"You know, Joe's secretary."

"Ah, yes, I didn't speak to her though."

"No, I know, but she has been fantastic. Faxing, e-mailing, phoning, and sorting out all the finance. She's oiled the wheels of our tour and made everything go smoothly."

Leddicus, distracted by the fabulous scenery, stared out of the window. The sun was hanging in a clear sky, and a golden light bathed the meadows. The distant craggy mountains were darkly silhouetted against the sun. Buzzards glided, almost motionless, riding effortlessly on the thermals as they waited patiently for their unsuspecting prey.

I interrupted his reverie. "Why did we end up at those churches then? What did Julie say?"

"She said I might like to try out some of the churches she had been to, and I did think they were interesting. It was pretty obvious to me that these people really are people of the way. But I still struggle with some of the structures and how they do things. It seems less natural than what I am used to. Perhaps that's because it's a different age. Our community was just us living out what we had been taught. We didn't see the church as being everything, but I think these people see it that way."

"You've lost me, Leddicus. Not sure I understand your problem, although something happened at one of the meetings that nearly scared me to death!"

"I didn't see you get sick!" Leddicus looked quite worried.

I laughed aloud. He still did not get some of the colloquialisms and had a tendency to take them literally. "No, I wasn't sick. I was very scared. One of the guys in the church came up to me as we were getting ready to leave. The one in Newcastle? Or was it Norwich? Anyway, one of those cities."

"What happened? Why were you scared?"

"This guy bowled over and launched straight in. 'Hello. Hope you don't mind, but I think God has something he wants me to tell you.' I didn't have a clue what he was on about so I just smiled politely and said okay. He said a lot of stuff, about how I had grown up and what I was planning to be. And then he wrapped it all up by saying, 'The problem is, when you get where you want to be, it will not satisfy you or make you content.' He was very accurate, and it frightened me. I'm sure he didn't know me from a bar of soap."

"You weren't sick, but you were dirty?" Leddicus asked.

I could tell he was winding me up. "No, wise guy, I just meant he didn't know me at all. We had never met, but he was telling me about my life, and he seemed to know it very well. Scarily well!"

Leddicus smiled. "I am glad God is still doing those things today."

This conversation was getting far too deep for me. I didn't want to pursue it any further. *Perhaps I should get out my laptop and do some work.* But I was intrigued about the structure issue Leddicus had mentioned earlier. That would be a good way to change the subject.

"What did you mean about the structure? How was it so different to what you were used to? Not that either of us can understand it. We only went to two meetings."

Leddicus screwed up his face in deep thought for a while and then took a deep breath. "The thing is, Jesus told us that, first and foremost, we should seek the kingdom of God, the community that I call people of the way. Today, what people seem to call the church have the job of doing what Jesus said, seeking God's kingdom. That's everything that's on Earth. It's all God's business. The kingdom is much bigger than the people of the way, and God is at work in his entire world. It seems to me, from what I observed in the churches we attended, although the people were lovely, they appeared more worried about getting people into their church buildings than seeking God's kingdom. Maybe I have it wrong, but that's how it looked to me. But for me, seeking God's kingdom is all about changing the world!"

"Wow, Leddicus, you definitely should be a politician. That was a heavy-duty speech!"

We both laughed.

"I am from a different world," Leddicus reminded me. "And you have often asked me why I am careful about what I say, even if I have the right words." He grew serious again. "I can never forget that I'm a follower of the way. Where I live, it's very easy to be killed for what I am saying, especially about the kingdom of God. I had two very close friends. We met regularly on the first day of the week and spent many hours discussing the way. One week when I was away, soldiers discovered where my friends were meeting and told everyone their gathering was against the law. Right there and then, they ran my friends through with their swords." He paused and took a deep breath.

"They were slaves, so it was easy for the soldiers to do this to them without any further consequences. It would be a bit harder for them to kill me without any questions being asked, not impossible though, but I would still risk my life by saying these things."

It just seemed like a story from history to me. To be honest, what he said didn't affect me deeply. "Why was it like that? Why were you safer than slaves?" I asked.

"I had the privilege of education. My father was a well-paid Roman official. I had been very fortunate. But Rome dominates the world. The Roman Empire is everywhere. It makes slaves of thousands and oppresses them. Caesar is called the son of god, and people worship him like a god. We celebrate Caesar's birthday, and it's supposed to be the Good News Day. Then along comes people like me, followers of the way, many of us slaves. We say Jesus is king, and he is good news. We also say he has risen from the dead and knowing this King Jesus can change your values, your innermost being, and your thinking. That is very threatening to Rome and

Caesar. That is why I am careful, but it doesn't mean I don't believe what I say or follow. I am just extremely careful so I can stay alive as long as possible."

"I can see how passionate you are about what you are saying. Perhaps we should let you talk in some of the churches as well as the universities. I doubt they would pay us very well unless we went to America, which brings me to something else I need to discuss with you. When we get back, Joe wants to talk to us about a tour in America, a TV documentary, a book about your life, and the possibility of a movie, all good money-making ideas. But what do you want to do next?"

Two deep creases formed between his brows. He took a deep breath and slowly released it slowly. He spread his hands out on the table and looked across at me plaintively. "Actually, I would like to go home to Caesarea. I really miss my friends, family, and, well, everything."

I took a sharp, involuntary breath, and my mind went blank for a moment. I looked across at him with what I hoped was a sympathetic face, but I knew I couldn't pretend all was well. "I don't think home will be anything like it was when you left, my friend. But here is my suggestion. How about we extend the tour for a couple of months to the USA? And then I promise I'll take you back to Caesarea."

I was concerned he might flip out when he went back to his hometown and saw it as it really was. I wanted to be sure that I built up my bank balance some more before I took that risk. I could sense he was still deeply confused and I wondered if he put on an act of acceptance of the situation as protection for his own mental well-being.

He looked at me. Aching sadness filled his face, but he nodded slowly.

"I don't think you will like what you find in Caesarea, and I'm not sure what we will do there or afterward." I tailed off, sensing that, although Leddicus was here and had been for some months, he just did not understand some things or perhaps did not want to face up to them. I had no idea what to do about that.

"America is a fun place, and the American people will love you."

"Okay, it sounds good to me." His voice was flat, devoid of emotion.

I checked my watch. I was amazed to see we were only forty-five minutes from London.

"Leddicus, let's eat. I'll go get us some coffee and sandwiches. It's not long now until we arrive in London."

He brightened a little at this. "Is Julie meeting us?"

I nodded and left him with that happy thought and headed off to hunt down some food.

We had just finished our late lunch as the train pulled into Euston. We piled off the train and there at the end of the station was the familiar sight of Julie Bright, sporting a bright red jacket and an even brighter smile.

Chapter Twenty

Bad News

Julie had booked us into the same hotel in Brentwood, she said it wasn't the nearest, but thought we might like a bit of familiarity. I would never have thought of that, but it actually did feel good. We dumped the cases in our rooms and met her in the lounge for coffee and a brief catch-up before she left us to relax.

"Our monthly meeting is on tomorrow. Want to come?" She poured us all coffee from the steaming cafetière.

Leddicus nodded vigorously as he spooned four sugars into his coffee. He had become quite a coffee drinker now due to my constant encouragement, but still balked at drinking it unsweetened.

"Okay," I said without enthusiasm. "Will you give us a ride, or shall we get a cab?"

"I'll come and get you. No problem."

The day dawned clear and sunny, and the traffic was kind to us. We arrived in good time to enjoy the buffet that was provided as a ritual. I was surprised to find that I actually enjoyed the meeting. This Saturday, there was a rock band that was reasonably talented and fun. Something else was going on in me that I could not quite define, some strange emotion, although I was rarely emotional.

Leddicus was in his element, looking happy and relaxed. Halfway through, they asked him to say a few words. I was not happy about that. We had not negotiated a fee. Did they think we were a charity?

Leddicus got up from his seat without hesitation and took the proffered mic. He didn't give his usual history spiel, but spoke with convincing fluency about finding out that God was still with him. He was quite honest about his situation, saying he didn't understand what was going on his life and, although his friends from the university were trying to find out, they were no nearer a solution. He said that, although he was separated from his original people of the way friends and his family, he felt at home in this new family. It felt the same, although he couldn't explain why. He didn't speak for long, and ended on a light note. "The best part of this strange new existence in which I have found myself is that I can make a lot of noise, use very odd technology, and talk openly without being caught and fed to lions!"

The crowd applauded him enthusiastically as he walked back to his seat. I was encouraged listening to Leddicus. I liked what I heard. He sounded more at home in his new situation than I had heard him before. I grudgingly admitted to myself that I'd had a good time. There was excellent food, a decent band, and quite a few normal people spoke to me afterwards. They seemed genuinely interested in me and appeared to care about what I was doing.

We arrived back at our hotel mid-afternoon, waved good-bye to Julie, and then settled down for some rest and relaxation. We had no agenda from now until eleven o'clock tomorrow morning when Joe was coming to meet us for brunch. It felt good to be free of any stress, and the thought of a lie-in was a delight.

Leddicus and I ordered burger and chips from the bar and ate it in the lounge.

"Joe is going to discuss the next leg of our tour tomorrow, but don't worry. I'll explain that you want to go home."

Leddicus covered his chips with ketchup and took a sip of Coke. He had certainly taken up some twenty-first century bad habits with a vengeance.

"Julie said she wants to come with us to my home. That's good, yes?" He said with his mouth full.

Julie had mentioned this in the car on the way home. In her usual inimitable style, she had jumped straight in and invited herself to Israel with us. Just in time, I had remembered that she could see my face in the rearview mirror and forced a smile.

"I guess," I said to Leddicus. I took a sip of the fine red wine I had treated myself to. It wasn't really what you should have with a burger, but what the heck.

"You don't want her to come?" Leddicus was getting to be an expert at reading body language.

"Seems like it's a done deal to me, Leddicus." I busied myself with my meal to avoid any more complicated questioning. This evening was all about winding down.

Joe arrived at eleven sharp, and we made our way to our usual table. I didn't remember inviting Julie, but she came anyway, saying she had given Joe a ride. She pulled up a chair and began making small talk with Leddicus. We all ordered brunch and then Joe kicked off the business session.

"What do you want first, the good news or the bad news?"

"Bad news first," I said.

He reached into his pocket and pulled out a news clipping. He smoothed it out on the table in front of us. I recognised that it was from what the British call "red tops." A picture of Leddicus was underneath the large headline, "Ice Man Fraud Revealed." The story continued with an in-depth interview and picture of his family in Newcastle-upon-Tyne.

I read out the first line, "Our on-the-spot reporter has found the family of the alleged two thousand-year-old man."

Leddicus jumped out of his chair. "They've found my family! Where?" He screwed up his eyes and studied the newspaper.

"This is your sister and brother." I tapped one of the pictures.

"But I don't have a sister, and I have no idea who that man is."

Julie joined in, "I didn't think you would. The same people who said the moon landing was done in a film studio wrote this piece."

Leddicus looked from me, to Julie, and back again in obvious confusion, and I saw a rare hint of irritation.

"Moon? My family is on the moon!"

"No, Leddicus, some astronauts went there in a rocket, but this paper said it was a hoax."

Leddicus put his hands on his head and sighed loudly. "Julie, what are you talking about? This is not my family. And what's the moon got to do with it?"

Julie looked wounded at the annoyance that Leddicus displayed, but Joe stepped in swiftly to rescue the situation. "This article is obviously rubbish, and Julie will be writing a very stiff letter to the paper refuting their claims, won't you, Julie?"

Julie nodded dutifully.

"We will also be making a complaint to the press association about this glaring lie that's been printed. Once the situation has been investigated and we are, of course, proved right, the paper will be writing a tiny apology. Then life will continue for us as usual." He folded the paper back up and tucked it away. "But I have no doubt that other papers will quiz Gerhardt about this in the next day or so. Julie, as well as the letter to this paper, please work on a press response that we can use for any enquiries that come in Gerhardt's direction."

Julie nodded again, but she was looking at Leddicus with ill-concealed annoyance.

"Why would they do this?" Leddicus shot back at Joe. Concern filled his face.

"To sell more papers," said Joe. "They print all kinds of wild accusations in the hope that they won't be sued. You're big news currently, a celebrity, so, of course, you'll get singled out."

I reached out and squeezed Leddicus shoulder. "And the good news?"

"It's more than good. I have a full two-month tour booked for the States, the same style as you have been doing in the UK, colleges and universities, but the best thing is that they are paying even more than their British counterparts."

"That is good news, marvellous in fact." I said. The disappointment at the negative press was receding rapidly.

"You fly to New York early next week, and Julie will accompany you, at least for the first few days before the tour commences."

"She will!" I was stunned.

"She will! A reputable publisher has offered us an advance for a book, and I'm reviewing the contract before we sign up, plus I'm sorting out the last details that will confirm the deal for a documentary. The film offer is still on the table, although not finalised. They are waiting to see how the book takes off, but it's looking positive. With all of this in the offing, I need an avid note taker, and Julie is that person."

I leaned back in my chair and gasped. "This thing is getting bigger than I ever expected!" I said to no one in particular.

Leddicus, who had been listening dispassionately while Joe briefed us, woke up and asked, "What's getting bigger?"

"You are," I said to him. "These are all money-making deals, and you are right in the middle of them. Are you willing to do it all?"

"Sure, I will come to this USA with you, and then you will all come home with me. Is that the deal?"

"Well, yes, sort of," I said, "but, as well as the trip to the States, there is also a documentary, a book, and a film."

Leddicus shrugged and gave a half-smile. "Okay." His earlier irritation was forgotten.

Joe laughed aloud and patted Leddicus on the back. "So far, so good. You fly on Tuesday!" He stood up and gathered up his briefcase and phone. "I suggest you have some time out today and tomorrow. I'll be in touch within twenty-four hours with the new contracts." He turned to Julie. "Okay to get a ride home?"

"Sure, no problem." She picked up her bag. "Do you want to have dinner with me tomorrow evening?" She smiled, but it didn't reach her eyes. Leddicus snapping at her, was, for some strange reason, still troubling her.

"Yes, of course," Leddicus responded immediately, speaking as usual for both of us when it came to anything to do with Julie. If he had noticed her emotional distance, which I suspect he had, he made no mention of it.

Left alone with Leddicus, I asked, "What do you fancy doing for the rest of the day?"

"I would like to go for a walk."

"Okay, where shall we go?"

"If you don't mind, I'd like to go alone. I need to do some thinking." He stood up, leaving me in no doubt that he was determined to do this, said good-bye, and headed out.

I sat back and closed my eyes. My brain was whirling at the success that was visiting me. What was happening was beyond my wildest dreams. After a while, I decided to go back to my room, get the most expensive meal on the room service menu, watch a couple of films, raid the minibar, and then get an early night.

The e-mail read:

All in place. She will obtain the information in the next few weeks that will fill in the gaps you mentioned. We must discuss how you will obtain the material. Call me at 23:30 tomorrow night. J.

The next night Eduardo was in his usual spot, perched on his large leather office chair and hunched over his computer. His mobile, on silent, skittered slowly across the desk as it vibrated with an incoming call.

"Joseph, you are working miracles."

"Thank you. I hope so. I have a plan on how to get the manuscript to you once it is in note form. She does not commit immediately to electronic means. She is rather old-fashioned, preferring a notebook in the early stages. Once the notes are typed up, then we must obtain them. I have just the person to get hold of them and transport them to you. All I need from you is a meeting point. The items will come to you by special courier."

"I will work something out and let you know. Once I have the material, I am probably only a month from completion." Eduardo hesitated. "You are sure about the contracts?"

"Trust me, my friend, have I ever let you down before?"

"Indeed no, but you know I like to get everything locked down. I like this life. I do not want any upstarts stealing it away from me."

Joseph gave a low chuckle. "You and me both, and I am making every effort to ensure that does not happen."

"By the way, I have changed my e-mail address and the server encryption provider. The new address is setaside@wind.it."

"What was wrong with your old system? Have you had any breaches?"

"None, but I hear on the grapevine that some good hackers are out there. I suggest you follow suit," Eduardo explained.

"Brilliant hackers are out there. What has this to do with you?"

"When I say good, I do not mean clever. I mean moral. They are working with law enforcers."

"Ah, I get your drift. Right, I will look into it."

"I suggest we go through this exercise regularly. Not a good idea to leave a trail. Now I must get on if I am to meet my self-imposed deadline. Yes, my friend, we will have dinner soon. It will be quite a celebration."

Eduardo gently placed his phone on the desk and changed his mind about working tonight. He was not tired, his energy never seemed to abate, he decided to go for a walk. Walking in the middle of the night was comforting and peaceful, when there were no people or children, whom he found even more intolerable than adults.

Chapter Twenty-One

The USA

The four of us were sitting in the hotel restaurant having a pre-tour breakfast. Leddicus and I were feeling refreshed after two days of rest and relaxation. Joe, Leddicus, and I had a huge full English, and Julie had her usual calorie-frugal fruit and yogurt. Joe had agreed to take the three of us to Heathrow for our late-afternoon flight, so this was an ideal opportunity to tie up final details for the trip.

After the plates were cleared away and the coffee poured, Joe hauled the statutory wedge of papers from his briefcase. We went through them one by one, and as usual, he had been thorough. After a while, Leddicus got busy pouring himself more coffee, fiddling with the sugar and milk, and paying no attention to the proceedings. He tried to stay interested in the business side of things, but he mostly faked it and swiftly got bored. These contracts meant we would all, including Leddicus, be earning a great deal of money, but he was just not interested. Apart from clothes, the occasional edible treat, and of course, his beloved laptop, he spent very little. Consequently, his bank account in the UK continued to expand.

Once all the contracts were signed and safely stowed in Joe's briefcase, we chatted about next steps following the US tour. We agreed Joe should continue to negotiate regarding the film possibilities and documentary opportunity. Joe was pretty certain that he could push for an increase in the offers being made on the back of the US tour.

"We can turn Leddicus into a money-making machine!" Joe quipped.

Leddicus looked up from stirring his coffee. "I don't want to be a machine. I like being human!"

We all laughed, except Leddicus, who gave us a bemused frown.

"Don't worry," said Joe. "You'll still be human, but if the book is a success and the film goes ahead, then the possibilities of making money expand. You can endorse products for example."

"Endorse? What does that mean?"

"Once the film has been released, people will recognise you even more than they do now. So you could say in a TV advert, 'This orange juice is the best. You should get some.' That's an endorsement, and you'd get paid for saying it," Joe explained.

"I could do that. No problem!" Leddicus said quickly. The frown disappeared as he held his coffee cup above his head. "This is good coffee. You should buy some."

We all laughed, and Joe slapped him on the back. "You're a trouper. That's what you are."

"Good for you," I said. "Let's leave Joe to work that out. In the meantime, the book deal is ready to be signed, and Julie wants to get started on that. We'll all get paid for that as well. Are you up for it?"

"Let's do it," Leddicus said.

Julie leaned over and gave him a hug. "I'm looking forward to doing this, Leddicus. I love to write. Before we make a move, I have one more piece of news. The red top has issued its apology, and as I expected, it was a tiny piece hidden away in the middle of the paper. They said they were given the wrong information. I have my suspicions that perhaps Pricilla Morrison is involved, but I can't prove it, and the paper will not give us its source."

"Well, it's better than nothing, and I'm sure you'll circulate it widely," said Joe. "I don't know what can be done about Morrison. Perhaps Leddicus can come up with an answer."

"Me!" Leddicus said. His eyebrows shot up. Surprise filled his dark brown eyes. "I don't know what I can do."

"Well, have a think," said Joe. "Something might pop into your head."

"Okay, I will," Leddicus said without conviction.

On that note, we concluded our meeting, piled our luggage and ourselves into Joe's car, and thus began the second tour.

As usual, we had a couple hours to kill while waiting for our flight. To pass the time, I hit on the idea of getting a world atlas to show Leddicus. I didn't know why I hadn't thought of that before. He was always fascinated about where he was, trying to understand the world and how it was interconnected. We sat in the coffee shop flipping through the pages. I pointed out place names I thought he might know, but Leddicus was struggling with the concept of the shape of the world.

"Is it flat or round?" He flipped between the front cover, which had a picture of a colourful globe, and the internal maps, which were flat.

We sauntered over to the nearest stationers, and I showed him the model of a globe I had spotted earlier when purchasing the atlas. I opened up the page with a map of America on it and then turned the globe around to show him the same piece of land. His expression showed me that understanding had clicked into place.

"Ah, that makes sense now. And what was written in the Jewish scrolls?"

It was my turn to be confused. "Jewish scrolls? They had maps in them?"

"No, no, it has these words in the book called Job. I saw them this morning when I looked in the copy of the scroll that is in my hotel bedroom."

"You have completely lost me now, Leddicus. What are you on about? There's a scroll in your hotel room?"

"There's a book in my room, and it has the same writing in it as the Jewish scrolls."

"Ah, I think you mean the Gideon Bible, but what's that got to do with the globe?" I scratched my head in frustration.

"In the book called Job, it says, 'God has hung the earth on nothing.' I always wondered what that meant, but when I look at this ball, it sort of makes sense to me."

My mobile chirruped at me. Julie had sent a text to say our flight had been called. We headed back to collect her and our luggage. As we walked towards our gate, it occurred to me how something that is initially strange and alien can rapidly become second nature. I remembered the first flight that Leddicus took and his wide-eyed fascination with every detail. Today, he headed towards the plane as if he had been flying all his life.

Although a hardened flyer, Leddicus had never done a long haul. As we waited for take-off, I talked him through all the new technology. He was particularly delighted with the TV screen embedded in the back of the seat. He had never lost his fascination of all things tech and wanted to know the function of every button and attachment. By the time the plane began taxiing to the runway, he was keen to get some use out of the TV. With his headphones on, he pressed hopefully on the appropriate control.

"It'll be an hour or so before they switch on the entertainment." I removed one of his earpieces so he could hear me.

He flicked through one of the flight magazines, but quickly became bored of adverts for perfume and jewellery. He turned towards Julie, who was craning her neck to watch the white cliffs of Dover pass by far below. The clear blue sky gave a perfect view.

"I saw an interesting programme about values last night," he said to her.

"What sort of values? Money? Stuff? Or life?"

"Life, that's the one. The values of life. In the programme, a man, who was an artist, was talking to another man who had something to do with ships. They were saying how you get values in life, but I think they got it all wrong, especially the man who was an artist."

Julie giggled. "I watched that, too. He wasn't an artist, he was an atheist, that's someone who doesn't believe in God. The other guy, he wasn't anything to do with ships, he's a bishop; that's someone high ranking in the Church of England."

An unfazed Leddicus ploughed on. "The artist man said we get our values from being human and how we were educated. Seems mad to me. My education and upbringing taught me ways to live and what it is to be human, and now I think most of the values I was taught were all wrong."

I leaned over and said to them both, "I know Leddicus in this mode. He can get very deep!"

Julie flashed a wide smile. "I know," she said without rancour, "but he is fascinating." She focused on Leddicus. "What do you mean when you say it's all wrong?"

"That's easy. When I became a follower of the way, following the teachings of Jesus of Nazareth, my values changed, my thinking changed, and my life changed. Some of the values he gave me would be mad to people in my world. For example, 'Love your enemies and do good to people who are bad to you.' That value had never been taught me and probably never would be."

"I see what you mean, and I agree. If there isn't a God, how can you get a trusted and consistent value system? An atheist would say a value system develops all on its own, but when has anyone ever suggested we should be good to people who are bad to us ever in the history of time?"

"Exactly!" said Leddicus. "A lot of the values I was taught came from Caesar, and he was totally corrupt."

I interrupted them, "The entertainment module is working now."

These heavy-duty conversations, for some strange reason, really got me rattled. I stuffed the headphones in my ears and switched on the TV screen. Leddicus quickly forgot about the debate and followed suit, flicking through the programs.

We arrived in New York in the late morning. Leddicus was very tired, and the time change puzzled him. As our taxi crawled its way through the lunchtime Manhattan traffic, I filled Leddicus in on the concept of jet lag and how best to counteract it.

"So we're not going to bed now?" He yawned widely.

"Nope, that would be the very worst thing to do. To limit the effects, you have to jolt yourself into the new time zone," I said.

We paid the fare and checked into the Marriot.

"The restaurant here has rave reviews," Julie said. "It's on the top floor and has panoramic views. Shall we eat here?"

"Sounds like a plan," I said. "Let's take a couple hours to shower and unpack. We can meet up at the restaurant for early dinner and enjoy the view while it's still light."

We followed the steward down the corridor to our rooms. Leddicus was the first stop. As he entered his room, I walked in after him and prodded him in the back. "No cheating!" I said with mock authority.

"What?" He plonked his case on the gargantuan bed.

"No taking a nap. You'll thank me tomorrow."

"Right, okay," he said blearily.

Julie and I waited for ten minutes in the restaurant reception before Leddicus appeared, looking very sheepish and breathless with shock at the speed of the lift. Julie grinned at me. We both knew what had happened. He would need copious amounts of coffee tomorrow. Julie had booked us an excellent table that took full advantage of the view. Leddicus snapped fully awake as he sat down and got sight of the view from the forty-eighth floor. He stared out for a full two minutes without saying a word, his eyes like saucers.

"I think I'm a bit dizzy," he said. "It must be the effects of the long flight. I feel like I am still moving."

"That's because you are!" Julie said triumphantly. "We all are! The restaurant is moving round, and you will eventually see views of the whole of Manhattan, including Times Square, and we'll be able to watch all the lights coming on right across New York as it gets dark."

"Incredible!" He stared back out of the window in awe. "How on Earth does that work?"

Neither of us said anything, and he looked with anticipation from me to Julie and back again. We just shrugged at him lamely and thrust a menu into his hands.

"Do you know how it works?" he said again.

"Google it," I said.

"But I haven't got my laptop here," he said in a mock whine.

To distract him from his engineering quandary, I pointed to the centre of the restaurant. "Have you seen that?" I pointed towards the chocolate fountain and the typical American overkill buffet, which could feed everyone in the restaurant for a year.

"Wow!" said Leddicus, instantly keen to get stuck in. He banished hidden cogs and gears from his mind.

Even though I was a little tired from the flight, my adrenalin kicked in as I revelled in this new experience. It had been a master stroke to arrive at the restaurant while it was still light. We were able to watch as night enveloped the city, turning it into a carpet of sparkling black velvet, glistening and winking as far as the eye could see.

After dinner, we decided to take a stroll in Times Square and experience the unique attack on our every sense. Sirens wailed, music blared out of open doorways, and delicious smells wafted from street vendors, all against the panoramic backdrop of signs that constantly ticked, winked, flashed, and blinked. Poor Leddicus was becoming dizzy as he stood twirling on the spot, staring at every corner from every angle. From ground level to as high as he could crane his neck, he tried to take in the hundreds of signs dazzling his vision.

We met up at ten thirty for breakfast, and all felt refreshed after a good rest.

"I have to go back to London in three days," Julie announced. "So Leddicus and I have our work cut out. I must capitalise on this time to get the outline material ready for the book."

"What do you need me to do?" Leddicus poured syrup over a huge stack of waffles.

"Answer lots of questions while I make notes and record the conversations."

"Can I eat first?" He grinned at us, daring us to say no.

Straight after breakfast, Leddicus and Julie found a quiet corner in the lounge, and I headed off to explore New York.

For the next three days, we settled into a routine. We took an early breakfast. After which, Leddicus and Julie would settle in the lounge. She would fire endless questions at him and make copious notes while I went exploring or worked in my room. I would meet them when they took a break for lunch, and then it was more of the same for all of us. In the evenings, we tried different American eateries.

At lunchtime on the final day, Julie announced. "I've enough to keep me going to make a good start on the book. Let's take the afternoon off to go sightseeing!"

We went to the Empire State Building. From there, we went to the remains of the Twin Towers and to check out progress on the new construction. I also managed to negotiate a private tour of the United Nations building by calling in a favour from a long-term acquaintance.

Leddicus struggled with the concept of the United Nations. "Rome rules everywhere. There is only one authority. Why would you consult nations on their opinions?"

While we waited for my acquaintance to arrive at the appointed meeting spot outside the building, we looked at the sculpture of a gun with a twisted barrel. I explained to Leddicus that this was a symbol of peace. The United Nations aimed to bring an end to all war. We had arrived about a half hour early so we wandered around the gardens and came across a sculpture of a man with a huge hammer raised above his head, ready to take an almighty blow to a fearsome-looking sword that he held in his other hand. The statue bore no inscription, standing bold and stark against the East River backdrop.

"I know what this statue represents. It's a verse in a Jewish scroll, but I can't remember it all," Leddicus said.

"Have we time to walk over the road, Gerhardt? I remember something from my last visit," Julie said.

I checked my watch. "We've got about twenty minutes before David is due."

"That should be enough time." Julie steered us across the road to Ralph Bunche Park in order to see the Isaiah Wall in the United Nations Plaza. And there, carved in the concrete wall is part of the Bible describing the statue we had just seen in the UN gardens.

Leddicus read it out very slowly, "They will beat their swords into ploughshares and their spears into pruning hooks. Nation will not take up sword against nation, nor will they train for war anymore."

We all stood in awe as we thought of the statue and the chiselled words on the wall before us.

"Come on," I said reluctantly. "We'd best make a move so we're not late."

My acquaintance, David Wakefield, turned up at the same time as us. After warm handshakes, he ushered us into the building. One of the best parts of the tour was being able, with use of David's pass, to access the main Security Council room and view the place where it is all decided, for good or ill, depending on your point of view.

The main United Nations forum room fascinated Leddicus, and he was still confused that representatives from each country had a seat and could take part in discussions on policy. He asked where Rome sat, and David walked over and pointed out the Italian seat. Leddicus also wanted to know if a seat were allocated for where he came from. He was shown the seats for Israel and Palestine. He wanted to know where on Earth the country was with the seat labelled Holy See. I explained that was Vatican City, which he had already visited on our trip to Rome. He looked very puzzled at that. He wandered from seat to seat, asking question after question. David checked his watch with barely concealed irritation. I knew he was on a tight schedule so I swiftly intervened, wheeling Leddicus out of the room and diplomatically suggesting a trip to his favourite venue for lunch. We were all bowled over by the visit, and grateful to have had the opportunity.

For Julie and Leddicus, New York had been hard work, but for me, it had been an adventure. I had explored so much of it while they worked. But all good things come to an end, and it was now time for Julie to go back to London. She waved good-bye to us from her taxi. An hour later, some very friendly people from New Jersey, where our tour was to begin, collected us from the hotel.

Eduardo slit open the package and pulled out the brand-new mobile. He plugged it in to charge the battery. He had located a source of new units. Some of them were of a very fresh variety. The first nine were ready for dispatch. He already had excellent transport links in place, a new and seemingly foolproof method. The final destination was London.

While he waited for the phone to charge, he put the finishing touches to the manuscript. He was almost ready to send it to the publisher. All that was needed were the essential notes containing the intimate personal details to bring it to life. Joseph had emailed to say that the courier would be en route within a few days. The up-front payment, which he split equally with Joseph, was in the region of £200,000, and that was just for the English version. He had already begun work on the Italian version and would thereafter commence the German translation followed by Spanish. His multi-lingual abilities engendered the only gratitude he felt for his violent and domineering father, who had forced him to learn all the languages spoken by both his parents.

Joseph had close ties with the film industry, and if sales were good, a movie deal was a foregone conclusion.

A powerful Kawasaki pulled up gently to the curb alongside a terrace of up market North London new build flats. The driver drew the bike up onto its stand beneath the thick foliage of a London Plane tree. The midnight streets were deserted, and there were very few lights showing from the windows of nearby homes.

He was clad entirely in black, and he did not remove his helmet as he moved swiftly through the shared courtyard and up the steps to one of the front doors, he quietly unzipped a pocket on the front of his jacket and removed a slender tool. This he inserted into the lock, and within 15 seconds the door swung open. To any casual observer, it was just a resident returning home early in the morning.

He did not remove his gloves or switch on any lights, he removed his mobile from his trouser pocket and switched on its flashlight. He checked each room until he found the one containing a desk and PC, and there, in a tray beside the keyboard sat a slim red notebook. He flipped it open, flicked through a few pages, and nodded to himself. He tucked it into a pocket on the inside on his leather jacket and stood silently for a moment, slowing his racing pulse, calming his breathing and listening.

No sound could be heard within the flat. He moved silently towards the front door, opened it a crack and checked each way along the street, it was still deserted. He cranked the bike back off its stand, but didn't push the ignition; instead he wheeled it to the end of the road where he placed it back on its stand, unlocked the small container behind the pillion seat and removed a sat nav, he clicked this into its housing on the dashboard and punched in the co-ordinates for Dover, then he fired up the bike.

For the USA tour, we used a similar format to the UK, and everything soon became a blur with us not really knowing when or where we were. Joe's office kept us on time and on track. The main difference was the hospitality. In the UK, at the end of most evenings, we would end up back at our hotel, grabbing a bite to eat from the room service menu. But in almost every venue, at the end of the seminar, the hosts insisted on taking us out to eat in fancy restaurants. It was fantastic, but my trousers were getting tighter and tighter. Even the salads added inches to your waistline here.

Leddicus did not take long to adjust to the new way of speaking English and could soon drawl with the best of them. He loved the hospitality and the fact that the Americans were much gentler with him with their questions and much less sceptical about his story.

We spent our time doing four things: sleeping, lecturing, eating, and flying. We criss-crossed the country from Texas to the Midwest and then back to the New England states. We even dipped once into Canada, where Leddicus would normally have quizzed me relentlessly.

"Why is it another country? Why do they use different money? Why is it the same person on this paper money as the money in the UK? Why is it different money? Why does it say dollar and yet has a different value to the American dollar?"

But by now, he knew that, whatever question he asked me, my response was always the same, "Google it."

On one of the rare free evenings during the tour, we were sitting on the hotel balcony and gazing out at the New England landscape when his mobile rang. He fished it out of his pocket.

"Julie!" His smile rapidly changed to a frown. He listened silently for a while and then handed the phone to me.

"Hey, Julie, it must be the middle of the night there. We've been having such a—" I stopped short as I caught a sob on the other end of the line.

"It's gone!" Her voice trembled. "I lost all the notes I had typed up for the book, and I lost the fifty pages I had typed for the start of the biography."

"Lost? How could you lose them? Did your laptop malfunction?"

"I don't know. They just disappeared from my files, along with a few other obscure documents."

"What was it? A virus?" I kept my voice calm, but I knew what this meant.

"I've had it checked out. The tech boys can't find anything wrong. They can find no trace. I've got a good virus protection program, and my laptop is firewalled, but that's not the worst of it."

"There's more?"

"I don't know how to tell you this. Joe was absolutely furious with me. I've never known him so angry." Julie stopped for a moment. I could sense her trying to regain control. "I've also lost my notebook, all the notes I made while I was with Leddicus. All Joe kept saying was, 'Why didn't you back it up, you idiot?' I've never backed anything up. I've never needed to before."

"How on Earth did you lose your notebook?" I asked gently and pointlessly, but was actually wondering how such an organised girl as Julie had lost all her work.

"I'm so sorry. I've let you all down. I don't know how I can make it up to you all."

"Look, Julie, this is terrible, but it can be fixed. When we are back, you can start again. I know that's wretched, but it just means it'll take more time."

"I hope you're right, but Joe kept saying timing is critical. We may not keep the monopoly if we don't strike while the iron is hot, and this is going to set us back months."

"I think I understand." Leddicus was hovering at my shoulder. "Leddicus wants to speak to you." I handed the phone back to him. He left me sitting on the balcony and wandered up and down the corridor as he chatted soothingly to the distraught Julie.

Over the next few days, we spoke a few more times. Julie went over and over it. She was torturing herself trying to discover what went wrong, but could reach no conclusion. The only answer was to start again. Julie had suggested this to Joe, but it did not seem to stem his anger. He kept saying that timing was of the essence. Someone else could pip us to the post. I didn't see how that could happen. We were the only ones with access to Leddicus.

When I compared the three-month UK schedule and the two-month States schedule, I realised the cunning Joe had packed in as many bookings as we had undertaken in the UK. No wonder I was beginning to feel ready for a break as the end of the tour approached.

I sat in my seat with a huge sense of relief as the plane revved up its engines, ready for the long haul back to the UK.

"Leddicus, you've done a great job. We've had a fantastic two months, and there's a lot to talk about."

"Yes, there is." He folded his arms and looked attentive and expectant.

"But I'm exhausted and just need to rest my brain, so, if you don't mind, let's have a quiet flight home."

His face fell, and he shrugged. "Okay, I understand." I was pretty sure he didn't. He had boundless energy and never seemed to need peace and quiet.

To ensure he was under no illusions, that I really did mean to have some quiet, right after the "remove seat belt" sign winked on, I stuffed on my headset, pushed the seat back as far as it would go, and closed my eyes. Almost immediately, I was fast asleep.

Chapter Twenty-Two

Bureaucracy Can Ruin the Best Plans

The flight back to London was smooth, uneventful, and peaceful. I even managed to grab a couple hours of sleep. As the plane taxied to its allotted bay, I surreptitiously switched on my phone and texted Julie.

"Here we are, safe and sound. Will our ride to the hotel be as smooth as the flight?"

I hastily put it into silent mode in case she replied before we disembarked. The obedient Swiss mentality was hard to shake. In less than a minute, I felt it vibrate in my top pocket.

"Welcome back! Am ready and waiting. As for a smooth drive, we'll see . . ."

The plane doors finally opened to the jetway, and we headed off towards passport control, which always seemed to be ten miles away when one is tired and hungry. We got in line and shuffled slowly towards the desks. It was finally our turn, and together we approached the waiting official.

"Stand behind the line!" the officer snarled at me.

"But we're travelling together," I exclaimed.

"One at a time! Stand behind the line! Wait your turn!" he growled ferociously.

"But we're together."

"If you don't stand behind the line and wait your turn, I will have an officer remove you!" he barked loudly.

The people behind me fell silent and stopped shuffling. I gulped back the words that were ready to spill out and stood meekly behind the line. Leddicus approached the desk and handed over his travel document.

"How long are you staying in the UK?" I heard the officer ask.

"Not very long. A few days. Then I am going home" Leddicus replied.

The officer turned the document over and over, scrutinising it closely. He then picked up the phone and made a call. A moment later, two burly men arrived. One of them picked up the travel document while the other one took a firm hold on Leddicus's elbow.

"Come this way, please," said the elbow-grabber.

I watched helplessly as they led him away.

"Next!" the officer snapped.

I hastily moved to the desk. "Where is my friend going?"

"He needs to answer some more questions." He didn't look up. He stamped my passport and shoved it towards me. "Next!" he snapped.

I stepped away from the desk. A cold panic settled into the pit of my stomach. Instinctively I headed in the direction that they had taken Leddicus, although the crowds had quickly blocked their destination from my view. I frantically scanned the perimeter walls for any official-looking doors. I noticed one with a "No Entry" sign on it and headed there. It opened into a small office, its walls plastered with posters about rabid animals and the dangers of untended packages.

A rather untidy official glared at me from behind his paper-stacked desk. "You should not be in here."

"My friend came through passport control. Two officers took him for further questioning. We're together. Could you please take me to him?" The words rushed out breathlessly.

"I can't give you any further information. Wait for him in the area beyond customs." He stood up and moved towards me. "This is an official area. You should not be in here. I can't help you." He opened the door and ushered me out.

The door closed behind me, and I leaned against the wall, my heart pounding, my brain rushing. This could not be happening. I stood for a while and took deep breaths to calm myself. I then went into auto mode and headed off to retrieve our cases. I stood blankly as the conveyor belt circulated. Our luggage chugged past my unseeing eyes before I focussed, shoved through the crowds, and grabbed them, plonked them on a trolley and headed down the corridor into the arrivals area.

Julie's welcoming face swam into view. She waved cheerily. "Where's Leddicus?" she asked as I reached her side.

"They got him. They took him for further questioning."

"Who got him? What are you talking about? You're as white as a sheet!"

"Officials at passport control. They frog-marched him off."

"What!" Julie took my arm and steered me towards a coffee shop. She bought the biggest takeaway coffee she could lay her hands on and thrust it into my hand. With her face set, she said, "Right. Keep up."

I gulped thankfully at the coffee, scalding my tongue and lips, as I rushed after her. She operated like a well-trained bloodhound, moving swiftly with notebook in hand, from information desk to information desk, official to official, and queue after queue, calmly questioning. She was always in control, investigative journalist par excellence.

After two hours, she had not flagged, but I had. We agreed to an intermission to dump the cases in the car and grab a sandwich. We sat in silence while she poured over her notes and made more notes, neatly bulleted on the pristine page. I was very thankful she was so firmly in control. I gulped down a large strong coffee to keep jet lag at bay and consumed a mammoth bacon baguette without even tasting it.

"I think I know where to go now." She sat back and sipped her tea. "So many jobsworth plonkers, so much cross information, but it all points to here. This office deals with illegal immigrants and passport anomalies." She tapped the last bullet point with her pen.

"Thanks," I said.

"What for?"

"For taking over. Sorry. I panicked back there." Embarrassed, I gave a slight shrug. I was so impressed with how she had handled the crises. She had never once got riled with the numerous irritating staff and officials she had spoken to. Her tone had remained calm and coaxing. Her broad smile never faltered.

She shrugged. "Don't give it a second thought. I'm glad I'm here, and this is what I do best." She pecked at her sandwich with thumb and finger and occasionally put a crumb into her taut mouth. She finally pushed it away. It was barely touched. "Not hungry. Do you want the other half?"

I shook my head. "No thanks. Shall we get on?"

"Yes, let's. We need to go to level two. I think we'll find Leddicus there."

After wandering around level two for twenty minutes, we finally found the right office. A young lady stood behind the desk, sullenly picking at her fingernails. Julie smiled that disarming smile of hers, and the girl's face softened slightly.

"We're looking for a friend of ours. He landed a couple hours ago, and he was held for further questioning."

"Name?"

"Leddicus Palantina."

The girl began checking through a very fat book that looked like a register. It seemed to take forever. "Ah, here we are. Palantina. He's been moved to a detention centre. Brook House. That's based in Gatwick."

"Thank you." Julie said graciously "Please could I have the address and telephone number?"

The girl scribbled the details on a tiny yellow post-it note and shoved it across the counter.

As soon as we had left the office, I burst out, "What on Earth? How can they do this? He's done nothing wrong. What craziness is this?"

"I know this place." Julie's calm exterior faltered a little. "It holds about thirty-five hundred people. It's where you get dumped if there are any problems with your travel documents. You can get stuck there for months. Those held don't have the rights that you or I have. The normal EU rules don't apply. We need to move quickly. Get him out before the paperwork gets stuck in an endless snarl-up." She clutched at her notebook. Her knuckles were white. "We must go." She strode off toward the car park. "There's no time to lose." She opened the driver's door. "You drive. Give me a minute to set up the sat nav. Then I can make some calls en route."

I was in awe and a little bit afraid of this element of Julie that I had never seen before. I knew I couldn't argue. I climbed behind the wheel and gritted my teeth. I was extremely tired and now faced a long drive.

"Don't forget that we drive on the left," she said stonily as she pulled her phone out of her bag.

"Sure." I gave myself a mental shake and a grim reminder that the only thing mattering now was that we must rescue Leddicus. I pushed away my tiredness, took a deep breath, and fired up the engine.

"At the roundabout, take the second exit." The sat nav commanded.

I'd never used one before, and I was reassured at how easy it was. Julie sat quietly for a while and let me acclimatise to the new car, the sat nav, and driving on the wrong side of the road.

"Bear right, and enter the motorway," the sat nav announced. "Continue for twenty-five miles."

Julie was immediately on the phone, making call after call. I was only half-listening. I was using the last dregs of my adrenaline to drive, stay awake, and obey the sat nav.

After twenty minutes, she laid the phone on her knee and leaned back with a sigh. "I think we're getting there. There are very strict visiting hours, so lots of strings to pull and arms to twist. Joe has some very powerful friends high up in government and the police. He's doing a ring-round now and will get back to us, hopefully before we get to Brook House."

The sat nav interrupted with more directions.

"You okay?" She patted my arm.

"I'll live. I could use some coffee, but I know there's no time."

Her phone rang. "Hi, Joe." She listened intently and said nothing for a while. "Great! Thanks! I'll call you when we've accomplished the mission." She jotted down something in her trusty notebook.

"Well, what gives?"

"He's pulled it off, good ol' Joe. The authorities are making all sorts of apologies and excuses. It was a mix-up, a misunderstanding. We can pick up Leddicus tonight. They're sorting the release papers now."

"Fantastic! That's great news!" I was suddenly wide-awake.

"But you know what makes me so mad I could spit?" She banged the dashboard with her notebook in a most uncharacteristic fashion. "We had the contacts, we knew what strings to pull, and we knew the people in high places who could make this happen. What about all the people who don't have those options? Who haven't got the contacts?"

Her anger caught me off guard, and I didn't understand what she was on about. I was furious that officialdom had caused all this nonsense, but happy and relieved that we were going to get

Leddicus. Her outburst left me confused. I didn't get what she was alluding to, but I was, after all, just an exhausted historian.

I thought that Julie's tirade was spent, but I was wrong. She was still wound up. "I've worked and reported on this stuff, and the worst thing is that my industry is partly at fault. Asylum seekers are held up as the scapegoat. They get blamed for every ill in society. The problem is, once they are branded as such, they are dehumanised. But what do the news moguls care? It sells papers, doesn't it?" The rhetorical question hung in the air."They're demonised and helpless. They're running away from terrible situations. They arrive here in the hope of finding a haven, but they end up in a detention centre because they answered one question wrong or their face didn't fit. Then instead of peace, they are crammed into a tiny room for months while their papers go round in circles." If Julie had been a smoker, at this point, she would have lit up. "What would have happened to Leddicus if Joe didn't have friends in high places?"

Again, I didn't answer. She was talking at me not to me.

"Oh, it makes me mad. It's so unfair! I did a couple pieces on one of the groups that protests about these centres and how asylum seekers are treated. I have tried to help. I'm sick of them being called scroungers and rogues! Goodness knows, many of them have already had such dreadful times, and then they are confronted with inhuman, faceless bureaucracy, and idiotic news stories saying how awful they are. It makes me rage!"

She ranted on and on, but I wasn't really listening. I kept my focus on the road and the sat nav. I truly did not want to get lost. I thought she was never going to stop, but the sat nav came to the rescue. "Destination in three hundred yards on the right," it announced calmly. Julie was suddenly silent.

I pulled into the car park and finally switched off the engine. I was so happy I could stop gripping the steering wheel, stop driving on the wrong side of the road, and Julie had finally stopped going on and on. It was getting on for midnight and drizzling. We both got out of the car, Julie walked to the door entry system and pressed the buzzer.

A voice crackled in the speaker, "We're closed."

"Yes, I'm sorry that it's late. We have come to collect Leddicus Palantina on the authority of—" A gust of wind snatched Julie's words from my hearing.

But I got the next bit, loud and clear, as it blared metallically out of the speaker. "I don't care who you are, who you think you have come to pick up, or whose name you quote. I don't care if the queen sent you. I answer to the governor, and he's gone to bed. I ain't opening this door unless he gets up and tells me to, so listen, missus, you come back tomorrow at visiting time!" The line went dead.

The wind was picking up. The drizzle turned into a heavy shower. I was getting drenched and began to shiver. I thought Julie was going to burst a blood vessel and I might have to restrain her from breaking down the door. Face red and eyes flashing, she stabbed at her phone keypad and began ranting at Joe. I opened the passenger door and beckoned to her, but she looked through me as she paced up and down, gesticulating in the rain. I got in and switched on the engine to get the heater working.

After about ten minutes, she opened the door, slumped into the seat, leaned forward, and put her head in her hands, totally spent. Her hair was clinging to her head. She was completely soaked.

After a minute or two, she sat up, got a wad of tissues out of her bag, blotted at her face and hair, and said tonelessly, "Nothing more we can do tonight. Need to find a hotel. The sat nav will find us the nearest one." She prodded at the screen and scrolled to a little icon, she pressed it and leaned back waiting as it found the location.

Half an hour later we were welcomed by a friendly porter who went to fetch the night receptionist. For the first time since I landed at Heathrow, something went right. The receptionist was a motherly lady who fussed and clucked at us. Within minutes, a jug of hot chocolate, two large whiskies, and sandwiches appeared as if by magic. Oh, the joys of five-star hotel! I was so happy this place was the nearest the sat nav could find. I took a slug of whisky to chase away the cold that had reached my bones.

As she let us into our rooms, this saintly lady whispered, "You're absolutely soaking dears. Leave all your clothes outside the door, and they'll be all ready for you first thing in the morning. You'll find a bathrobe in the wardrobe."

At two thirty, my head hit the pillow. A minute later, I was unconscious.

Chapter Twenty-Three

It Is Who You Know

Although I didn't get to bed until two thirty, I was wide-awake at six thirty. I showered, donned the voluminous, fluffy, five-star robe that was on the heated rail in the bathroom, and peeked outside my door. There, as promised, was a blue bag containing all my freshly laundered clothes. By seven fifteen, I had ordered the biggest fry-up on the menu and was wondering what the day held. *Would we be successful in our mission to release Leddicus?*

"Good morning, sir! full English with extra bacon!" The cheerful waiter, smiling broadly, placed my food on the table. I nodded and thanked him without much grace. It always seemed to make one feel much worse when other people were happy and you were gloomy.

Julie arrived just as the waiter was leaving. She waylaid him and ordered her usual frugal fare. I would never understand how people managed to be so strict with their eating habits. I was sure I saw a glimmer of disapproval as she surveyed my huge fry-up.

"Morning," I said through a mouthful of sausage. "Why are we up so early when the place is so near?"

"Sleeping is hard when your friend is in prison and you might be able to get him out."

I nodded. "I was so exhausted last night. I thought I would sleep forever, but here I am."

"Can't believe the service here. It's marvellous. Such a relief to have all my clothes back clean and dry." The waiter breezed up and greeted her equally cheerily. She smiled and thanked him.

She checked her watch for the third time since she had sat down.

"Do you know what time the centre opens?" I asked.

"Not until nine, but visiting isn't until ten, so we have to kick our heels until then."

"It's such a blow what happened. We had the best time in the States. We went to so many places. We were both looking forward to a break. Leddicus thoroughly enjoyed himself." I paused to pour some coffee from the cafetière the waiter had just deposited on the table. "Very odd how things worked out. In America, I thought he would struggle, but he took to it like a duck to water. I thought he would be at home in Rome, and he couldn't get away quick enough."

Julie just nodded, letting me ramble on.

"I took him to some of those churches you suggested. Not my scene, But as you thought, it would be a good idea, I went along for the ride. He understood them a bit, but he mostly struggled with the way things were organised. It confused him. He liked the people and understood what they said to him, but I didn't, not in the slightest."

Julie gave me an ironic smile. "You're the historian, as you often tell us. I would have thought you had worked some of that out by now."

"What's it got to do with history?" I asked defensively.

"If Leddicus and we are right about his date of birth, then he would have been part of a church that is quite probably nothing like it is today. He doesn't even use the word Christian, although I'm sure he understands what it means. Rather, he talks about the way. The word Christian was used much later and not when Leddicus was around originally. Second, you have to realise that the early church was very subversive. That's why Leddicus is often so careful when talking about it. In his day, he could easily have been put to death for what he believed. The church would probably have been non-institutional and non-hierarchical, a much more organic set up, empowering people from below. By 112 AD, Pliny, I think he was a Roman governor, wrote to the Caesar of the time and said, 'These followers of Jesus are everywhere. They have turned the world upside down, and our temples are closed. I am killing as many of them as possible, and still they multiply, but what else can I do?' That's why Leddicus is struggling with the so-called organised church of whatever ilk it is."

"Okay, Julie, thank you for the history lesson. Bit early for this, and your lectures are longer than the ones I get from Leddicus when he gets started."

At first, her face fell until she caught sight of my face. Then she grinned at me. "All right, sarky, shove me over that coffeepot."

"Coffee! Easy now." I teased.

She ignored my dig and poured a cupful. "I need to be on form when I do battle with those jobsworth morons at the centre."

"Did you ever find out what happened to your notes?" I asked.

She shrugged gloomily, "No, it's a complete mystery. I tried to do some of it from memory, but it was hopeless. I've never worked that way."

"It just doesn't make any sense. You are so organised."

"I pride myself on it. Joe seems okay about it now, but was cool with me for quite a few weeks while you were away."

"What's his beef anyway? It's your work, and you're freelance, aren't you?" I topped up her coffee.

"I know, but it's a vital key to what is rapidly becoming Leddicus Ltd. It's likely to be a huge money spinner, getting the book published and then, if the sales are high, a movie deal. All of that is on hold now."

"I can see how a file can go missing from a laptop, but your notebook? That's what I don't understand."

She just shrugged. "I always put it in the same place when I get home, right on top of my desk. When I lost the Word documents, I went to get it straight away. I turned my flat upside down. No joy. It makes my head ache thinking about it. Let's change the subject."

We chatted about trivia while waiting for the time to tick by. Both of us regularly checked the time. We requested more coffee and toast just for something to do. Julie checked her watch for the twentieth time and then stood up.

"I'll be down in ten minutes. I'm going to freshen up. Then let's get out of this place and go get our man. I have flights booked for Caesarea Philippi for tomorrow, and we are going to be on that plane."

I called after her, "I'll pay the bill and meet you in reception."

We pulled into the car park at ten minutes to the hour. Julie pushed the buzzer, and as predicted, another jobsworth was at the end of the phone, "Visiting time is at ten."

What sad people. It's only five minutes to go, but they won't open the door. I could sense the bile beginning to rise in Julie. Her face was fixed and pale. I wondered where calm Julie had disappeared to. An explosion would not help our cause.

"Hey, Julie, it's only a few minutes. Let's be patient." She took a deep breath, and we wandered up the path alongside the building to pass the time.

By the time we got back, it was just after ten. I pressed the buzzer.

"Enter," said the officious voice.

The door clicked, and we pushed it open into a small reception area. Behind glass panelling, rather like in a bank, sat a grim-looking, middle-aged man in need of a shave.

"Yes," he said.

"We have come to collect Leddicus. Leddicus Palantina." Julie said quickly.

The man pulled up a small hatch. "Papers."

"What papers?" said Julie.

"Collection papers."

I saw her shoulders go rigid, so I stepped forward, "Please, can we see Mr. Palantina?"

He looked up. "Papers." His face barely moved.

This was getting tedious. "What papers?" I said calmly.

He looked me in the eye. A curious mixture of boredom and defiance, his monotone voice informed us, "Visiting papers from you and collection papers from her."

"I'm sorry. I didn't know I needed any papers. I was with my friend at the airport yesterday, and I understand he was brought here. I would very much like to see him."

"Need papers," he said in the same monotone.

Julie was exasperated. "Yeah, yeah, it's more than your job's worth to do anything at all without papers, isn't it?"

He shrugged, unfazed. "Them's the rules, lady."

She moved over to the other side of the reception area, pulled out her mobile, and started punching at the keys. She was soon talking to Joe, updating him on the situation.

The monotone guy actually raised his voice. "Oi! No mobiles in her. It's not allowed."

She pulled the phone away from her ear and snapped, "I don't doubt it! Not without papers!"

She turned her back on him and continued her call to Joe. When she finished, she turned round and glared at the man behind the screen.

There were a couple chairs set against the wall, and Julie sat down on one of them. I walked over and sat down beside her.

"What now?"

"We wait. Joe said to hang on while he finds out what's holding things up. He's surprised at our reception. He was promised everything was in place. He's making some calls now. But quite frankly, I would like to punch someone." She glared darkly at monotone man.

Unblinking, he stared back at her. "I need your papers. And no more phone calls."

Julie looked at him or rather looked through him and didn't say a word. I admit I felt out of my depth. When I glanced at monotone man, I got the impression he felt the same in the face of this total defiance. From Julie's perspective, he was surplus to requirements. She would no longer be dealing with him.

He kept looking over at Julie, then at me, and then back to Julie. He was blinking furiously, perhaps casting around for something to say that did not involve papers. Every now and then, he would open his mouth, but no words came out. He would shift in his seat. Every time he looked over at Julie, she stared back at him blankly. I'm not sure if he were afraid or what he felt, but he certainly did not know how to deal with the situation. The minutes ticked by, and the tension mounted.

From behind the only other door in the reception area, I heard footsteps coming down the corridor. The door swung open, monotone man jumped out of his seat, and he stood almost to attention.

A tall, angular man walked in. His lined face smiled down at us as he extended a hand. "Very sorry for the delay. I'm the governor in charge. I have only just become aware that you are here when I received a call from our government official. Would you please follow me?"

We walked behind him down a long, grey corridor, starkly lit with regulation fluorescent strips. He opened a door, ushered us into his office, and asked us to take a seat.

The governor cleared his throat. "Again, my apologies. This is a most unusual case." He picked up the phone and spoke into it quietly. Almost immediately, we heard a knock on the door. A uniformed guard entered the office.

"Thank you, George. Would you please take these people to the common room to meet with Mr. Palantina? Then can you bring them all back to my office?"

We stood up and dutifully followed George along the depressing grey corridors. He eventually led us into a large room filled with people. Some were sitting chatting, others were drinking from paper cups, and many just sat there and stared into space. It smelled of dirty laundry and fish. There in the centre was Leddicus, surrounded by a gaggle of what could only be described as the United Nations. As we moved closer, we could see that they were trying to teach him to play cards. It was all very noisy and good humoured.

We approached the table, and Leddicus finally noticed us. A huge smile spread over his face. He jumped out of his chair and said to the group, "Here are my friends!" He beckoned to us. "Come and meet all my new friends!" He began introducing them one by one, so many names, so many different nationalities. It became a complete hubbub as everyone began speaking at once, greeting us in their own language. Leddicus fetched two more chairs and insisted we sit down and have coffee with his new friends. That was the last thing on either of our minds, but the people were so welcoming, and Leddicus was so persuasive that we hadn't the heart to refuse.

Everyone started talking at once, and I let it wash over me, smiling and nodding mechanically, but not hearing any of it. Julie was more gracious. She made small talk with everyone as she sipped at a paper cup filled with the most disgusting coffee imaginable. I noticed a small group of children in the corner, sitting quietly on the floor. There were about nine of them. They could not have been more than five or six years old, all girls. They made no sound. Their eyes were dark-circled and haunted. One small, skinny, dark-haired girl sat hugging her knees and rocked back and forth. In her hands, she had a grubby linen handkerchief, which she twisted and twisted and twisted as she stared at the wall.

I eventually managed to cut across the noise and confusion and put my hand on Leddicus's shoulder. "We need to go and see the governor now."

Julie quickly noticed my cue and started to head toward the exit. She smiled, waved at everyone, and said again and again, "Nice to meet you." Leddicus hugged everyone and followed us out. I swear he looked sad to be leaving.

George was waiting for us in the corridor, and we followed in the direction of the governor's office. It didn't seem to take nearly as long on the way back, and we barely had chance to ask Leddicus if he were okay before we were back in the room with the governor.

As we entered, the governor looked up from his desk and motioned for us to be seated. "I'll be with you in just a moment." He looked down and continued to read and write. He seemed a little uneasy, perhaps embarrassed. A small bead of sweat glistened on his temple.

He scribbled on the form before him for a while. He eventually looked up. "Apologies again for the mix-up. Most unfortunate, your friend phoned me, and now we are trying to ensure that this does not happen again. I hope you are not planning to leave the country in the near future as we must send Mr. Palantina's travel document to the home office, where he will be given an ILR. I just need Mr. Palantina to sign here. Then he can collect his belongings, and you can be on your way." He slid the paper towards Leddicus and handed him a pen. With his other hand, he picked up the phone. Again, George appeared immediately.

The governor continued to speak, but this time to George, "Please take Mr. Palantina and his friends to collect his belongings. He is free to leave now. Here is the discharge form for the front desk." He picked up his pen, looked down at the neat stack of papers on his desk, and began to write on the top one. The exchange was concluded. It seemed the governor could not wait to be rid of us.

Leddicus had signed the document, which George now held, and we obediently stood up and followed him out of the office. During this whole time, none of us had said a word. We had not been given the opportunity. The governor had rattled away at us. His clipped comments bombarded our ears like a verbal machine gun. He had somehow even managed to maintain Julie's silence.

As we walked past Mr. Monotone, Julie gave him her sweetest smile. We stepped from the grey gloom into the fresh air, and I stopped, leaned against the wall, and heaved a huge sigh of relief as the tension ebbed away. Only then did I realise that I had grooves in the palms of my hands that my fingernails had made.

"I feel like I am waking up from a nightmare," I said. "What on Earth was all that about? I have no idea what that governor guy was talking about. Who is the friend that phoned? What is an ILR? And why can't we travel?"

"Let's just get going," Julie responded. "We can talk as we head back to civilisation."

We loaded Leddicus's case into the boot and clambered in. Julie gunned up the engine.

"Leddicus, how are you?" She edged her way onto the main road.

"I'm well, thanks," he said in his usual unruffled manner.

"And how did they treat you?" Julie asked.

"Most people were nice to me, but some of the ones in uniform treated me most strangely. They said they knew I was the iceman and gave me a plate of ice cubes for my meal. I tried one, but it wasn't very nice. I don't mind them in Coke, Gerhardt, but on a plate? Not nice at all." He rubbed at his stubbly chin. "Some of the people who were not staff were very kind. One said he came from a small island called Sri Lanka, and he made me what he said was his national dish. He said that it would be hot. It was! It made me cough!"

Julie and I laughed at the thought of Leddicus sampling curry for the first time.

"It did make me sad, though, talking to some of the people. Most come from places where there is war and lots of fighting, and they all seemed to be trying to escape terrible things. They asked what I was running away from and didn't understand when I said nothing. They asked why I was there. I told them I had no idea. They were puzzled by that, but then, so was I."

We laughed again at his simple pragmatism. He had taken it all in his stride, and his experience did not seem to faze him at all.

"I don't think the staff were being particularly kind to you. In fact, it was quite cruel what they did, but it sounds as if you were okay with the other people there." Julie patted his shoulder. "It's good to have you back."

"I second that!" I said. "One thing I wondered, Leddicus, that group of children in the corner. Where were their parents? They looked rather terrified."

"Finding out about those girls was the worst thing about my visit. They came in about four days ago. They were discovered in crates in a lorry carrying bananas, the same crates used for the bananas. Heartbreaking."

"Gosh, the things some people will do to get their children to this country," I quipped.

"Don't joke like that, Gerhardt. Unscrupulous men stole those children from their families to be sold as slaves," Leddicus said quietly. His face was dark.

"Slaves! What work could those tiny kids carry out? And slaves in England? I think the authorities would have something to say about a six year old doing the dusting."

Julie sighed heavily. "You are such an idiot. You do walk round with your head in the clouds! Think about it. Do I have to spell it out to you?"

I opened my mouth, ready to snap back at her, when a cold chill ran down my spine. "Oh, hell! No!"

"Sadly, yes," said Leddicus. "I couldn't believe it either when I found out. I went and sat with them when I first arrived. Not one of them would speak. They had been there four days, and social services still had not been able to find foster homes for them. I couldn't sleep thinking about them."

We drove along for a while in silence. The full horror of what we had seen and heard percolated into our consciousness, a reality none of us wanted to believe but could not erase from our memory.

"Julie, what was all that stuff the governor was going on about?" I asked after a while to lighten up the atmosphere. After all, there was a positive side. We had rescued our friend.

"Not totally clear, but my guess is that the friend he referred to was probably someone in government that has intervened at Joe's request. I've dealt with those types. They can be quite imposing. Maybe the governor wanted shot of Leddicus to avoid making waves. They had already detained Leddicus by mistake. Then blocking us from seeing him last night obviously did not go down well. Add that to all the phone calls that were flying back and forth between

Joe and people in high places, it all starts to look very bad on the governor."

"I'm glad I'm in history and not politics!"

"Us turning up this morning and being stonewalled by Mr. Monotone, although I wanted to thump him, probably strengthened our case."

"And the travel document?" I felt more relieved the further away we got from that awful place.

"That's very good news. ILR. Indefinite leave to remain. Means he can pretty much come and go as he wants. It's almost like a full passport. It seems they want to avoid further embarrassment down the road. Stamping his documents ILR gets Leddicus, Joe, and all those powerful people off the governor's case."

"Hey, buddy," I said to Leddicus, "no more worries when we travel!" I was delighted.

"It's great for Leddicus and us, but very frustrating for all those people stuck in there who haven't got powerful friends to help them cut through the bureaucracy and will continue to suffer at the hands of Mr. Jobsworth and Mr. Monotone."

I was getting ready for Julie to launch into another tirade, but there was no time for that. We were pulling up outside the hotel. This place was becoming our second home. We decided to celebrate the release of Leddicus and end of Team Ice's second tour with a trip to a good restaurant.

"Well, Leddicus," said Julie, "I'll have to postpone our trip to Caesarea Philippi until your travel documents are released. It seems you'll have time to get a better look at London after all. In which case, I'm going to take you to see Boadicea."

"Who's that?" asked Leddicus.

"You'll see." She grinned.

Chapter Twenty-Four

What a Time

Since we had rescued Leddicus, Julie had returned to her usual calm and efficient persona. She arrived punctually the next morning. She looked radiant and ready to keep her promise to take Leddicus to meet Boadicea. I didn't want to do another tour of London, but was concerned about her influence on Leddicus and the effect she would have on him without me around.

My Leddicus paydays could be threatened if she took him under her wing. Did I want to trail round London? No! Did I have pressing deadlines? Yes! I had stern e-mails from the magazine and university. Did I trust Julie? No! Although I found her very useful, I could not escape this nagging feeling she was trying to steal my pay cheque. These thoughts went round and round as I hacked into my sausages and mixed them with beans and scrambled egg.

As I popped the mixture into my mouth, Julie said, "Are you cross with me, Gerhardt? You're glaring at me as if I'd stolen your breakfast and put you on bread and water."

That caught me so off guard that I swallowed hard. It went down the wrong way, and I ended up having a coughing fit. I coughed so hard that I had to mop my streaming eyes and drink a large glass of water. During which time, Julie clucked over me with concern, and Leddicus fell about laughing. I eventually regained my composure and managed to speak.

"Cross? Who me? No, I was just wondering if I ought to stay here today. I have a ton of work, and I am being hounded to meet deadlines, but I didn't want to leave Leddicus to you to look after for the whole day."

"Well, you are a grown-up, aren't you, Leddicus?" She smiled warmly at him. Leddicus was hungrily pushing grapes, toast, and jam into his mouth and didn't reply. Perhaps because he didn't want to replicate my coughing fit. Instead, he nodded enthusiastically. "We'll be fine. If you need to work, that's okay, I'll play guide and host to our Roman." She patted my shoulder and laughed. "You really have no need to worry."

I gave a wan smile and shrugged. "Okay then. I'll stay here and work while you go and meet Boadicea. I wonder how long we'll have to wait for those travel documents to be released. I'm sure Leddicus is keen to go to Caesarea Philippi, aren't you?" I said to him.

"I am. I can't wait to be the tour guide for you and show you around my town. It will be good for me to play host to you two for a change."

"Are you coming, too?" I asked Julie. My heart was sinking.

"Yes," she said firmly. "Don't you remember? I said that weeks ago when the idea was first mentioned."

"Okay, so when do we book the tickets?" I sighed.

"You are losing the plot, aren't you? Have you forgotten I already booked them? I've put them on hold with the travel agent until the documents come through?" She leaned forward to pick up her handbag off the floor. "You're very distracted today, Gerhardt. Perhaps you should rest, not work. The governor said it could take some time, but Joe said he'll chase it up if it's too slow in arriving. Let's just relax a little. Leddicus had a rough time the last forty-eight hours. Let's be a bit patient and try not to fret about it."

Well, that put me in my place. I bit my tongue to avoid snapping at her. They both stood up, and prepared to leave.

"I hope you get through your work, Gerhardt," Leddicus said. "I will tell you all about this foreboding sea person when I get back."

Julie and I laughed at that, and the tension eased a little. I poured a third coffee, more to avoid the inevitable than the need for another drink. I sipped at it, delaying putting my nose to the grindstone and thinking about all the time and energy I had put into Leddicus and all the money I had earned from the tours. I still could not shake this feeling that Julie was trying to muscle in on my property. Even though I had spent so much time with her, I still did not trust this London newshound.

Back in my room, I reluctantly fired up my laptop, but once I got down to it, I made good progress. I completed the two articles that *Archiv* was chasing me for. Finally back in my stride, I fired off the two thousand-word unit to the uni, which was already three weeks overdue. There was a brief e-mail from Mr. Calabro indicating I had done a good job so far and I only needed to e-mail him once a week in future. *Suits me just fine.*

At around four thirty, feeling very smug and self-satisfied, I treated myself to a pot of English tea, accompanied by scones, jam, and cream. I settled into a large leather armchair, cup in one hand and newspaper in the other, when Leddicus dropped into the seat opposite me with a loud thud.

I peered at him over my paper. "How is Boadicea?"

"She is very well, thanks. Sitting in her chariot opposite Big Ben. Julie also took me to see some Briton who had tried to fight us Romans, as if they had a chance!" He laughed at his own joke. "We had a very good day." He busied himself and splurged jam and cream onto one of my scones.

"Where's Julie?" I was only half-listening and still trying to read my paper.

"She's gone to some meeting or other. She just dropped me at the door. She said she was running late. But it's good she's gone. I wanted to chat to you about an idea I've got."

Leddicus paused long enough to take a huge bite of his messy scone and then carried on with his mouth full. "I want to invite Pricilla Morrison over, you know that lady from the Vatican, and give her a personal interview. What do you think?"

"What do I think?" I almost exploded and slammed my paper down onto the table. "I think that's a terrible idea. Who put you up to such a crackpot idea? Julie Bright, I'll bet!"

"No, no!" Leddicus said hastily. "You've got it all wrong. It's not her idea. Julie thought it was mad, too. But I insist. I think it's a good idea, and I've asked Julie to arrange it. I understand Pricilla is in the UK at the moment."

"I need to speak to Julie!" I yanked my phone out of my pocket and started punching in the number.

Julie answered after the first ring. "He's told you then!" She didn't even say hello.

"How did you guess?" I asked.

"I can see the fumes from here!"

"What do you think?"

"I think it's a bad idea, but for some odd reason, he's on a mission with this one. He's like a dog with a bone. So insistent."

"It's not just a bad idea. It's a terrible idea." I glared at Leddicus. He just gave me a calm half-smile.

"I agree! It is! But he just won't leave it alone. He's been on about it most of the day. He would not budge. There was no way I could persuade him to change his mind."

"What shall we do?"

"I was going to call you after my meeting to fill you in. I've already been in contact with Morrison. She's coming to the hotel tomorrow after lunch. I'm sorry, Gerhardt. I think we just have to let him have his head with this one and be around to pick up the pieces. I have to go now. I'm so late. I'll call you this evening." The line went dead.

"You crazy Roman!" I put my head in my hands.

Pricilla Morrison arrived at two thirty, just ten minutes after Julie met her in reception and escorted her to the quiet corner in the lounge where Leddicus and I were sitting. Leddicus had learned impeccable manners in such situations. As Pricilla Morrison approached our group, he stood up, gave her a big smile, and put out his hand. Morrison did not take it. Leddicus stood there feeling rather foolish and quickly retreated back to his chair.

"Well, let's get on, shall we?" Morrison took over the proceedings. "I want to deal with this as a professional interview, but I need to say first of all, Mr. Palantina, that I do not like you. Not one little bit. So let's just stick to a professional interview, shall we?"

Leddicus looked crestfallen and disorientated, but he smiled graciously at Morrison. "I am pleased to meet you at last. Please, go ahead and ask the questions you would like me to answer."

I noticed Julie looking down at the floor, biting her lip, and tapping the arm of the chair in an effort to keep quiet.

"Where do you really come from?" Morrison snapped.

Leddicus took a deep breath and remained calm. "I thought everyone already knew that. I have been saying it over and over again."

"Yes, yes, of course," Pricilla interrupted. "For your tour publicity. But where do you really come from?"

Leddicus looked at me, almost in despair, so I intervened, "Well, perhaps it does not fit with what you want to write, perhaps it challenges your belief system, and maybe you don't like Leddicus, although I have no idea what he has done to deserve your treatment of him."

Morrison opened her mouth, but I didn't give her chance to respond.

"It's common knowledge where he was found, on which mountain, and by whom. The why and how of the mystery is still a matter of continuing research and debate. If you have a problem with that, then you need to take it up with the professional authorities involved. If you have come here to personally attack Leddicus in the hope of receiving an answer that will fit in with your expectations and theories, then you have wasted your time!" I was more than happy with my articulate response, delivered very quietly and with great emphasis on the word "professional."

My controlled tirade had given Leddicus a chance to think, and now he looked at Morrison. "What do you really want from me?"

"The truth!" she spat at him.

"I have only ever told the truth, but you obviously do not believe me. I can only tell you what has happened to me. I can only give you a straight and honest answer to your question. But it seems that is not the answer you want to hear."

Morrison leapt up out of her chair. "I thought this would be a waste of time. I am not staying here to listen to this rubbish!" She grabbed her things off the table, stood up, and turned to me. "And as for you, Gerhardt Shynder, I still think you are pulling a fast one much like you pulled a fast one and arrived one year later than you should at university and completed your degree in two years, not three. Don't think this is the end of it because it isn't. You're just a bunch of crooks. This is a scam. It's just one big fat gravy train!" She turned on her heel and Marched 'rapidly through' the revolving doors, leaving them almost whirring as she disappeared to find her taxi.

As soon as the revolving doors stopped spinning behind her, we all burst into peals of laughter, drawing glances from the other residents sitting in the normally quiet lounge. After quite some time, we managed to control ourselves, and the laughter died down.

"Unbelievable. Can I write up this story for my paper? Don't you just hate it when people say they are professional, but don't possess an ounce of professionalism or even common sense? Poor woman, I doubt she even knows what day it is!" Julie was on a roll. "The only thing I don't get, Gerhardt, is why she attacked you. What was that about your university and being late? What is she on?"

"I have no idea," I said. "I did have to retake my exams at school to get into the university I am at. I didn't quite get the right grades first time around, but so what? And how does she know that? I would have thought that was confidential. Very strange. I don't know what else to say."

"I am so sorry!" Leddicus looked at us, shamefaced. "You were both correct. That was not a good idea."

Julie was quick to respond. "No, it wasn't, but you're forgiven, Leddicus. You must admit it was a giggle, and it's given me a good story. I am going to write up this meeting, at least the interview with you, Leddicus, if you don't mind. I still can't get my head around her having a go at you, Gerhardt. Maybe you have some hidden secret. It will make a good story for the press and keep Leddicus in the news."

"Write it up if you think they'll bite, but keep my name out of it!" I said.

"I don't mind," said Leddicus. "And what exactly does professional mean?"

"If you are referring to Miss Morrison's use of the word, then it means 'I am well and truly up my own backside,'" Julie said. "I vote we go get a drink. What say you lot?"

We didn't need any persuading and swiftly decamped to the bar. As Leddicus took a sip of his wine, I could see that telltale crease between his eyebrows.

"What's bugging you?" I asked.

He shook his head and shrugged. "I've let you both down. I was a bit naïve, I suppose. I thought that if she were out of the gladiatorial arena of the press scrum, she might be more amenable, more approachable. I feel pretty dumb now."

"Don't say we didn't warn you!" Julie and I chorused.

"And I still don't understand what professionalism means."

"Poor Leddicus, I'll explain another time. As Julie said, it was a laugh, but ultimately, her behaviour was very offensive. For now, let's put the rude Miss Morrison out of our heads, have a drink, and relax."

Leddicus grinned. "Okay, you're right." He raised his glass. "Let's drink to a successful tour and my escape from prison."

We chinked our glasses together and soon forgot Morrison. We settled down by the bar, ordered up some snacks, and spent a delightful few hours discussing everything under the sun with the exclusion of the formidable Miss Morrison.

Late into the evening, Julie reluctantly made her departure. "I have heaps of work tomorrow, so you'll have to manage by yourselves."

"Fine by me. I could do with a lazy day." Leddicus and I walked with her to the exit.

As Julie's taxi pulled away, Leddicus opened his mouth to speak, and I knew exactly what he was going to say.

"Google it!" I said before he had said a word.

"How did you know what I was going to say?" He looked peeved.

"I am a total genius," I said.

I snuggled down into bed, luxuriating at the thought of a long lie-in, a late breakfast, and no deadlines. The most taxing thing would be explaining to Leddicus the meaning of the word professionalism, that is, unless he was Googling it at that very minute.

Chapter Twenty-Five

Tel Aviv-Yafo

Leddicus and I had agreed to meet at ten thirty. That was as late as we could risk arriving before the waiters started clearing away breakfast and preparing for lunch. By coincidence, we reached the top of the stairs at the same time. As we stepped from the stairs into the lobby, we both stopped in surprise. Not only was Julie sitting there, but Joe was alongside her.

"Joe, what a surprise!" I said as we walked toward him. "What on Earth brings you here? Not bad news, I hope."

"No, just the opposite." Joe reached into his briefcase and pulled out a large brown envelope. "Surprise, surprise!" He handed it to Leddicus, who immediately began tearing into it.

He pulled out the contents and gave a big smile. "Someone has sent me back my papers with my picture on it. That's nice."

"Much better than nice," Joe said. "I've already had a peek at it, and there's a very important addition." He took the papers back from Leddicus, flipped them open, and tapped the bottom of one of the pages. "See this stamp here. It may not look too impressive, but it says 'indefinite leave to remain.'"

"What does that mean?" asked Leddicus.

"Fantastic," Julie piped up. "It means you can travel and come back to the UK whenever you want to, and they won't stop you and put you in a detention centre again."

"It wasn't so bad. Most of the people were all right, apart from some of the ones in uniform. I didn't like how they spoke to me," Leddicus said.

"You might think it's okay, but I found it very stressful. I don't ever want to go to that place again!" I said. "Anyway, this little stamp means we can make plans to visit your hometown." I turned to Joe. "What do you reckon?"

"Yes! Yes, please!" Leddicus clapped his hands.

"Go for it." Joe picked up on Leddicus's keen desire to get there. "But I hope you'll come back soon. Shall we get a coffee and something to eat? Then I can tell you what's going on, and you can let me know what you want to do."

Julie hugged Leddicus. "At last, we're on our way."

In all the excitement, we had missed breakfast, but the waiter willingly served us coffee and a plate of croissants. Leddicus was obviously keen to get going as soon as possible. He had a distant look in his eye, and he wasn't paying any attention to the conversation as Joe updated us on the outcome of the American tour, where the finances were at, and how he and Julie planned to salvage the loss of Julie's vital electronic and hard copy book preparations. He also outlined plans for a second UK tour. He had started receiving approaches from schools and church organisations. Although not as lucrative as the previous tour, it would keep Leddicus in the public eye.

Leddicus had been sitting there, impatiently waiting for a gap in the conversation. As soon as Joe sat back and took a bite out of a croissant, he jumped in, "When? When are we going to my home?"

"Julie, can you give me the details of the booking you have on hold? I'll get my office onto it," Joe said, "and get them to locate a guide. When's a good time for you to fly, Julie? This pair are freewheeling now, but you have deadlines."

"Sunday or Monday is best for me."

Leddicus pulled a face. "Why do we need a guide? It's my country. I know it like the back of my hand."

"Trust me, Leddicus. It's better to have one." Joe pulled out his phone and made a quick call to his personal assistant to ask her to reschedule the flights.

As soon as Joe had made the call, Leddicus relaxed. "Why are we flying?" he asked me.

"I thought you realised. There's no other way to get there unless you swim."

"I don't fancy that, so I guess flying is better. I don't mind as long as we get there."

Julie asked Leddicus and me if we wanted to go to her meeting on Saturday. As I was up to date with my work, I agreed. I didn't particularly want to, but truth be told, I was beginning to get cabin fever.

It made a pleasant change to be away from the hotel. People, as usual, surrounded Leddicus and Julie. I didn't feel part of it, but everyone seemed very friendly, and I found myself wondering what they had. I was not really in the mood for chatting, and I was just enjoying my bowl of homemade soup, accompanied by a giant-sized hunk of crusty bread when a young lady came and sat beside me.

"Hi, Gerhardt, isn't it?"

"Yeah," I said through a mouthful of bread.

"I'm Jenny. Jenny Latimer."

"Hi, nice to meet you," I said automatically. As I ate my soup, she began chatting to me, asking me about my life before Leddicus arrived on the scene. She seemed genuinely interested in finding out about me, which was quite odd. In the last few months, no one had ever talked to me about me. If they were talking to me, it was always about Leddicus. Against all the odds, I was having a good time, and I felt a little sad when it was time to depart. Jenny was very interesting and interested in my thoughts and ideas. Before I had thought it through, I had given her my mobile number, something I never did unless it was a business contact. She walked out to the car with the three of us.

"I'll text you," she said as Julie pulled out of the car park.

We finally flew out of Heathrow at five o'clock Sunday evening, bound for Tel Aviv, and arrived in Israel around midnight. The airport was packed, and queues formed at the immigration desks. It was quiet. No one seemed to have the energy to talk. The lines of shuffling people looked straight ahead with grey, morose faces. Many made no attempt to stifle bouts of yawning. We all gradually moved towards the line of desks containing the usual suspects, stern, uniformed officials stamping papers and making very little conversation.

I yawned and rubbed my eyes. As I looked up, I noticed a couple of official-looking men gradually moving along the line. They were speaking to people, but I couldn't make out what they were saying. They moved from person to person, coming nearer, and I strained my ears to try to catch what they were saying. When they were about ten people away, I caught the word "Palantina" and then my name and Julie's. My heart sank. I remembered the poker-faced official at Heathrow who had frog-marched Leddicus away to the detention centre. We had nowhere to run. We just had to stand there with our hearts pounding and wait for them to reach us.

"Mr. Shynder? Miss Bright? Mr. Palantina?" We acknowledged we were who they were seeking. One of the uniformed officials turned to the other men and said something I didn't understand. They all moved towards us. "Come with us." One of them said.

"What's this all about?" Julie whispered to me.

"We're going to the dungeons," I said rather inappropriately.

Leddicus was looking like a rabbit in the headlights. The officials walked us smartly to the end of the line of desks where all that could be heard was muffled thuds as officials stamped passports. I noticed one young lady sitting in a nearby booth was not stamping any passports. Above her was a sign announcing "Diplomats and Crew." Our captors were heading directly toward her. As we drew level, one of the men with us smiled at her.

"We found them. Thanks," he said.

Before we knew it, we walked straight past her smiling face without even showing our passports.

I drew alongside one of the men. "Excuse me, what's this all about?"

Before he had a chance to answer, another man approached our group and shook hands with everyone.

One of the other men turned to us. "Welcome to Israel. This is Kaalim Malouf. He will be your guide during your stay, and we hope you will enjoy your time with us."

The three of us were stuck dumb, but the ever-practical Julie soon found her voice. "Thank you very much. It's good to be here. Where can we collect our luggage?"

Kaalim turned to her with a broad smile. "Ma'am, that is all taken care of. It has already been retrieved and placed in the bus that will take you to your hotel. Please follow me." He swept his arm forward theatrically and led us out of the terminal.

The heat hit us, and our faces were soon glistening with moisture. Kaalim led us along the terminal perimeter to a large, shining luxury minibus, and we all clambered into its cool interior.

"This is a rather nice dungeon," whispered Julie.

"Now this is the sort of reception I like," I said.

Up to this point, Leddicus had not said a word. He had just trotted along behind us, looking rather confused by it all, but now, as we sped along the modern road toward the centre of Tel Aviv, he exclaimed, "Are you sure we are in the right place, It all looks very strange to me. The only thing that's right is the weather."

"Let's get some rest, Leddicus, and we'll see how it looks later once we have slept," I said to calm him. I was too tired to get into a big debate. I knew he was uncomfortable, and I was not surprised. I still had the Rome experience in the back of my mind.

The hotel was luxuriously perfect, and the rooms were exquisite. The sumptuous surroundings and attentive staff blew Leddicus away. As it was so late, we had a quick nightcap and went to our rooms with the agreement to start early, but not too early. Our guide would join us for breakfast at the hotel.

Chapter Twenty-Six

The Coliseum

Surrounded by brightly coloured brochures and scribbling into a small spiral-bound notebook, Kaalim was sitting at the table in the restaurant. He looked up as we entered and flashed us a broad, white smile. He dipped his head a little as we approached. His profusion of long, curly dark hair skimmed his shoulders, mingling with a paradoxically neat, trimmed beard.

"Why do we need a guide? This is my land," Leddicus whispered to me before we reached the table.

"He's got transport. Be nice to him," I hissed back as we took our seats.

Julie and I greeted Kaalim warmly. Leddicus nodded at him sullenly. Breakfast was buffet style, and it was a feast of such variety and colour that the choice overwhelmed us. Leddicus, as usual, heaped his plate. Since our trip to the States, such choice no longer perturbed him. I noticed Kaalim had a couple of dirty plates at his elbow so I assumed he had arrived early and already eaten. While we pondered on the spread before us, he simply refilled his cup with more strong black coffee.

"I want to go to Caesarea, and I want to enter via the coliseum. I would like to show my friends that place first," Leddicus said firmly as he tucked into his breakfast.

"No problem," Kaalim agreed. "And after we have been there, I will share with you the plans I have to show you many of the other fascinating places in this amazing country," he said proudly.

I always forget how air-conditioning shields you from the real weather. In the short walk from the hotel to Kaalim's vehicle, my shirt was sticking to me in thirty-five degrees. I was already becoming thirsty. "Kaalim, I need to just nip back to the hotel and buy some water for us. Can you hang on a minute?"

"No problem, my friend. I have plenty of water in the car in a specially refrigerated container."

"Excellent. It seems you have thought of everything. Thank you." I grinned at him and climbed into the front seat alongside our guide.

We drove along a smooth road and looked out into the sweltering streets. The sun shimmered down mercilessly on the glistening buildings. Kaalim parked near to the entrance. We walked towards the coliseum and entered the building past the rugged two thousand-year-old stones.

My history gene started whirring, and I was soon absorbed in the fascination of the place. I was delighted. This era had been my love since I was a child. We walked up what was perhaps originally the back stairway access, and it brought us almost to the top of the coliseum, which opened out hugely in front of us.

Leddicus looked puzzled. "What has happened to it? It's in such a bad condition since I was last here."

"Why does each section have two doors, Leddicus?" Julie changed the subject.

"No, not two doors." He laughed. "The other opening is . . . erm, Gerhardt . . . What is that machine that makes all the noise in the bedrooms?"

"You mean the air-conditioning?"

"Yes, yes, that's it. Those openings are the coliseum's air-conditioning."

"Air-conditioning in ancient Rome? No way!" Julie said. "How on Earth does it work?"

"A couple of slaves are usually here, and their job is to put thick cloth in cold water and hang it over this opening, alongside the door. Then they use large fans from this side, which blows through the wet cloth, cooling the air. On some days, when the wind is in the right direction, the system works all on its own."

Julie was astonished and curious. "But there's no roof on the building. I don't see how that would work."

Leddicus shrugged. "I don't know how. It just did."

"Simple physics, my dear Watson." I crossed my arms and imitated a lecturer. "Warm air rises, and cool air sinks. If you push cold air into this round building, even though there is no roof, the lower you sit, the cooler you will be."

"Yes, that's true. On very hot days, I sit in here and am quite comfortable, but come on, I want to show you something. You go and sit at the very top of the building. Look." He pointed. "Right up there. I'll show you something amazing."

We set off climbing up the steps to the very top tier as Leddicus bounded down the stairs to the front Kaalim smiled indulgently. He was a guide pleased to have happy tourists in tow. We reached the top and sat down on the stone seats.

Leddicus took a bow and strolled back and forth across the stage and then turned toward us and raised both his arms dramatically. "Hello, up there! You know how I have used your microphones on all the tours we have made, but here I am talking to you without one. I'm not shouting. In fact, I am speaking very quietly, yet I know you can hear me perfectly, can't you?"

Julie and I broke out into spontaneous applause. "Amazing!" Julie said. "Can you hear us?"

Kaalim chuckled at our surprise. No doubt, he had performed this trick for other tourists.

"Follow me. There is more. Come on." Leddicus was completely enthused as he headed out of the building through a door by the end of the stage.

It took us quite a while to make our way down the many stairs from the top to where the door was. We moved out of the coliseum and marvelled at the huge ancient pillars and structures surrounding us as the dazzling sun sweltered overhead. A few people were around with cameras clicking away, but Leddicus was nowhere to be seen.

"Leddicus! Leddicus where are you!" Julie called out a few times.

The nearby people looked at her blankly each time she called, but Leddicus did not appear. The time ticked by. We wandered slowly around, past the ancient public toilets with their stone seats and enormous pillars stretching far above us, and peered at ruined temple structures, expecting that Leddicus would appear at any minute, but still he was nowhere in sight. This was getting beyond a joke, we were getting hotter, and our water bottles were rapidly emptying. After an hour of looking in doorways and behind pillars, we were getting seriously worried.

"Perhaps we should go back to the hotel," Julie suggested, "and report Leddicus to the police as a missing person."

"Let's keep looking a little longer," Kaalim said. "Perhaps we should split up and look everywhere again."

After another fifteen minutes, I was beginning to think it was hopeless. We had peered in doorways, behind pillars, and in every nook and cranny without any success.

"Quickly! Over here! I've found him!" Kaalim shouted.

Julie and I rushed to where the guide was kneeling, and there was Leddicus, lying on the ground behind a large pillar quite close to the coliseum. He lay very still. His arms shielded his head. His dark curls clung to pale cheeks as the sweat trickled down his face. I quickly checked his pulse to see that he was alive. As if to confirm that life was still in him, he groaned softly.

"Leddicus! What's wrong, Leddicus?" Julie gently pulled his arms away from his face.

His eyes were open, but not focussing. He didn't speak. Kaalim and I took an arm each, pulled them around our shoulders, and half-dragged, half-carried him back to the car. Leddicus slumped into the backseat and remained motionless and silent as Kaalim drove like a wild thing back to the hotel.

We heaved him out of the car and placed him on a sofa in the coolness of the reception area. Kaalim immediately went to the front desk and spoke rapidly in Hebrew to the receptionist, requesting an emergency doctor. While we waited for the doctor to arrive, we managed to get Leddicus up to his room and lay him comfortably on his bed. His face was as white as the sheets. I was exhausted.

He's deadweight. I immediately regretted the thought. Leddicus lay motionless staring at the ceiling. The doctor arrived after about fifteen minutes and gave him a thorough examination: pulse, temperature, and blood pressure. He peered into his eyes and tested his reflexes. I had a flashback to the hospital room in Italy, where I had first met Leddicus. He had that same catatonic expression on his face, as though he was seeing but not perceiving, as if in a state of shock.

After a while, the doctor put his instruments back in his bag and looked at us. He shook his head. "I can find nothing wrong with him. All his vital signs are normal. I would say he is in shock. Please tell me what happened to him."

"How long have you got?" I quipped.

The doctor did not smile, but smoothed at his bushy hair and looked at me intently. I felt as if I were back at school so I gathered my thoughts and told him as briefly as possible, from the beginning, about the mystery that was Leddicus. As I spoke, the doctor's eyebrows crept higher and higher, and there was an almost imperceptible shake of the head.

When I had finished, he rummaged in his bag and handed us a bottle of pills. "Give him one every four hours." Then he took a small notepad from his case and wrote a name, address, and telephone number on it. "This is a friend of mine, a psychiatrist. He is an excellent practitioner, and I suggest you take Mr. Palantina to see him as soon as possible."

"What about hospitalisation?" Julie interjected.

"I trust you have good insurance. Britain and Israel have no reciprocal health arrangement, but I don't think the hospital will do any more for your friend at the moment than I have already done. I will check again tomorrow. It is essential you keep him well hydrated."

As the doctor closed the door behind him, I looked at Julie. "Health insurance? Did anyone think of that?"

She looked forlorn. "In all the excitement, I forgot. I'm so sorry."

"Well, can't do much about it now." I shrugged. "It's not your fault. I didn't think of it either."

We gently pulled Leddicus up into a sitting position. Between us, we managed to give him one of the pills and some sips of water. He did this instinctively, without any indication that he was aware what was happening. For the next day or so, we milled around the hotel and popped in frequently to check on the staring, drowsy Leddicus. We gave him as much water as we could and continued with the medication programme, but his condition didn't change.

At lunchtime on the third day, Julie and I sat in the hotel lounge with coffee, a plate of sandwiches, and very little appetite. We sat silently staring into space.

After a while, Julie sighed. "What a dreadful thing. Poor Leddicus, we really must get him back to London."

"That will be tough." My head was in my hands. "But if we organise a wheelchair, it's probably possible."

The doctor had been back two or three times, but seemed to be saying nothing new, apart from telling us he had left his bill at reception for us.

Julie put her hand on my arm. "I have some friends just outside London. I spoke to them today, and they are willing to accommodate Leddicus while he recovers. Let's get the flights booked as soon as possible."

I nodded, rather defeated by the whole situation. "I'll sort the flights." I stood up. I headed to my room to fire up my laptop. The food remained untouched.

After booking the flights, I came back downstairs to join Julie. As I walked through reception, I saw Kaalim with some other tourists in tow. He turned to them, said something, and then came over to me. "Your friend? He is recovering?" He enquired.

"No change I'm afraid, we're heading back to London. We leave in two hours."

The ambassadors who had greeted us on our arrival appeared at the hotel an hour later. They were full of concern and commiserations. They had taken care of everything, including having two sturdy male nurses in tow. The nurses placed Leddicus gently into a wheelchair and transported him to a minibus which was equipped with a small lift that folded out of the back door. At the airport, we were whisked through passport control to the waiting aircraft and into a special area set aside for travellers who were using a wheelchair.

The two ambassadors, who had escorted us right on to the plane shook hands with us warmly. "Nurse Goldhirsch will accompany you and Mr. Palantina on the flight to ensure that he arrives safely back in the UK."

We thanked them profusely and took our seats. The nurse settled in beside Leddicus and fastened the specially adapted seat belt. In the UK, we were swiftly escorted to a waiting taxi, which took all three of us to the house where Leddicus would be staying.

A slim, dark woman opened the door and hugged Julie. "Welcome to our home." She pushed the door wide open to accommodate the wheelchair.

We sat down in the living room for a few minutes to make introductions.

"I'm Diane Jones, and this is my husband Jonathan."

"Pleased to meet you. I'm Gerhardt, and I appreciate you taking in a complete stranger."

Diane disappeared into the kitchen for a few minutes and reappeared with a tray containing a pot of tea and homemade fruit cake.

"That's kind of you," I said. "I'm suddenly ravenous."

Jonathan turned to me. "Our local doctor is on his way, he should be here very soon. Also, I have some friends nearby who have plenty of space in their house. They are willing to put you up if you wish, then you can be near Leddicus."

"Thank you," I said through a mouthful of cake. "That sounds like a good option."

Julie managed to get half a cup of tea into the patient and then Jonathan and I took Leddicus upstairs and settled him into the spare room. We had just sorted him out when the doorbell rang. A moment later, the doctor stood in the doorway to the bedroom. He spent a while examining Leddicus and then asked, "Is he on any medication?"

I pulled the bottle of pills out of my pocket and handed them to him.

He squinted at the label. "Antidepressants. Quite strong ones. I recommend you cease this medication within two weeks, or Mr. Palantina could become dependent on them. He is very dehydrated, are you managing to give him fluids?"

"Yes, a little," I said.

He reached into his bag and pulled out a wallet containing Dioralyte sachets. "Mix the contents of one of these into any drinks you give him, and try to get more fluids into him. I'll come back tomorrow evening and see how things are going." The doctor shook our hands and headed on to his next patient.

I looked at Jonathan, and he put his hand on my shoulder. "Try not to worry. We'll look after him. We both have nursing experience." He took the sachets from me. "I'll make sure we get more fluids into him."

Julie stood up as I entered the sitting room. "Shall we call a taxi? Are you ready to go?" I nodded and briefly told her what the doctor had said.

I turned to Jonathan and handed him my business card. "Call me at any time if you need me."

Diane snapped her mobile shut. "The cab will be here in five minutes. Here's the address of our friends."

David and Josie were equally as friendly as the other couple were and lived about a mile from the Jones's home. It was a large, rambling house, and other people seemed to be living there. Josie led me upstairs to a bright, clean bedroom and then showed me to a kitchen on the same floor.

She opened up the refrigerator. "Plenty of food and drink in here. Help yourself, and please stay as long as you need."

I followed Julie out of the house to the waiting taxi. She sat in the back and looked at me grimly. "Call me in the morning, and we'll decide where to from here. I'm too tired to think right now."

The taxi pulled away, and I stood watching until the taillights faded from sight.

David offered me a cup of tea, but I declined. "I'm exhausted. Would you mind very much it I called it a night?"

"No problem," he said. "Sleep well."

I splashed water on my face and slowly brushed my teeth. I was completely drained. I climbed into bed, but sleep evaded me. I lay for a long time staring into the darkness.

Chapter Twenty-Seven

Switzerland

Diane and Jonathan had tried hard to get fluids into Leddicus, but it hadn't worked as effectively as necessary. Their efforts had helped to stabilise the dehydration, but not improve it. Twenty-four hours after his first visit, the doctor put his foot down and called an ambulance. Leddicus was transported to the local hospital. For the last four days, he had lain staring at the ceiling with drips sticking out of his arms and nurses regularly testing and monitoring.

We visited him every day, but there was no change. One evening as we were leaving, I stopped by the nurses' station and asked to speak to the sister. I didn't get much out of her, not being a relative, but I did ask about the antidepressants. I was reassured to hear that Leddicus was no longer being prescribed them.

Each evening, I stared listlessly at my e-mails. They were piling up, and the pressure was on. If I were to finish my doctorate and graduate, I had to get my head in gear. The only way to do that was to get away, get back to Switzerland, get back into study mode, and ensure I completed what was required. I couldn't face not meeting the deadlines and having to add on another year. Leddicus was not going anywhere. I had to put myself first now. There was no other choice.

On the fourth day, I said to Julie, "I have to get home. There's urgent stuff I need to attend to. I'm sorry to leave Leddicus, but I have no alternative."

She folded her arms and leaned against the bar. We had stopped for a quick drink after leaving the hospital.

"Gerhardt, it's fine. Don't worry. I'll look after him." Her words were encouraging, but her body language said something entirely different.

"Do you want to grab something to eat?" I asked, but didn't really have my heart in the offer.

"Can't. Got an early start. I need to get going." She drained her glass and slipped on her jacket. "What time is your flight?"

"Early tomorrow." I followed her out of the pub, and we climbed into her car. We drove in silence to Dave and Josie's. "I'll keep in touch," I said as I got out the car.

Julie just nodded, gave me a half-smile, and drove away. I had too much to sort out to be ready for the morning to worry about her disapproval. She wasn't the one facing the prospect of extending her studies for another year. I pulled my case out from under the bed, started packing, and instantly forgot all about her.

Bathed in hazy sunshine, Zurich loomed into view. As the aircraft continued its descent, I felt a wave of relief to be home. It would be good to be back at the university and get into a normal routine. I couldn't wait to get stuck into my remaining assignments.

I hailed a taxi, and it took me a few streets away to where my faithful Audi was waiting. It fired up immediately. *What a great car. So reliable that it starts up on the first turn after months of lying dormant.*

I was looking forward to sleeping in my own bed in St. Gallen and making arrangements for my graduation awards, which would go ahead once I produced the essential work. I turned onto the A51 and headed toward my parents' home. My mother was cooking me dinner to welcome me home.

I kept in touch with Julie every couple days, but the news was always the same. No change, no change, no change. One evening as I was sitting in my favourite restaurant a few blocks from my apartment, I had a thought. I flipped open my mobile and called Julie.

"Latin!" I said immediately.

"Hi, Gerhardt. And how are you?" she asked.

I ignored her sarcasm. "Latin! That might reach him. When I first met Leddicus at the hospital in Italy, he was in a similar state, nowhere near as bad. He was eating, drinking, and moving around, but he looked totally out of it."

"I still don't understand."

"When we went to Rome, he became very withdrawn and uncommunicative, and he had a very distant look in his eye. Perhaps those were warnings of something bigger that might kick off in the wrong situation. His trip home finished him off."

"What has Latin got to do with it?" Julie asked. I could hear the frustration in her voice.

"The way I first got him to start communicating in Italy was Latin. When the doctor spoke to him in Latin he looked and smiled. Perhaps you could draw him out in the same way."

We finished the call, and I poured myself another glass of wine. Julie was such a bloodhound. She would never give up once she was on the scent, and I knew that, even now, she was on the internet searching for Latin phrases. The waiter placed a large plate of mashed potatoes and sausages before me. I picked up my knife and fork with relish.

Three weeks later, I was sitting in the university canteen drinking coffee and catching up on my reading when my mobile rang.

"It's working! It's working!" Julie was bursting with excitement.

"Tell me more."

"I've been learning a few Latin words and phrases, as you suggested. Each evening when I visit Leddicus, I'd try them out on him. I was losing hope, as it seemed to have no impact at all. This evening, I went through the same routine, and he focused on me. I could see the change in his eyes. Then he said, 'Hello, Julie' in English. I almost fell over backward. I managed to get him to sit up, and he slowly started to talk to me. He's very weak, but he's definitely back in the land of the living. I've told the medical staff, and they're starting him on some proper food and making arrangement to remove the drips. They've made an appointment for a psychologist to visit him later today."

"That's fantastic news. Well done. I knew you could do it. Was he making any sense when he spoke to you?"

"Yes, very slow but perfectly lucid. He asked about you, and he would like to talk to you. He has his mobile if you want to call him."

After I finished at the university for the day, I pulled out my mobile to make the call. It occurred to me how little I had thought of him through the intense days at university and the long evenings pounding out work on my laptop. I realised now that I actually missed him, and I was looking forward to hearing his voice.

"Gerhardt. Good to hear your voice." His voice sounded rather feeble, but it was unmistakably the old Leddicus.

"You, too, Leddicus. You gave us all quite a scare."

"I guess I did, but it was an even bigger scare for me, that is, until I blacked out."

"What can you remember?"

"Feeling very shocked when I saw the state of the coliseum, but at first, I just pushed it aside. I was so excited to be there and show you my trick on the stage, but then, when I went outside and saw how decayed everything was, I woke up from my dream, and everything slipped away from me."

"You woke up from a dream. I'm not quite following you."

"Ever since I met you in Italy, I felt I was in a dream, and I believed, if I went back to Caesarea Philippi, it would wake me up. When I saw the decay and ruins, it hit me that I was awake. What I saw could only mean that I truly am two thousand years old. I don't remember anything after that."

"I think I understand, although as I've said before, I'm no psychologist. You believed all the tours, lectures, time you spent with Julie working on the book, and meetings with Joe. You thought that was all part of the same dream."

"I guess so. It sounds crazy to say it aloud. But I think that is perhaps how I coped with everything. The last few weeks are a blur until I heard Julie saying hello to me in Latin. At first, it was as if she were far away. I could hardly make out the words. A bit like when someone speaks to you and you are deeply asleep. She kept speaking in the far distance, and she gradually seemed to be moving closer to me."

"Then what happened?"

"I don't really know. I guess I just woke up yesterday when she came in and said hello in Latin. I heard her clearly and could see her, and I finally managed to speak. You should have seen the look on her face. It was as if she had seen a ghost."

We both laughed at that, but I could hear his voice was cracked and weary.

"Have your people come up with anything yet? Are they any nearer discovering why this happened to me? How I ended up in that block of ice?"

I rubbed at the stubble on my chin as I wondered what to tell Leddicus. Then I decided that the truth was the only option.

"It's not encouraging. I've been ploughing through it since I got back. They've produced huge tomes of documentation. You have kept quite a number of physicists, Biologists, Historians, and other boffins very busy. They have carried out extensive research, but every avenue they have gone down has drawn a blank." Leddicus didn't respond. "You still there?"

He sighed. "Yes, go on."

I hesitated. I didn't want to send him back into shock.

"Gerhardt, I know what you're thinking, but I'll be alright. I can handle it. Go on."

"Okay, my friend, this is where it's at. They've gone through your genetics with a fine-tooth comb and have done every test in the book on your blood, skin samples, and DNA, also on the articles you had with you when you were discovered, but they're still no nearer to a solution. The problem is you're a first, a one-off. If they had a few more ancient guys to compare you with . . ." I tailed off, suddenly worried about what my news was doing to him.

"Oh, dear, since I woke up in this hospital bed, I have been hoping they had found an answer. It's very disappointing to hear they still don't have a clue."

"There is some good news though."

"Let me hear it. I could use some good news."

"They all believe, to a man, that you are not a fake."

Leddicus laughed at this. "Nice to know I'm not a nutcase at least." He paused. I could hear his laboured breathing. "I'm sorry, Gerhardt. I'm rather tired. Will you call again soon?"

"You can bank on it," I said.

Relief washed over me as I finished the call. He sounded like he was returning to his old self, but stronger emotionally now that he had accepted his situation. After a couple weeks of proper food and physio, he should be back to normal physically. I pushed my hands through my hair and suddenly felt invigorated. My mind started working overtime as I formed a plan to celebrate.

"Hey, Julie, I want you all to come over for my award ceremony. Do you think you can sort it?" I dropped this into one of our catch-up conversations.

"When is it? And who do you mean by all?"

"It's about five weeks away. I'd like you and Leddicus to come, of course, and Joe and Jenny."

"Jenny?"

Julie had no idea that Jenny and I had been texting and calling since we had met at one of Julie's Saturday meeting. I still didn't know why I had never said anything.

"You remember, Jenny Latimer from your church group."

Julie gave a little sarcastic giggle. "Aha, that Jenny. You're a dark horse. Sure, I'll include her in the group. Anyone else?"

"I can't think of anyone, but you can invite whoever you like. The more, the merrier. I've had a look at few of the hotels. A good place to stay would be the Continental on Stampfenbachstraße. It's central, not too pricey, and I'm sure you could cut a deal for a group booking. Do you think Joe would pay for everyone out of the central Leddicus account? A tour reunion?"

"Leave it with me. I'll have a chat with him." She laughed.

"What's so funny?"

"Nothing. I'll call you in a couple days."

By the time they came to Zurich, it would be a couple of months since I had seen any of them. I was already looking forward to it. During the last few days, I felt like a cloud had lifted. I pulled out my phone and sent a text to Jenny.

Chapter Twenty-Eight

The Reunion

I was not a particularly excitable character, but despite my usual pragmatic attitude, I was quite excited as I drove to Zurich airport to meet my friends from London. I arrived in plenty of time and settled myself at a table with an unhindered view of the incoming flights board. I plunged the handle down on the cafetière and poured myself a coffee.

Julie had told me that Jenny had jumped at the chance of coming to Switzerland. As I sipped my coffee, I began to get cold feet. Texting and phoning was one thing, but meeting up in person was an entirely different can of worms.

We were all staying at the Continental in central Zurich. During the weekend, I had a tour of the city planned. On Monday, it was the presentation at my university. I had missed the main awards ceremony due to the Leddicus tours. My lecturers and a few other colleagues had decided to have a special presentation for my friends and me. I was looking forward to this opportunity of stepping out of university life with a bit of a flurry. Once the formalities were over, I had booked a table at a rather posh restaurant in Appenzell. I wanted to revisit a sport I had missed in the last few weeks, introducing Leddicus to something new. I thought fondue would be just the ticket. The restaurant I had chosen was recommended for this Swiss specialty.

An hour later, the board flashed up the flight number with "Landed" alongside it. It was bang on time. I watched impatiently for the sign to change from "Landed" to "Baggage in Hall." I paced up and down for about twenty minutes. Then there they were, heading towards me, smiling, and waving.

I managed to cram the rather large quantity of luggage into the boot. *What a lot of it there was just for a long weekend.* Fortunately, Joe was coming in on a later flight, which meant there was room for all of us in my Audi. We clambered aboard and headed off to the hotel with everyone talking at once.

They were all delighted with the hotel. After congratulating me on my choice, they headed off to freshen up and do a bit of unpacking. I sat in reception with a long, cool lager, waiting for Joe to arrive. Just as everyone arrived back in reception, my phone rang.

"Joe, where are you? I thought you would be here by now."

"I'm sorry, Gerhardt. Something urgent has come up, and I will have to delay."

"But you will be able to come?"

"Not today, I'm afraid. I . . ." he hesitated. "It's bad news I'm afraid. I can't say more than that at this stage."

"When do you think you will be able to come over?" I was so disappointed. I wanted the whole crew there.

"I will keep you posted. E-mail me the details of your graduation. I will do my utmost to get there for that."

"What's happened? Can you say?"

"At this stage, I don't want to until my fears are confirmed."

"Well, good luck, and keep in touch." I cut the call.

Three pairs of eyes stared at me full of questions.

"What's going on? Is Joe all right?" Julie asked.

"He's wouldn't say what it was. Only that it was bad news."

We sat down on the sofas in reception. The excitement was ebbing away.

"I hope you don't mind me butting in," Jenny ventured, "but we're here now. Perhaps we should try to make the best of it?"

"That sounds sensible to me," said Leddicus. "What plans do you have for us, Mr. Shynder?"

We headed off into the Zurich afternoon sunshine and wandered along the streets at a leisurely pace, with me pointing out places of interest. After a couple hours, we all piled into a small restaurant and ordered a late lunch.

As the meal drew to a close, I checked my watch. "I have to go and collect my parents. It's about an hour-long round trip, and there's no way you lot can all fit into my Audi. Let's meet up back at the hotel in a couple hours."

"Sounds good to me," said Julie. "Don't worry about the bill. I'll sort that out. You get going. Leddicus and I will find our own way back."

I stood up and headed out of the restaurant, and Jenny followed.

"Okay if I tag along?"

"Of course," I said. "Good to have the company."

"Are your folks staying at the hotel tonight?"

"They are. They wouldn't miss this for the world, and they're very keen to meet Leddicus."

The journey passed quickly. Although initially I felt rather nervously uncomfortable the feeling gradually ebbed away. I was surprised how easy it was to chat to Jenny.

"So good to meet you, Mr. and Mrs. Shynder." Jenny smiled warmly and shook them by the hand.

My mother looked at me quizzically, but made no comment. I popped their bags in the boot, and we headed back to the hotel. Jenny sat with my mother in the back. They were soon chatting away as if they had known each other for years. My father got in the front with me. As I drove, I brought him up to date on plans for the weekend.

The evening was a great success. The hotel restaurant had an excellent à la carte menu, something for everyone. I could see my parents hanging on every word Leddicus said. He was on good form, waxing lyrical with funny stories from our tours. He even managed to add some humour as he described his collapse in Caesarea Philippi. I was pretty impressed at how he had broadened his knowledge in the past few weeks. When he was recovering in hospital, he had brought himself up to date with current politics, western and European, and he expounded his world opinions with clarity and conviction.

Joe called me in the middle of the evening. Although he sounded grim, he said he would be making every effort to be at the graduation. He remained tight-lipped about the reason for his delay.

There was a party atmosphere as we arrived at the university the next morning. Determined I was not going to miss the inevitable graduation photos, I had hired a gown and mortar for the occasion. Before we piled into the taxis, I made everyone check that cameras had not been forgotten. Leddicus was soon snapping away on his brand-new smartphone and ribbing me about my attire.

The principal presented me with my doctorate, and everyone stood up and applauded. I was grinning from ear to ear, although I did forget to throw my hat in the air. My department had laid on drinks and canapés. The room was a hubbub of chatter, and I made a point of speaking to everyone and making sure Jenny, as the newcomer to both groups of people, was included. I soon realised I had no need to be worry about her. She seemed to have a way of effortlessly engaging with everyone she met. I think my parents were a little overwhelmed with the whole event, but they were also, quite obviously, glowing with pride.

As the afternoon wore on, I spotted Leddicus on his own for the first time since I had collected everyone from the airport. I had some plans I wanted to run past him. I could leave it until the next day, but I was keen to get his thoughts, find out if he liked my ideas.

We sat in the corner of the room, Leddicus with the inevitable plate piled high with an array of nibbles and a large glass of red wine and me with a glass of sparkling water. I didn't want to get tipsy on this auspicious day. *Well, not yet at least.*

"Congratulations, Gerhardt. It's great to share this day with you. Before you say anything else, I want to ask you something. Will you join me in London for another celebration? And I need a favour."

"We should celebrate. You've come back to life twice now, and what was the favour you wanted?"

"That's not the celebration, although it is pretty amazing. Apparently, when you get married in this culture, you need a best man. So that's the favour. Will you be the best man?"

"Well, if I'm going to best man, I at least need to know who is getting married."

"Me, of course!"

My throat grew dry, and my hands began to sweat. "To whom?" I said slowly.

Leddicus looked surprised. "To Julie of course!"

For a moment, I couldn't speak. This was the worst outcome possible. My pulse was racing as anger rose up and destroyed my euphoria.

I kept my face straight and my voice level "Of course, I would be honoured to be your best man." Inside, my brain was yelling out one phrase, "Julie has won!"

Leddicus was so animated that he didn't notice my distinct lack of enthusiasm on receiving his news. He just carried on chatting, "I have some more news. I have a job."

"A job? What do you mean?"

"Remember the UK stamped my travel document ILR. Not only can I travel, I can work. And now I have a job."

I sat there stunned. I could find no words. My worst fears were being realised. I was losing everything because of that wretched girl Julie, and my initial instincts had been spot-on.

Leddicus interrupted my thoughts. "I think we could say that woman has won!"

I couldn't believe what he was saying. Out of the fog invading my brain, I said, "Yes, she has. Julie has won."

"What are you on about? I'm talking about Priscilla Morrison."

"The Morrison woman. What has she got to do with anything?"

"It's a bit complicated. I need to go back to the beginning. When I became a follower of the way, I remember being told that Jesus said we should first of all seek the kingdom of God. Even though I am new at everything that is twenty-first century, I thought I should still be doing that. I think I have found out exactly what I should be doing here."

I was still angry and not really paying attention. "I still don't see what that's got to do with Morrison?"

Leddicus spoke calmly. I was sure he had now sensed my tension. "Priscilla and my time at the holding centre were the catalyst. For me it brought modern-day slavery into sharp focus. I couldn't get those children out of my head or my dreams."

I shrugged. "The catalyst for what?"

"There's more slavery today than there was then. You really have forgotten what our research revealed, haven't you? Well, I'm going to work for a charity that's trying to put a stop to it. They are working closely with law enforcers to bring those who trade in human misery to justice. I feel it's my destiny, my purpose, to be a small part in the fight against this evil. I think, as a follower of the way, it's the right thing for me to do." He laid his hand on my arm. "Everything has changed for me, my friend. I have to make a new life here. I hope you understand."

I could feel everything slipping out of my grasp: the tours, the film, and the book. I needed to act quickly. *If only Joe were here, he would know what to do.*

Julie joined us, and Leddicus slipped his arm around her shoulder. He looked at her proudly. "What do you think of it?" She held out her left hand to display a dainty diamond ring.

"Very nice," I said with little enthusiasm. "Congratulations. I hope you'll be very happy. Please excuse me. I need to circulate."

The room was very crowded. I didn't realise I knew so many people.

As I was pushing through the crowd, a lady said, "So you are still enjoying the benefits of your con job!"

I swung round, and there facing me was Pricilla Morrison. I was already angry. And now this! I couldn't help myself and snapped at her. "How did you get in here? This is university property. You have no right in here."

"Oh, don't I?" she snapped back. "You are quite wrong. I'm a member. I studied here!"

I was speechless, and I took a deep breath. "So that's how you knew about me coming here one year later. What year were you here?"

"One year ahead of you. Don't you remember?" She glared at me. Her voice was a low growl.

"I need to sit down." I pushed my way to the edge of the room. I found a chair and flopped into it. Pricilla, the pain, had followed me through the crowd and sat down next to me.

"I don't know you. I thought I knew the names of all the students in the year above."

"I changed it!" she snapped again. "When I moved to Rome. But what's worse, you don't even remember my face!" she spat the words out at me. "You don't remember going out with me for two months. You don't remember taking me out to the year-end proms and all those things you said to me on the way back to my flat?"

I stared at her in horror. The light was slowly dawning. The years fell away, and the familiarity of her face popped into my brain. The alcoholic memory loss cleared like thick mist on a sunny day. The sharp reality hit me. Now I know why she had the knife in and was twisting it hard. I slowly regained my composure. Her eyes held mine. Full of hate, they bored into me. She was talking of something that had happened years ago as if it were yesterday. I was dealing with an unbalanced freak. I decided to tread softly.

"I'm sorry I didn't recognise you," I said calmly,. "I had no idea you were now a journalist, but you need to know something. Leddicus is the real deal. We are telling the truth."

Morrison was not listening. She glared at me, just the way she had at the hotel. Fury filled her eyes. She stood up and marched out of the room. I watched her elbowing her way through the crowd, and then I heard the huge oak door slam so loud that it rattled the windowpanes. I leaned back in the chair, closed my eyes, and took some slow, deep breaths.

Just then, the door swung open, and there stood Joe. His face was dark, and he held a large parcel under his arm. Leddicus, Julie, and I quickly gathered round him, all talking at once. I led the group over to a table on the edge of the room, away from the hubbub.

"I have some dreadful news." He turned to me. "I'm sorry to rain on your parade, but I thought you should know as soon as possible." We all fell silent as he placed the package on the table and slowly drew apart the brown paper. There in all its glory was a hardback book, *The Leddicus Enigma* by Edgar Crabtree.

Leddicus and I started talking at once. Julie sat back in her chair with her hand over her mouth. Her eyes were brimming with tears.

"How could this have happened? I thought we had exclusive rights," I said.

"We do up to a point, but you must realise that anyone can write a book." Joe glared at Julie.

I jumped to her defence. "Joe, you know damn well that it wasn't her fault. You've given her enough of a hard-enough time. Lay off her."

His face softened slightly. "Okay, okay, but this was my fear all along. There is so much stuff out there about Leddicus. Whoever this author is, he has got his act together and produced this ahead of us."

While the conversation ran back and forth between Joe and me, Julie ran her fingers over the cover of the book, slowly turning the pages and scanning the text. She suddenly let out a gasp. "This is my stuff. This is what I wrote. This was in my notes!"

"What on Earth are you talking about?" Joe snapped.

"This bit here about his early childhood days. This has never been in the press. I should know. I have every cutting ever produced about Leddicus."

We sat there dumbstruck. The reality was slowly dawning on us.

Joe broke the silence. "You mean your laptop was hacked?"

"It can be the only explanation," she said wearily.

"And your lost notebook?" I asked.

"It must have been stolen." She shuddered.

"Don't we have copyright? And who is this Crabtree guy?"

"You can't copyright every item in the press. As for Crabtree, I've been in touch with all my publishing contacts. They can tell me nothing. It seems this is his debut biography. He is apparently somewhat of a recluse and shunning all publicity."

We sat discussing it with heavy hearts. The conversation went round in circles.

"Don't I get any say in what's written about me?" Leddicus asked.

"I'm getting that checked out with my lawyers, but as there is no character defamation and as you are a worldwide celebrity, it would seem not," Joe replied.

Julie looked distraught. Leddicus stood up and took her gently by the hand. "Walk with me." Concern filled his eyes.

I sat stunned, the full implications of what had happened swept over me, this was financial disaster for us all, I could hardly bear it, after a few moments Joe touched my arm and I looked up at his distraught face.

"Joe, my hospitality has completely deserted me. Can I get you something to eat?"

"A stiff drink would be good," he said.

I rustled up a couple of large whiskeys from the makeshift bar. We drank in silence.

"This is a complete disaster. We are ruined." I said. "Do you want a top up?"

He handed me his empty glass. "Not ruined exactly. Just much poorer than we anticipated."

Twenty minutes later, Leddicus and Julie returned. They had a bottle of Champagne and four glasses. They both looked more relaxed.

"Something terrible has happened, and we need to find out how and see what can be salvaged," Leddicus began, "but we are forgetting that there is much to celebrate. Gerhardt has successfully graduated. I am yet again back from near death, I have a job, and best of all, Julie and I are getting married." He popped the cork and caught the sparkling liquid in the proffered glasses.

"Is this the end of the dynamic duo? Will we ever go on tour again?" I asked Leddicus.

"You can depend on it." He said as he filled my glass.

"Be sure you keep in touch." I said.

"You can always get me on Facebook." He chinked glasses with a beaming Julie.

The Back Pages

My publisher suggested that back pages are not in vogue for fiction novels. But it's hard for me to relinquish my maverick tendencies, so against the proffered advice, here they are anyway.

I hope you enjoyed the story. The following section is for:

Those people who watch a film and then want to know how it was made

Those of you who read a book and want to know what inspired the author to write it and how it was inspired

If you are not one of those people, then you should stop reading now.

I'm not one of those people. I don't read notes at the bottom of pages, look up source references, or dive with glee into tomes that nestle at the back of nonfiction books. But I know many people who are of that persuasion, so here, with my compliments, are some answers to the burning questions that those people have been asking as they have read the story.

While writing the book, I have done some research. Of the many places mentioned in the story, I have first-hand experience. It has long fascinated me how things change, not just due to me growing older, but what I experience as I move in and out of different cultures. Cross-cultural perceptions and experiences can seem alien and inexplicable.

I once had a Kenyan friend who had obviously never heard of Archimedes law and never before seen a bathtub, having only experienced a shower. He was staying with some English friends, and he thought he would try out this newfangled idea of lying in a small pool of warm water. He filled the bath to the top and climbed in. To his horror, the Water, displaced by his body, swooshed over the sides of the bath, poured under the door, and down the stairs. His hosts, fearing he had drowned, knocked urgently on the bathroom door. He was so embarrassed that he remained silent for a long time. This inspired even greater concern to those knocking on the door. He only broke his silence when he feared they would break down the door.

Herewith the back pages. Enjoy!

There Really Was an Iceman
The Man in the Ice by Konrad Spindler, published by Weidenfeld and Nicolson London.

The Argument between Leddicus and Pricilla Morrison: The Facts
Two children are trafficked every minute. Two girls per minute are taken as slaves, and it's growing. **Two to four million** men, women, and children are trafficked across borders and within their own country **every year. More than one person is trafficked across borders every minute**, which is equivalent to five jumbo jets every day. This trade earns twice as much worldwide revenue as Coca-Cola.
Source: Stop the Traffic UK, *www.stopthetraffik.org*

Report from Assist News on the Slavery Issue
ASSISTNews-owner@thomas.sheperd.com by Danjuma1@aol.com
Filed: 28 February 2010 04:39
Subject: Indian Rescue Mission story
ASSIST News Service (ANS): PO Box 609, Lake Forest, CA 92609-0609 USA www.assistnews.net, assistnews@aol.com
Save me! Help me get out! An unheard midnight cry of a victim girl forced into prostitution at a brothel in Mumbai, India
Indian Rescue Mission rescues this girl along with 15 other victim girls.
By James Varghese
Extract from copy by Special Correspondent in India for ASSIST News Service
INDIA (ANS)—Tears rolled down from the eyes of 15 year old Pooja, as she expressed her interest to come out of the brothel to an Undercover Operative (UO) on investigation in a brothel in Mumbai red light district on February 25, 2010.
Acting on information provided to Indian Rescue Mission (IRM), by a confidential informant about minor girls in prostitution, an UO was sent inside brothel Garden alias 307 at Kamathipura red light area at the midnight of February 24, to verify the provided information.

Local pimps surrounded him on his way into the brothel with a promise of good girls for sex, but refusing, the UO got inside the brothel and asked for other girls. The Manager brought out well-dressed innocent girls for customer viewing. Among them UO saw a terrified, depressed girl. Paying money to the Manager, the UO engaged the girl and took her inside the sex room—a move which was part of investigations, but with strict instructions given not to have sex.

Pooja thought of him as a usual customer desperate to have sex, but seeing the disinterest he showed made the girl more comfortable and hence she began to open up. She began to sob bitterly and requested him to help her get out from the bondage of musclemen at the brothel.

From information obtained by the UO, it became known that Pooja was trafficked from West Bengal state and was sold to Mumbai's prostitution flesh industry hub Kamathipura, one of the biggest red light areas in India, and was kept in a place where she was guarded by strong musclemen who do not allow her go anywhere from the brothel.

For further details and to sign a petition to end child trafficking visit the Indian Rescue Mission website at http://rescuemissionindia.weebly.com. You can also e-mail them at indianrescuemission@gmail.com

Other Slavery Facts

When the first abolition bill passed in 1807, four million people were enslaved. Today the number is estimated at twelve million. According to a news release, in the new biography *Once Blind*, author Kay Marshall Strom employs the legacy of John Newton to call attention to twenty-first-century slavery throughout the world. **Source:** Assist News Service, www.assistnews.net

"**Love146** works toward the abolition of child sex slavery and exploitation through prevention and aftercare solutions, while contributing to a growing abolition movement. Slavery is still one of the darkest stories on the planet but for Love146, the hope of abolition is a reality. Love146 believes in helping grow the movement of abolition while providing effective, thoughtful solutions. Love146

believe in the power of Love and its ability to affect sustainable change. Love is the foundation of the organisation's motivation."
Love146 was founded in 2002 (as Justice for Children Intl.). In the UK, Love146 is a registered public charity (UK Registered Charity Number 1137048). In the US, Love146 is a 501(c)(3) nonprofit organisation.
Source: Love146, www.youtube.com/watch?v=NME1-ZiJPXY

The Gerhardt and Leddicus Discussion on the Train
Training notes prepared for Kenya Leadership training for church leaders by Simon Markham in his Kingdom Notes for Lecture use:
The challenge is therefore to be kingdom-minded. This quote from Howard Snyder is a useful summary, "The church gets into trouble whenever it thinks it is in the church business rather than the Kingdom business. In the church business, people are concerned with church activities, religious behaviour and spiritual things. In the Kingdom business, people are concerned with Kingdom activities, all human behaviour and everything God has made, visible and invisible.
Someone has also said, "The Kingdom is a dynamic greater than the church. If you pursue the church you won't find the Kingdom, but if you pursue the Kingdom you will find the church."
Source: Simon Markham Kingdom Notes Leadership Training Kenya
Tyndale Bulletin 46.2 (1995) 337-356.

News Report that Julie Bright Shows to Gerhardt on the Way to the Airport
Bug could hold key to alien life
In an experiment which could come straight from a science-fiction film, scientists have awoken a tiny bug found deep under the Greenland ice from a 120,000-year sleep.
They believe the unusual purple-brown bacterium, named Herminiimonas glaciei, could hold clues to life on other planets. The frozen microbe came back to life and started to replicate after being gently warmed over 11-and-a-half months.

But there is nothing to fear, say scientists—the bug is not harmful to humans, which is just as well as it is so small it passes straight through safety filters used in labs and hospitals.
H. glaciei—a fiftieth of the size of the food bug E.coli—belongs to a rare family of 'ultramicro' bacteria that live in extreme environments.
It was found in ice samples taken from 3km (two miles) under Greenland.
Dr Jennifer Loveland-Curtze, who led the US team at Pennsylvania State University, said: 'These extremely cold environments are the best analogues of possible extraterrestrial habitats. The exceptionally low temperatures can preserve cells and nucleic acids for even millions of years.'
Source: *London Metro*, 14 June 2009, http://www.metro.co.uk/news/684584-bug-could-hold-key-to-alien-life

Julie's Rant about Detention Centres
Correct at time of publication
At present, there are a total of 3,105 bed spaces in Immigration Removal Centres (IRCs) and Short Term Holding Facilities (STHFs). A planned increase of 1,300 bed spaces will bring the capacity to 4,405. A sizable number of prison bed spaces are occupied by persons at the end of criminal sentences (have reached their release date) and continue to be detained as immigration offenders await deportation or transfer to a detention centre. UKBA no longer releases the numbers of those held in prison as immigration offenders.
Source: http://www.ncadc.org.uk/about/capacity.html

UKBA Detention Capacity (16 March 2009)
At present, there are a total of 3,085 bed spaces in Immigration Removal Centres (IRCs) and Short Term Holding Facilities (STHFs). A planned increase of 1,726 bed spaces will bring the capacity to 4,385.
Source: NCADC voluntary organisation, which provides practical help and advice to people facing deportation on how to launch and run anti-deportation campaigns, www.ncadc.org.uk/resources/addresses.html
Brook House IRC

Perimeter Road South
Gatwick Airport
Gatwick
West Sussex
RH6 0PQ
Source: UK Border Agency (correct at 14 April 2008), http://www.ukba.homeoffice.gov.uk/managingborders/immigrationremovalcentres/

Children in Detention/Removal Centres, as per Leddicus experience when detained
Source: http://www.guardian.co.uk/uk/2009/aug/30/children-detention-yarls-wood http://www.dailymail.co.uk/news/article-132725/Asylum-children-held-detention-centre.html http://news.bbc.co.uk/1/hi/education/8518742.stm

Sending Letters in the Ancient World
Although there was no official postal system, I did hear that it took two days for the senior Roman officer on Hadrian's Wall in Scotland to get a letter back to his wife in Rome during the Roman occupation of Briton. They say, today, it takes three days, excluding e-mails, of course.
C.J. Hemer offers the suggestion that the "sequences of journeys implied by Philippians are more easily explained within the facilities offered by the presence of Christian couriers in the imperial service to and from Rome (cf. Phil 4:22)". In a footnote, he continues, "The journeys implied between Rome and Philippi were probably not all private and sequential, but part of a continuous passage of Christian intelligence by frequent travellers along the whole route." The proposition is that there were Christian slaves and/or freed men of Caesar's household who, as tabellarii (couriers), used the facilities of the imperial post and who could be imposed upon while performing their official duties to carry private letters and news between Paul imprisoned in Rome and the community of believers situated at Philippi. The proposition rests on the number of journeys implied in the text of the letter.
Source: C.J. Hefner, *Sending Letters in the Ancient World: Paul and the Philippians*, Stephen Robert Llewelyn

The early church was subversive, noninstitutional, organic, and empowering from below. Pliny the Younger said, "They turned the world upside down."
Source: Quote by Stuart Lindsell

Pliny the Younger
C. Plinus Secundus, called Pliny the Younger to distinguish him from his uncle, was governor of Bithynia in Asia Minor about 112 AD. He wrote to the emperor Trajan to seek advice on how to deal with the problem of Christians in his province. He recounted to Trajan in his letters that he had been killing so many; he was considering whether he should continue killing anyone who professed to be a Christian or only certain ones. He explains he made them bow down to statues of Trajan and "curse Christ, which a genuine Christian cannot be induced to do." In the same letter, he says of the people who were being tried:
They affirmed, however, that the whole of their guilt, or their error, was, that they were in the habit of meeting on a certain fixed day before it was light, when they sang in alternate verse a hymn to Christ as to a god, and bound themselves to a solemn oath, not to do any wicked deeds, but never to commit any fraud, theft, adultery, never to falsify their word, not to deny a trust when they should be called upon to deliver it up (Epistles X, 96).
Source: Rome and the Christians, from *The Letters of the Younger Pliny,* translated by Belt); Radice, copyright © 1963, 1969 by Betty Radice, 293-295. Reprinted by permission o[f] Penguin Books Ltd.

Nonfiction Books by the Same Author

Leadership and . . .
Twelve thousand copies in print and now on its third print run
Latest publication by iUniverse
ISBN 978-1-4401-2662-8 $10.95 £6.50

Attracting Training Releasing Youth
Six thousand copies in print and now on its second print run
Latest publication by iUniverse
ISBN 978-0-595-50858-7 $13.95 £7.00

Jacob: A Fatherless Generation
Published by Rainbow Publishing
ISBN 1-903725-17-8 $ 9.99 £5.99

Hello Is That You God
Published by iUniverse
ISBN 978-0-595-42346-0 $9.95 £5.00

Culture Clash
Published by iUniverse ISBN 978-0-595-50707-8 $14.95 £7.55

Available from all good booksellers and iUniverse